Just Friends

TIFFANY PITCOCK

Swoon READS

Swoon Reads | New York

A SWOON READS BOOK

An imprint of Feiwel and Friends and Macmillan Publishing Group, LLC
175 Fifth Avenue, New York, NY 10010

Our books may be purchased in bulk for promotional, educational, or business use. Please contact your local bookseller or the Macmillan Corporate and Premium Sales Department at (800) 221-7945 ext. 5442 or by e-mail at MacmillanSpecialMarkets@macmillan.com.

Library of Congress Cataloging-in-Publication Data
Names: Pitcock, Tiffany, author.
Title: Just friends / Tiffany Pitcock.
Description: First edition. | New York : Swoon Reads, 2017. | Summary: Told from both viewpoints, after Jenny and Chance, a bookworm and a popular heartthrob, pretend friendship to save a doomed assignment, they are shocked to find a real friendship—and more—developing.
Identifiers: LCCN 2016038313 (print) | LCCN 2017017892 (ebook) | ISBN 9781250084026 (Ebook) | ISBN 9781250084057 (trade paperback)
Subjects: | CYAC: Interpersonal relations—Fiction. | Honesty—Fiction. | High schools—Fiction. | Schools—Fiction. | Family problems—Fiction. | Humorous stories.
Classification: LCC PZ7.1.P614 (ebook) | LCC PZ7.1.P614 Jus 2017 (print) | DDC [Fic]—dc23
LC record available at https://lccn.loc.gov/2016038313

Book design by Liz Dresner

Feiwel and Friends logo designed by Filomena Tuosto

First Edition, 2017

10 9 8 7 6 5 4 3 2 1

swoonreads.com

TO MEME AND TO MOM.
TO KASEY PERRY-LOVELL,
BECAUSE I ALWAYS PROMISED I WOULD.

CHAPTER 1

Jenny

The classroom door swung open.

Every head in the class turned to see a boy with messy blond hair walk in. He gave a nod to his classmates before handing Mrs. Tanner, the slender Oral Communications teacher, a slip of paper.

"Late on the first day, Mister"—she looked closer at the slip in her hand—"Masters?"

"Car trouble, ma'am," he assured her.

She shook her head disapprovingly. "Don't make a habit of this."

"Wouldn't dream of it." He winked before heading to the only open seat in the room.

He collapsed into the seat next to Jenny Wessler. Jenny glanced at him out of the corner of her eye as she chewed the end of her pen. She knew who the boy was, of course. He was the one and only Chance Masters. He'd spent his high school career carving out the most scandalous reputation he could.

"Anyway," Mrs. Tanner called the class to order. "As I was about to say, for your first assignment you will each interview the person next to you, and then perform a dialogue together about your summer vacations for the class. Any questions?"

"Um, yeah." Kelsey Molar, a perky blond, raised her hand. "Can we switch partners?" She looked at her partner, Danny Jennings, with disdain while Danny just continued to slumber in his seat.

"No, sorry, Kelsey, but I pick partners in my class. It's the first day of your junior year. It's one of your last chances to meet new classmates," Mrs. Tanner explained. "Could you wake Danny, please?"

Kelsey prodded Danny awake with her pencil, then glanced over at Jenny.

Jenny met her eyes, shrugged, and mouthed, "I wanted to be your partner."

Jenny watched as Kelsey gave a weak smile and turned to start the project. *I better start, too*, she thought as she looked to Chance. He sat slouched in his desk, his blond hair tousled just so and his brown eyes shining wickedly. He flashed what could only be called a smirk and said, "Ready to go, partner?" in a voice that could convince even the most grounded girl to run away with him.

Luckily, Jenny had no time for him. "Look," she began in her no-nonsense voice, "I really, really like having all A's, so no playing around. You have to take this seriously. I want to start the semester off right."

"Well, you're no fun. I bet you're the type who excitedly packs her backpack the night before the first day because you just can't wait for school to start." He sat up and produced a notebook. "Let's get this over with, then, Little Miss Really-Likes-Having-A's."

"I am not . . ." she hedged, blushing slightly. The truth was, of course, that she was exactly that type of person. She tried to hide her blush by looking over at Margaret Lester, who—with every perfect hair in place—was interviewing the brainless Max Gregs.

"Ah." Chance followed her line of sight. "Margaret Lester. She's not quite the perfect angel everyone seems to think," he said matter-of-factly.

"How would you know?" Jenny turned back to him. "She only moved here at the end of last year."

"Because we went out," he said with a shrug. "We met at a party, and one thing led to another. . . ." He trailed off. "You might want to write this down, since the interview is over something we did during the summer."

"I can't get up there and tell the class how you hooked up with Margaret."

"Why not?"

"Seriously?" She looked skeptical. He was a gross pig, just like everyone said.

"Okay, I see your point." He scratched his chin. "Well, I also broke into an abandoned gas station with my cousins, and then we went skinny-dipping with some girls they knew, but I'm betting you won't say that, either."

"No." Jenny set down her pen. "Did you do anything school appropriate?"

"Um, let's see." He pretended to look thoughtful for a moment. "Nope."

"Of course not." Jenny was feeling a little uncomfortable with him. She'd heard that he got around, but she didn't expect it to be true. She also couldn't help but think of her own pathetic summer; she'd locked herself in her room and read the entire time.

"Let me guess: You did nothing fun?" He raised one eyebrow.

"I've always wanted to do that," she blurted out.

"What?" He looked taken aback by her bluntness. "Have fun?"

"No, raise one eyebrow," she explained, feeling lame.

He just nodded and went to sketching on a blank page in his notebook. Jenny bit her bottom lip and looked around the room; everyone else was well under way with their interviews. Mrs. Tanner sat at her computer, playing solitaire. Jenny glanced back to Chance as he absentmindedly doodled. "Chance?" she asked.

"Yeah?" He looked up, his eyes surprisingly sweet.

"How many girls have you slept with?" The question sprang from her lips before she could contain it. She quickly looked away from him and blushed. *How could I be so stupid?* she thought. *You can't go around asking people those things!*

He let out an amused chuckle and said, "That's none of your business, Little Miss Really-Likes-Having-As."

"Sorry." She fidgeted with her pen.

"Do you always wear your hair in a ponytail?" he asked. He gestured to the tangled mess of brown hair she had shoved back in an elastic band.

"Yeah, it's a bitch to straighten," she admitted.

His eyes lit up. "Aha, so you're not perfect. Now we're getting somewhere."

"I never said that I was perfect," she mumbled, feeling insecure. "I just try to be."

♥ 4 ♥

"Yeah, you do seem like the type who is desperate for approval."
He returned to his doodle.

Anger flared as Jenny snapped: "Hey, you don't know anything
about me. Don't pretend to."

A lazy smile formed at Chance's lips as he looked up at her through
his blond bangs. "Relax, Little Miss Really-Likes-Having-As. I know
nothing of your life and I'm okay with that." He flipped to a clean page
in his notebook and started writing frantically. "You did give me an
idea, though, so maybe you're good for something."

Jenny stared at him in confusion. "What idea? What are you writing? We don't have time—"

"Relax," he said again. "I've got this covered, seriously. When she
calls on us, just work off of me and we're golden."

Jenny glanced around the room at all the other partners huddled
close together, writing out scripts for their dialogues—and then back
to Chance. Was Chance Masters really asking her to trust him? Doubt
clouded her mind as she tried to sneak a peek at his chicken scratch.

"You look like you're having an episode," Chance informed her.
He reached out and pushed at the corners of her mouth, forcing them
up. "At least look like you enjoy my company. I kind of have a reputation to uphold. Girls love me."

"Oh, trust me, I'm aware." She jerked away, trying not to let it show
how much his touch affected her. Her heart pounded in her throat as
she watched Mrs. Tanner work her way back to the front of the classroom. "Chance, she's going to call time, and we're not ready."

"Yes, we are," he informed her, closing his notebook. "We're ready
and we're going to have the best dialogue."

"We don't have a script," she reminded him in a frantic whisper.

"Yes, we do." He smirked.

A nervous sweat began to form on her neck and back. "Then would you kindly fill me in?"

"It'll work better this way," he assured her as Mrs. Tanner called the class to order. "Besides, it was your idea."

"What was?" Jenny asked again, frantic.

"Pretending to know you," he whispered back.

Before Jenny could reply, Mrs. Tanner called up the first group: Kelsey and Danny. They had a snooze-worthy discussion about Kelsey's trip to Colorado and Danny's quest to sleep for seventy-five hours straight. All through it, Jenny kept throwing worried glances at Chance, but he seemed as calm and collected as ever. Finally, after five more groups, Mrs. Tanner called on them.

Chance sauntered to the front of the classroom, causing all the girls to pay attention. Jenny meekly followed him, cold sweat drenching her hands. She glanced from Chance to Mrs. Tanner and back again, waiting for this whole thing to blow up in his face. Chance shot her a wicked grin, cleared his throat, and began.

"Well, it was actually pretty fortunate that Jenny was picked as my partner," he told the class. "We spent most of summer break together, since our families are pretty close."

Jenny tried to control her expression, but she was sure the confusion in her eyes gave them away. She didn't know where he was going with this. Mrs. Tanner was nodding approvingly, while the rest of the class looked between Chance and Jenny, trying to figure out how such a friendship was possible.

"You see, Jenny came over the second day of vacation and helped my brother and me decorate for our annual summer cookout, like she does every year." The class nodded, as if this was old information. They were actually buying it.

"Yeah," Jenny jumped in, trying to go with the flow. "I got there at, like, eight in the morning and no one was up. I had to bang on the door for at least ten minutes."

"Well, we like to sleep." Chance grinned, happy that she was playing along.

"You told me to get there at eight," Jenny tossed back, surprised at how easy it was.

"By 'eight' I mean, like, 'twelve.' You should know this already." He turned back to face the class. "Anyway, after barging into our home at an ungodly time, Jenny and I spent the next few hours attempting to put up those tiki-torch lantern things."

"Which is not the easiest task when Chance's brother keeps blowing them out." Jenny sighed, enjoying herself. "We eventually gave up and just went with tiny American flags. It's more traditional anyway."

"After that, we fought over who would light the grill. It's usually me—"

"Actually, we're supposed to take turns," she reminded him.

"I did it the last two years in a row." He crossed his arms, a playful spark in his brown eyes. "Obviously you just don't remember it right."

"Oh please." She tilted her head and smirked. "I got sick two years ago, remember? Your mother accidentally put expired eggs in the cookies and I spent the whole day throwing up. You stole the grill from me my year."

"Whatever, it's my house and my grill." He turned back to the class. "We were fighting over who got to do it, and suddenly—"

"The lighter broke when Chance tried to tug it out of my hands," Jenny finished. "He tends to break a lot of things."

"I broke your Barbie sunglasses when we were seven. Get over it, Wessler."

"You ran them over with your bike, Masters."

"Well, you shouldn't have left them in my driveway," he said, as if that solved everything.

"Anyway, back to the story," Jenny continued, loving the way the class seemed intrigued. She couldn't believe they were actually buying it. "We ended up getting banned from the house while decorating continued."

"We went to Jenny's house instead." Chance took it from her. "We ended up just spending most of our time there, honestly."

"Well, I was kind of trying to cook things for the party." Jenny sighed again. "You just came with me to annoy me and eat my food."

"Not to annoy," Chance corrected. "To relieve you from boredom."

"Either way you word it, a distraction is still a distraction."

Before Jenny could pick the story back up, Mrs. Tanner called time. The class clapped as they had to after every dialogue, and the two made it back to their desks. The rest of the partners went up and spoke, but Jenny didn't pay them any mind. Her thoughts were all on Chance and how easy it was to get up there and play make-believe with him. Hell, she half believed their lie herself.

She looked over to find Chance looking back at her. He smiled his boyish grin and gave a thumbs-up. She returned the gesture and the grin before giving her attention back to the speakers. After everyone was done and Mrs. Tanner congratulated the class for their hard work, the bell rang, signaling lunch.

Kelsey came up as Jenny was shoving her books into her backpack. With a cautious look at Chance, Kelsey whispered, "I didn't know you and Chance knew each other."

"Oh, yeah." Jenny smiled, keeping up the charade. "We used to live next to each other when we were little."

"Now that you mention it, I think I used to see him around once or twice." Kelsey nodded eagerly, her blond curls bouncing around her face. "You must've mentioned him at some point."

From the corner of her eye, Jenny saw Chance looking at them. She smiled and continued packing. "Totally."

"Well, I'm going," Kelsey said, sensing that Jenny didn't want her there. As soon as the bubbly blond left, Jenny turned to look at Chance. A smirk formed at her lips.

"Well, I apologize for freaking out," she said. The boy leaned against the edge of his desk and smiled, encouraging her to continue. "Obviously, you were able to handle things. I should've just relaxed."

He shook some hair out of his face and laughed. "Thanks, Little Miss Really-Likes-Having-As. Coming from a model student like you, that means something."

"Don't push it, Masters," she threatened, pointing a finger.

He reached out, grabbed her accusing hand, and shook it, smiling what she was beginning to think was his signature smile. "Jenny Wessler, this is clearly the start to a beautiful friendship."

"And that is an overused line." But she smiled back anyway.

Chance slung his backpack over his shoulder before offering her his arm. "Wessler?"

Is this still part of the game? she wondered. After a moment's hesitation, she laced her elbow through his arm, blushing slightly. "I'm going to regret this one day, aren't I?"

"Fat chance," he scoffed. "Apparently, you've had years to get away from me."

A knot twisted in the pit of her stomach, excitement welling up in her. "I guess I haven't learned my lesson yet."

THE WALK TO lunch was awkward. Jenny very seldom walked down the hallway with anybody, let alone arm-in-arm with Chance-freaking-Masters. People, it serves to say, were taking notice. Jenny could feel the eyes on her and Chance and hear the whispers. "So . . ." she began. "This is new."

"You're terrible at conversation," Chance said as they turned into the cafeteria. It was a big room, with rows and rows of round gray tables and gray folding chairs around them. Two long lines wrapped around the walls, people in line for either choice A or B for their lunch. Chance and Jenny sidestepped through the throngs of people, seeking out a table. Jenny typically preferred to sit in the back, by the stage area. It was quieter there and people generally left her alone. She knew from observation, however, that Chance liked to be in the middle of things. He usually sat in the center of the caf, at the same table as all the other outgoing kids. Sure enough, he was leading her there now. Jenny could already make out Leslie Vandercamp, a petite redhead who could barely sit straight under the weight of the twenty or so statement necklaces she had piled on. Leslie was sitting by her best friend, Emelia Vargas, a nice and stunningly beautiful blond. They were both talking vehemently to Drake Sellers.

"You don't mind, do you?" Chance asked, gesturing to his table. He must've sensed her unease.

Jenny thought about it for a moment. How many chances did a girl get to sit at the so-called popular table, escorted arm-in-arm by a hot guy? Not many. At least, not as many times as teen movies had led her to believe. If life were a teen movie, then this would've been just another Tuesday.

Jenny often ran into these moments in her life. She called them Robert Frost moments. Two choices were presented to her: one that would change everything and one that would keep everything the same. Obviously, her gut instinct was to keep everything the same— to never step outside her comfort zone. As soon as she figured out which choice that was, she knew she had to take the other one. Always take the road less traveled.

Chance was the road less traveled.

So she put on a smile, tightened her grip, and said "Not at all," before dragging Chance to his own table.

Lunch had just begun, so the table wasn't full yet. There were still a few scattered empty seats, and Jenny chose the only two that were side by side. She plopped herself down, unafraid, pulling Chance down next to her.

A sharp voice brought her back to her senses. "Is this your new girlfriend, Chance?"

She whipped her head around, realizing it was Leslie who had asked the question. "Oh, it's not like that."

Everyone at the table burst out laughing, causing Jenny to bristle. "It's not," she asserted. She turned to the blond boy next to her, looking for affirmation. "Right, Chance?"

Chance, looking annoyed at the laughter, nodded vigorously. "That's right. Jenny here is my oldest friend, *not* my girlfriend. I'm sure I've mentioned it."

"I've never seen Chance be friends with a girl before, not that I remember," Leslie continued. She tucked her hair behind her ears, flashing her ring-adorned fingers. "Nothing against you, Jenny. I'm just saying that this is news to me."

Jenny knew what Leslie was delicately trying to say. Jenny wasn't a loser, per se. She had the splash of notoriety that came with being top of the class, but that was about it. She didn't really make time for anything outside of studying, which, honestly, suited her just fine. She got invited to the parties, but she never went. Everybody knew that.

Chance, on the other hand, didn't just *go* to the parties; he typically *threw* them as well. She and Chance were two stars that orbited around each other but were never supposed to intersect.

"I don't know, I think I've seen them walking at the park together a few times when I've taken my niece to the playground," Emelia chimed in with a shrug. Her long blond hair was piled on her head in a messy bun, a few strands escaping and hanging in her eyes. "They like to hang on the swings and stuff."

Jenny and Chance looked at each other, wondering what the hell Emelia was talking about. It was true that Jenny liked to hang out at the park swings a lot after school, but she had never seen Chance there. It was clear from his expression that he'd never seen her there, either.

Drake piped up, startling Jenny. He looked between her and Chance. "So, how did you guys first meet?"

Everyone knew Drake Sellers: He was the tallest guy in school and was in a band called The Bleeding Axe Wounds. He played the guitar and sang and could cause a girl to melt with only a smile. His blue eyes caught Jenny's green ones, and she couldn't help but blush a bit as he smiled and said a quiet "Hey."

She also couldn't stop her eyes from traveling down his throat to the sparrow tattoos that decorated his collarbone, peeking out from under his lavender V-neck.

"Hey," she replied. One conversation with Chance Masters and suddenly she was on Drake Sellers's radar.

Oh God. There was no getting out of this.

"Ah, well . . ." Jenny trailed off, cursing her Robert Frost moment. Screw Robert Frost anyway, what did he know about the road less traveled? Because the road less traveled now led straight to public humiliation. The next time she had to make a choice that might affect her life forever, she was just going straight home. She looked at Chance, pleading for help. He was the one who had gotten them started back in class, after all.

"It's such a story. . . ." Chance passed it to her. It was obvious, to her at least, that he didn't know what to say, either.

"But Chance tells it better. . . ." She threw it back. There was no way she was doing this alone.

"All right, all right, I'll tell," he began, flashing her the same smile he had during their presentation. "My family moved here when I was seven, and I got all depressed because I was new. But it turned out that I had this neighbor who had a kid around my age. I decided to journey out to meet her and, of course, she was a brat."

"Hey!" Jenny interrupted crossly. "She was a freaking genius; she was an adorably precocious child. We ended up becoming best friends."

"That's it?" Leslie asked, sounding disappointed and a little disbelieving.

"Well." Jenny picked up the story then, feeling a little more confident than before. She finally had an idea forming in her head—a story taking shape. "Not at first. Like he said, I was better than him—"

"Hey!"

"But one day I happened to climb the tree in my backyard to get a Frisbee I'd thrown up there."

"She ended up getting stuck—"

"And I started screaming for help—"

"So I came running from my backyard—"

"And he climbed up the tree, too—"

"And I ended up getting stuck right along with her." Chance sighed, laughing to himself.

Making up this story was filling Jenny with adrenaline. Her nerves disappeared as she looked around at the enraptured faces of the people seated around her. They were listening to her—actually listening. Their hungry eyes flashed between her and Chance, trying to picture them as children stuck in a tree. Suddenly, Jenny wanted the story to be true.

"He started screaming like a little girl," Jenny told their audience, a smile on her face. She looked over to see that Chance was smiling, too.

"I don't like heights," he admitted.

"We were stuck for thirty minutes before anyone heard us."

"She still doesn't like to go outside."

"Why would I go outside and get all hot and sweaty when I could just curl up inside with a good book?"

"Ugh," Chance groaned dramatically, rolling his eyes. "You and your books. Remember the summer the last Harry Potter novel came out? You dragged me to that midnight release party and forced me to drink that God-awful, lukewarm butterscotch-and-root-beer monstrosity that Barnes and Noble tried to pass off as butterbeer."

"I thought it tasted nice!" Jenny defended, her heart hammering with excitement. She could see the strands of their fake past weaving together right in front of her, forming a cohesive timeline now. "Besides, I wasn't the only one who wanted to be there."

Chance held up his hands innocently. "I have no idea what you're talking about."

"I wasn't the one who begged my mother to draw a lightning-bolt scar on my forehead in eyeliner before we left."

"That totally did not happen, and if it did, it was a very manly eyeliner lightning-bolt scar." Chance laughed, and Jenny found that she quite liked the sound of it. "Also, I wasn't the one who won the last book for free by defeating everyone in the store at Harry Potter trivia."

"You say that like it's something I should be ashamed of, but it's not."

"Do you remember how mad all those people who preordered it were when you got to cut in front of them in line?"

"Oh my God, I can still see their faces." And she could, in her mind's eye, imagine what those fictional people's faces might've looked like. Kids in round Harry Potter glasses would've narrowed their eyes as she was led in front of them, clutching their cardboard-and-hot-glue wands in anger and jealousy. One or two Hermione cosplayers would've whispered, "That's *so* not fair." Most important, though, she could picture Chance, a little younger than he was now, watching her with pride as she won.

"Wow," Drake interrupted them. "You guys bicker like a married couple." Just like that, the spell was broken.

"We get that a lot." Chance shrugged, leaning back. Jenny leaned back, too, realizing that they'd both been unconsciously leaning toward each other during their exchange.

She wondered how Chance felt about this. He seemed comfortable next to her, his eyes bright and his smile easy. He seemed to instinctively turn toward her as he talked, even when he was addressing other people. Then again, so did Drake. Maybe it was a boy thing.

"THIS HAS BEEN an eventful day, huh?" Kelsey said as they climbed into her Toyota Camry.

"Yes, it has." The first day back from summer was always a super-stressful one for Jenny, even without the sudden friendship with Chance. Kelsey knew that Jenny always stressed over where her new classes were and what the teachers would be like.

Kelsey complained about it every year, too. Jenny loved the routine of it.

Jenny had first met Kelsey in sixth grade. The town was so big that they had four elementary schools that ran from kindergarten to fifth grade. Sixth grade was the start of middle school, when all the students started going to the same school. Jenny had been alone and anxious, separated from her elementary friends. Luckily, she'd met Kelsey when they'd both joined the Future Problem Solvers of America team. After that they kept meeting up in extracurricular activities—Quiz Bowl, Writing Circle, Art Club. Anything they could sign up for, they did. It wasn't until halfway through the school year that they both realized they were only joining so many clubs as an excuse to be friends.

"So . . ." Kelsey began, a more serious note in her tone. "Which clubs are you joining this year?"

"I don't know," Jenny said, not wanting to shoot down her friend. She knew Kelsey was only trying to help her, but she didn't feel like joining clubs anymore. The enjoyment was gone from it. She'd much rather stay at home. "I'm thinking about it."

"I suggest Writer's Circle; it's usually fun. There's always an open spot for an alternate on the Quiz Bowl team, too," she said, glancing back to the road. "I'm going for head of the Student Advisory Board this year. Can I keep you in mind when I'm eventually elected and have to assign people to fund-raisers?"

There was no doubt in either of their minds that Kelsey would win. Kelsey was the most organized person that Jenny had ever met. "I promise to work at least one fund-raiser with you," Jenny conceded. One event wouldn't be too much, right? She hung out with Kelsey all the time at one club or another, but they'd never extended too much beyond that.

Jenny always kept to herself, but she was trying to be better. That was why she'd sat at Chance's table, after all. It was another Robert Frost moment, and agreeing to help was the road less traveled.

Chance. She'd briefly forgotten about him and their newfound friendship. Would it continue? Was it real or was it just a fluke—a stunt pulled to pass a dumb assignment and nothing more? It had been so *easy.* Jenny had never clicked with someone with such ease. *It's the fake past,* she decided. *It's easy to talk to someone when I don't have to be myself.*

She had a feeling the magical evening was over and it was time for Cinderella to return from the ball.

She knew what would be waiting for her when she walked through her front door: the same thing that had been waiting for her every day for the past four years. Her mother would be in the kitchen, on the phone with one of her work friends. Jack, Jenny's twelve-year-old brother, would be in his room playing Xbox, and Jessa—only four years old—would be in the living room watching TV. That's the way it always was. Her house had been unchanging since the divorce. Jenny suspected her mother was bending over backward to provide the kids with a stable routine.

"All right," Kelsey said as they pulled up in front of Jenny's house. "I'll pick you up tomorrow."

THE LIGHTS WERE on in the living room when Jenny let herself in the door. Sure enough, she could see her mother sitting at the island in the kitchen. The only thing out of place was the absence of a phone in her mom's hand.

The divorce had aged Jenny's mom. Her long brown hair now looked a little thinner, and her green eyes were surrounded by crow's feet that hadn't been there before. She seemed ultimately smaller than she did in all of Jenny's childhood memories, but maybe that was what happened when you grew up. Maybe your parents just deflated.

"Mom?" Jenny called, dropping her backpack onto a maroon arm-chair by the door. Jenny's mom turned around, startled, holding Jessa.

"Oh, Jennifer, you scared me," she said as she continued to rock Jessa. "Why don't you come in here for a second?" Now Jenny could see her little brother, Jack, his brown hair messy as always, sitting across from their mother. "I have something I need to discuss with you and your brother."

Oh . . . oh no. Family discussions are never good.

Jenny reluctantly trudged into the kitchen. She took a seat by her brother, who—thanks to his recent growth spurt—was almost as tall as she was.

"So . . ." their mother began a little awkwardly. "I'm not sure how to explain this, so I'm just going to jump right in. I met someone. His name is Phillip and he's a gym teacher. We met at Jack's last parent-teacher conference and seemed to hit it off. He asked me out, actually, but I wanted to talk to you two before I made any decisions."

Wait, what?

For the first time in years, time seemed to move forward in their house. Jenny could see the change that came over her mother as she said Phillip's name. She seemed alive for the first time since the divorce.

Did Jenny mind if her mother dated? Of course she didn't. It had been years, and her mother deserved some happiness in her life. Was Jenny weirded out by the thought of her mom going on dates? Of course she was. Jenny herself didn't even go on dates, and she was seventeen.

It was Jack who spoke up first, however.

"Of course it's all right, Mom," he said, sounding much older than he actually was. "You're an adult. You can date whoever you want."

"Jackie's right," Jenny piped up, placing an arm around her brother's slim shoulders. "As long as he's nice, then it's fine."

Jack bristled under her touch. "Don't call me Jackie. I'm not a little kid."

"But Jackie's such a cute name." Jenny reached out, pinching his cheek. He'd lost the baby fat over the summer, playing baseball and jumping on the trampoline, making it harder to condescendingly pinch his cheeks than it used to be.

"Mom, she's patronizing me again," Jack complained, but stopped short at the sight of their mom. Jenny turned to see what he was looking at and slowly let her arms drop from her brother.

Their mom was sitting there, holding Jessa, with tears in her eyes as she watched her children. "Thank you" was all she said.

WHAT DO YOU really think about Mom dating again?" Jenny asked her brother thirty minutes later as they sat in her room. She sat on her bed, geometry homework in hand, as he lounged in her computer chair, absentmindedly browsing reddit on her PC.

"I hate it, of course," Jack said simply, not even turning around to face his sister. "I don't want my parents seeing other people. And what if he hurts her like Dad did? There are too many variables here, and I hate it."

"You told her you were fine with it, though."

Jack shrugged. "We can't hold her back from living her life."

"Are you sure you're only twelve?"

"I'll be thirteen in a few months, you know that."

"I was being sarcastic, Jackie."

Her brother grimaced, stepping away from the computer dramatically. "Just for that, I'm going back to my room."

"Fine, go. See if I care." But she was teasing and he knew it. He left, leaving her to her homework.

Things were different now, definitely. Her mother was dating and time was moving forward and her life was changing and Chance—oh God, Chance. What the hell was Chance? She pushed her schoolbooks to the floor and sprawled out on her bed, looking up at the ceiling. What was she going to do about Chance—if anything? Would this all blow over tomorrow?

She had felt so *alive* carving out a fake past with him at lunch. She had felt like a different, unpredictable person. She *liked* that feeling, and she wasn't sure if she was ready to let it go yet.

Things could be changing right now, she thought. *This could be the start of something different*—something good. Do I really want to give it up just yet?

Lying there, in her same old room looking at the same old ceiling, she could easily imagine a different life, where Chance had always been there supporting her and arguing with her at the same time. She could imagine him sitting at the computer chair like her brother had done, talking out her problems with him for years on end. She could easily insert him into her entire life and not even blink. It was almost seamless.

To her, at least. She had no idea how he felt. She figured she was probably a minor annoyance or a momentary source of entertainment that he'd toss aside come tomorrow morning.

After all, it wasn't like she even knew him.

CHAPTER 2

Chance

Chance woke up to the smell of burned eggs. And to yelling. Lots of yelling.

That was normal, though. The yelling, not the eggs. He was beginning to wonder if he could even sleep without the dulcet tones of his mother screaming at his father. It had become his regular lullaby lately. He could hear them, muffled through the walls, their voices straining.

Chance couldn't take it anymore. Not even wrapping his pillow around his head could drown them out. He had to get up. Their yelling had already given him a headache.

He tried to think of a time when yelling wasn't his alarm clock, but he honestly couldn't remember that far back. They always yelled— it was their thing. Some parents did karaoke. Some parents played bridge. Some did drugs. Chance's parents yelled. About everything.

Buying groceries? They fought about it.

What to have for dinner? They fought about it.

Money? Religion? Politics? What to watch on TV? They fought about all those, too. The worst fight had been three years ago, when his brother, Levi, up and left for college without a word. It was no wonder that he hadn't been back home since then.

Chance finally pried the pillow away from his ears and sat up. He could always drown them out with a shower.

When he slipped into the hallway he saw that his brother's door was wide open. Levi had hardly ever been home when he had lived there, always trying to be out of the house as much as possible. Of course, when he was out, their parents would argue about where he was and how he was bringing them some type of shame. Levi couldn't make a move without drawing their parents' ire.

Chance and Levi weren't the closest of brothers. They never had been. Levi had always been so much older and taller and cooler. He didn't have time for Chance once he got to high school. Chance still looked up to him, though. Levi always seemed, above all else, undeniably *cool*.

Chance made sure to close the bathroom door loudly, interrupting his father mid-sentence. They quieted down a bit after that, not that it mattered. Chance couldn't hear them over the roar of the hot shower anyway.

Levi is the lucky one, he thought as he washed his hair. *He got out—just left without a second thought. I would give anything to be able to do that.*

THE BEST DAY of Chance's life was the day he got his car. It was a lovely black 1999 Dodge Charger, and it was his pride and joy. Sure, it was secondhand (more like fourth-hand, to be honest), the passenger-side window didn't work, and the upholstery was seriously ripped up, but it was his escape.

It also meant he could drive himself to school. He didn't have to rely on Levi or his parents.

He was embarrassed to admit it, but he felt like he was in a music video whenever he drove it. One of those indie music videos with girls in knit caps and boys with ukuleles. The type that accompanies movies about manic pixie dream girls saving the boring male protagonist from himself. It was dumb, but he loved it.

He thought about Jenny Wessler suddenly, her face flashing behind his eyes. The way she had looked seated next to him at lunch, lightly blushing. The way her brown hair curled in its ponytail, the ends just brushing her shoulders. She had seemed so *nice*.

Chance could use some nice in his life.

He knew their minor interlude was finished, however. It had burned bright for one hour, and then it had burned out. That was the way it was. It was the way it *had* to be. He couldn't complicate his life any more than it already was. Besides, she seemed like the type who didn't live in a constant state of yelling. He couldn't drag her into his mess.

Although he had to admit: Nothing had ever come as easily as their game of make-believe.

He saw her the moment he pulled into the parking lot. He would've liked to swear that she wasn't the reason he parked by the library, instead of behind the science building like he always did, but he knew the truth.

She was walking from a maroon car, her messenger bag bulging at her side. *What does she have in there, the whole damn library?* Her hair was down today, and she wore a light-blue polo shirt. The color looked good on her; it went well with her pale complexion.

He was out of his car and catching up to her before he even realized what he was doing. "Jenny!" he called, causing her to turn around. "Hey. I think we should continue to be friends."

She looked up at him. "We're friends?"

"Damn, Wessler, that's cold. I thought we hit it off yesterday."

She blushed, turning away. "I only meant that I didn't realize everything yesterday was real."

He hadn't, either, not until he'd said it. "Of course it was real. You're my oldest friend, Jenny."

She laughed, "Oh sure, the tree and Harry Potter and all that."

"You couldn't have made me sound a little manlier in our origin story?"

"You can't rewrite the past, Chance."

Now it was his turn to laugh. "Oh, of course. I forgot that the past is set in stone." They had reached the side entrance to the cafeteria now. That was where everyone hung out before the first bell rang.

A few people looked at them curiously as they made their way across the room. Chance even caught a few people wearing *what the hell?* expressions. Which was odd. It wasn't like it was unusual to see Chance with a girl. Most of his friends were girls, really, and it wasn't like he didn't date.

"People are staring," Jenny whispered to him, drawing herself closer.

"We don't have to walk together if it bothers you," he told her.

"Are you kidding? This is exciting." But she didn't sound wholly convincing.

Kelsey came out of nowhere. One moment it was Chance and Jenny, the next they were almost on top of the blond. She was taller than Jenny—at least five-eleven—and her blond hair was in orderly curls. "Jens! I was wondering where you went. . . ." Her voice trailed off as she caught sight of Chance. "Oh, Masters, it's you. I should've known."

"What is that supposed to mean?"

Kelsey shrugged.

She doesn't like me. It was as if she was nearly trying to shield Jenny from him.

"Sorry about that." Jenny shrugged. "We got to talking."

"I see," Kelsey said. "You left me at the mercy of Danny Jennings."

"Still?" Jenny asked in disbelief. "He hasn't taken the hint?"

"We were partners on one assignment. I mean, Lord, it doesn't mean we're freaking soul mates."

"Yeah," Chance spoke up. "Letting an icebreaker assignment rule your relationships is just stupid."

"Exactly!" Kelsey exclaimed, blind to the sarcasm in his voice.

He felt Jenny shake beside him and looked over to find her suppressing her laughter.

"The boy shaves his head!" Kelsey went on. "Like I could ever date someone with a buzz cut. I mean, my gosh, I have standards!"

Jenny snickered.

Note to self: Stay away from buzz cuts.

The bell rang then, cutting Kelsey off mid-rant. "If he waits outside my first block class, I am telling the counselor," she muttered as she walked away. "Oh, and Jenny?" she called over her shoulder. "The Student Advisory Board is voting on their president this afternoon. See you there!"

Then there were two.

"So . . ." Jenny said, tugging on the strap of her messenger bag. "I have American Lit."

"Oh, I have Geometry A. I guess we should"—he opened the door in a sweeping gesture—"go to class?"

She gave him a small wave good-bye and pushed past him, making her way out the door. She paused, turning to look at him. "It'll be fun," she told him.

He quirked an eyebrow. "What will be fun?"

She smiled, big and wide. "Being your friend." Then she was gone. Chance watched her leave, unsure of the feeling building in his chest. She was right; of course, this *was* going to be fun. Now that he was sure this was what he wanted, he was dedicated.

Jenny Wessler was going to be his new best friend.

CHAPTER 3

Jenny

I don't understand why we're reading *Hamlet* in American Lit. I mean, I just do not get it," Jenny said to Kelsey as they made their way down the English hall. "*Huck Finn* I get. *Walden* I get. But *Hamlet?*"

"Mrs. Princeton says it's because she believes that every English novel can be linked back to Shakespeare," Kelsey told her. "That's not it, though. They require the English department to teach a Shakespeare play every year."

Jenny snorted. "They do not. I would've noticed if we read one every year."

"Really, think about it. Which have you read and when?"

Jenny thought about it. "Freshman year was *Romeo and Juliet*, then we read *Julius Caesar* and that was sophomore year . . . now *Hamlet* . . . everyone knows the seniors read *Macbeth* . . . and crap, you're right!"

Kelsey shrugged. "I know the inner workings of the school like the back of my hand."

Jenny moved over just in time to dodge a couple barreling through the crowded hallway, their hands clasped. She looked over her shoulder, watching the two until they disappeared around a corner.

"Don't you just hate hallway PDA?" Kelsey asked, glaring after the couple.

The only boy Jenny had ever held hands with was her brother, back when he was too young to walk alone in a store. What would it be like to hold hands with a boy she liked? To want to be together so badly they'd hold on to each other in a crowd just because they didn't want to lose a second of contact? She finally turned away, only to spot another couple up ahead, leaning against the lockers, talking so closely their noses were practically touching. *When did everyone pair off?* she wondered as she looked away.

"It's not too bad," she told Kelsey as she spotted two girls holding hands by the water fountain. "I like PDA. The idea that they like each other *so* much that they . . ." She trailed off as Kelsey's eyes narrowed suspiciously. "What?"

"This doesn't sound like you," Kelsey said. "What gives?"

To be honest, Jenny had been thinking about dating ever since she found out her mother was doing it. It was like a wake-up call, and now suddenly she was so *aware* that everyone seemed to be dating except her. "It's nothing," she told Kelsey. She didn't want to bother her friend with her family drama. Jenny hated being a burden.

"Ah," Kelsey said knowingly. "I know what this is about. Or, rather, *who* it's about."

"What?" *Kelsey knows my mom is dating?*

"It's Masters, right?" Kelsey ignored her protests, continuing on. "Look, you've known him for a long time, so I don't have to tell you about his reputation. It's bad, Jens. I wouldn't do it if I were you. That isn't a frontier worth exploring."

"This isn't about him."

"Suuuure," Kelsey laughed. "It's okay, we've all been there at least once in our lives. He's attractive, but he's not boyfriend material. I don't want him to hurt you."

Jenny stopped walking, causing the person behind her to mutter angrily as they stepped around her. "I'm not talking about Chance," she insisted. She *hated* when people told her what she was thinking or feeling. "I wasn't even talking about myself."

This brought Kelsey up short. "Oh. Um, I'm sorry, I just assumed . . . Who were you talking about, then?"

"Never mind," Jenny said, looking at one of the digital clocks posted in the hall. "We're going to be late for class. C'mon."

Jenny marched into Oral Comm just as the bell rang, Kelsey trailing behind her. She wasn't in the mood to deal with class right now. Kelsey's warning still rang in her head.

Sure, she knew that Chance was dangerous. A person doesn't earn a rep like his without being a little wild, but Kelsey's warning was ridiculous. From what Jenny could tell, Chance was a good person, and he was definitely fun to be around. It wasn't like Jenny was going to marry him; they were just hanging out. Besides, they weren't like that.

Okay, true, the thought of hanging out with him after school sent her nerves into overdrive, but that was because he was still new. It wasn't because of his reputation—though now that Kelsey had brought it up, Jenny couldn't help but think about it. She tried her best to calm her frazzled nerves as she thought of a hundred and fifty ways in which being Chance Masters's friend could go wrong, but she must not have been as composed as she thought, because not even five minutes into class she found a note fluttering onto her desk.

What's wrong with you? the note read in unfamiliar scrawl. It took her a moment to realize it must be from Chance.

Nothing, she wrote back.

The note was back in seconds. *Bullshit.*

I was talking to Kelsey. She stared down at the words, afraid to pass it back. She didn't want him to think something was wrong with her. Finally she marked it out, the lead of her pencil making indents on the paper. *It's seriously nothing.*

She surreptitiously watched him as he opened the note, taking stock of his reaction. He didn't believe her, it was obvious. He sat there, pencil poised over the paper, but he didn't write anything. He eventually wadded up the note and shoved it in his bag. That was the end of that.

She half expected him to get up and leave without a word when the bell rang, but he didn't. He loaded up his backpack and waited by her desk for her to do the same. "Ready for lunch?" he asked.

"Um, yeah." She trailed him as he left the classroom. She couldn't help but notice the way his shoulders filled out his faded green T-shirt or the way his blond hair slightly curled at his collar. "I'm sorry about that with the note—"

He turned back to look at her, confused. "What? Oh, you don't have to be sorry about that. You don't have to tell me anything you don't want to."

"Oh." She felt relief wash through her. After Kelsey speaking for her, she found it refreshing that Chance let her speak for herself.

He didn't ask her again what was bothering her. They went through lunch at his table, and they talked energetically, but he never brought it up. It was like . . . like he didn't expect anything from her, and as a result she didn't have to try. Like the day before, talking to him came easily. Her words flowed off her tongue and her smiles were easy and frequent. Chance made her feel relaxed and, well, she rather liked that.

"Earth to Jenny," Chance said, waving his hand in front of her face. She had paused, halfway through the cafeteria door. People behind her were making impatient noises. "C'mon, Little Miss Really-Likes-Having-As."

Then Chance grabbed her hand and dragged her through.

CHAPTER 4

Chance

We should have a secret handshake. Everyone who has been friends since elementary school has a secret handshake."

Jenny rolled her eyes. "That's ridiculous. We don't need a secret handshake. That's too much trouble. I thought the point of this was to make up things on the fly."

"It is, but say that someone came up to us and was like, 'Do you guys have a secret handshake?' And we tell them yes and try to make it up on the fly, then we'll only embarrass ourselves."

"No one is going to ask us if we have a secret handshake."

He looked at her seriously. "You don't know that."

"And if anyone ever asks our secret handshake, then making it up on the fly will be fun." She led Chance to his table now, not even pausing to contemplate going to her old one. Jenny had assimilated so fast, Chance was impressed. She took her seat between him and Drake with ease.

Honestly, she looked like she belonged there.

"So, Drake," Jenny began, turning to the tall boy to her right. "How's your band doing?"

Kelsey, who had just approached the table, groaned as she set her tray down. She had slipped into their lunch group as easily as Jenny had, but seemed to hate Drake's band. Chance liked that about her.

"Oh God, don't ask about his band," Kelsey complained. "I'm sure you're trying your best, Drake, but you sound like every other pseudo-intellectual rich boy with a guitar."

Drake brought his hand to his chest in mock pain. "You wound me."

She shrugged. "It's true."

It *was* true. Chance had been to enough of their shows to know.

"I'm sure that's not true," Jenny defended. "Everyone's always talking about how great your shows are."

"That's because you haven't heard them yet," Chance assured her.

Drake glared at him. "Don't listen to Jackass over there. You should come to practice sometime and check us out."

Chance didn't like the way Drake was looking at Jenny, his eyes skimming over her hungrily.

Jenny thought about it, biting her lip. "That would be fun," she told him, before turning to Chance. "What do you think, wanna go to band practice sometime?"

That's my girl, Chance thought as Drake's face fell.

Leslie plopped down at the table then, her chair dangerously close to Chance's. He nearly choked on her perfume as she reached past him to steal a few fries from Drake's tray. "Don't worry, Jenny. You'll have a chance to see them live. Drake is playing my Halloween party."

"No, I'm not," Drake said. His eyes slid from Leslie to Jenny, lingering on her as she took a sip of her water.

Leslie sank back into her seat. "You've gotta do it," she said before popping a fry into her mouth.

"Are you gonna pay me?" Drake asked.

From there the conversation switched to The Deplorable State of Modern Music and The Act of Doing It for the Art. Chance tuned most of it out. He had very few opinions on music. If it was catchy, he liked it. If it was annoying, he hated it.

The bell rang suddenly, loud and shrill, making him jump. It was time for third block already. The day was going by too damn fast. Soon, he knew, he'd have no choice but to head home, where things were only getting worse.

He didn't want to go home.

"Hey, Jenny?" he said, stopping her before she could leave the table.

"Yes?"

"Wanna go to the park after school?"

She didn't even hesitate. "Sure, if you'll give me a ride home afterward." And just like that, he had plans with Jenny.

"CHANCE!" JENNY'S VOICE rang out, breaking him from his thoughts. She half jogged across the parking lot to meet him. "Sorry I'm late. I had to catch up with Kelsey and tell her to head home without me."

His face lit up at the sight of her—he couldn't help it. "No problem. You ready?"

The two crossed the street, chatting idly about their last two classes. Chance barely even noticed his feet carrying him to the rusted red swing set that sat to the right of the amphitheater. Back when he was a child, the swings used to sit in a pit of rocks, but over time the rocks had been replaced with chunks of rubber. He guessed that was safer. He took the right swing, the one that some high schoolers had repeatedly tossed over the top to make the chains shorter. Jenny took the one next to him.

It was a beautiful, if small, park. It had a giant walking track that wrapped around it, and it was cut in half by a small creek that was running low from lack of rain. It only had a few bits of playground equipment: a jungle gym, the swing set, and a giant fake climbing rock. It was simple, but Chance enjoyed it.

"These swings used to seem a whole lot bigger when I was younger," Jenny remarked, kicking off with her feet.

"I remember I used to come here after school sometimes back in fourth grade because my parents were always late picking me up," Chance told her, slightly pushing himself forward with the toes of his shoes. "I would section the place up and pretend it was Neverland."

He wasn't sure why he was telling her this. He had never told anyone about this before, but somehow within minutes of being near Jenny it was all pouring out.

Jenny stopped swinging to look at him curiously. "Neverland?"

"Yeah." Chance nodded. He pointed straight ahead of them, to the awning-covered picnic tables used for children's birthday parties. "That over there was Pirate's Cove because that's where the birthdays happen, and—"

"—and birthdays mean growing older, which is akin to piracy in Neverland," Jenny finished for him.

He smiled ruefully. "Yeah, that's right. See that big fake rock that kids climb on over there?" He pointed toward the parking lot. "That was Skull Rock."

Jenny laughed. "Naturally."

"Hey, nobody said I was original. The other awning all the way at the bottom of the hill there was Blind Man's Bluff, the creek that runs at the bottom of the hill over there was Mermaid Lagoon, and the water fountains over there were the Indian Camp."

"What about the swings?" Jenny asked, setting off again, kicking up some bits of rubber as she did so.

"Hangman's Tree, of course, the hideout of the Lost Boys," Chance answered as if it were obvious.

"You sound like you were quite the imaginative little boy."

"You should know—you were there." At least, he wanted her to have been. Maybe his games wouldn't have been so sad if he'd had Jenny to share them with. Instead of a lonely little boy running around, playing Peter Pan to ignore that his parents had forgotten him, he could've just been playing. Peter Pan needed a Wendy. Chance needed Jenny.

"Was I?" Jenny asked, playing along. "What was my role in all of this?"

"You were a Lost Girl, of course." He thought about that for a moment, before adding: "Not in the Alan Moore way, either."

"Was I bossy?" she asked.

"The bossiest."

"What did we do on these adventures?"

He pushed up, swinging a little higher. "We rescued princesses, of course."

"Oh, naturally." She sped up, her swing matching his. He looked over just in time to catch her brown hair trailing behind her as she rose.

"Did I participate in the rescuing?"

"You were the best at it," he told her. "I always got distracted by the pirates. You were the one who came up with the rescuing plans."

"I like this story," she replied. "I can picture it all so clearly."

Good, he thought, *so can I.*

They swung for another thirty minutes or so, talking of whatever popped into their minds. Eventually Chance's legs grew tired and he decided to stand up and push Jenny's swing instead.

"You don't have to do this," she told him as he pushed her forward.

"It's fine. My legs needed a rest, anyway."

"I didn't play any games like that as a kid," she told him. "Like Neverland, I mean."

"What did you do?"

"I didn't like to go outside much. I mostly followed my mom around, pretending to do all the big-girl chores."

He let out a bark of laughter. "Why does that not surprise me?"

"I liked it. It made me feel like I was doing something productive."

It must've been nice, growing up in a home where she could do stuff like that, Chance thought. If he had tried that, his mother would've yelled at him for always being in the way and doing everything wrong.

Her phone went off then, startling them both. She stomped her feet frantically, trying to stop her swing. Chance reached out to grab the chains, steadying her as she pried her phone from her pocket.

"Hello?" she said. "Oh, hi, Mom. No, I'm at the park across from the school. I thought you'd still be at work. I can be home soon." She looked over her shoulder at Chance, her expression apologetic. "It's no problem. See you soon. Love you."

Chance let go of the chains, already turning to pick his backpack up off the ground. "I take it that we have to go?"

"Yeah," Jenny said, getting to her feet and grabbing her backpack. "My little sister, Jessa, was running a bit of a fever so Mom came home from work early. She wants me to come watch Jessa so she can cook dinner."

So Jenny wasn't an only child? *Interesting.*

Chance's Charger was still parked by the library, where he'd left it that morning. The black paint shone in the afternoon sun. Unfortunately, so did all the dirt clinging to it. *I should really get that washed.*

"I guess you've never been in my car before, huh?" Chance said as Jenny eyed it skeptically. He was wary of people judging his baby.

She circled it, scrutinizing it as she did so. "Of course I have," she said after she reached the passenger's side again. "I helped you pick it out."

Now it was her turn to make up a story. Chance unlocked the door, slipping into the driver's seat. "You did?" he asked after she climbed in.

"Mm-hm." She nodded. "You were unsure about it, you see, because it's so run-down with its ripped seats and messy floorboards. I was the one who convinced you it had character." She reached into her front pocket, producing a small tube of lip gloss. She flipped down the front visor so she could use the mirror. Chance watched as she applied the gloss—some cherry-red flavor, by the strong smell of it.

She pursed her lips once before leaning up and pressing her lips to the mirror. She pulled back, revealing a single perfect kiss mark. "I marked my territory, see?"

Damn. Jenny definitely knew how to play the game.

Chance's eyes lingered on the kiss mark. "As my oldest friend, you always get shotgun."

She nodded, slipping the lip gloss back into her pocket. "Now everybody knows that."

He had to admit, the sight of her kissing that mirror made his heart hammer. He wasn't even sure *why*. For one, he had done a lot more than kiss other girls in that car. And yet none of them had gotten his heart going like Jenny and that mirror had.

Maybe it was because, in the back of his mind, he knew that this was the start of something bigger than those other things. That kiss mark wasn't a hasty hookup in the backseat of a car; it was precise—it was *planned*. It was, well, kinda permanent. Many people would pass in and out of that car, but that lip print would stay.

Jenny would stay.

CHAPTER 5

Jenny

"Plum or Black Cherry?"

Jenny looked up from her perch on her mother's bed, surveying the two shades of lipstick that her mother held. "Black Cherry," she said at last.

This was weird. Even Jenny had to admit that this was weird. She'd only found out a week ago that her mother was dating, and now she was helping her pick out a lipstick color. She wasn't supposed to be helping her mother get ready for a date. This wasn't daughter territory. Jenny decided to grin and bear it, though, because that's what a good daughter would do.

Her mother stood at the foot of her bed, leaning down to check out her reflection in her vanity mirror. She had chosen a simple black A-line dress with thick straps and a pair of shiny black kitten heels. Jenny thought she looked great. She also knew that Phillip would think so, too. She wasn't sure how she felt about that, but her mother's happy glow was undeniable. She hadn't looked this excited since she told Jenny and Jack about being pregnant with Jessa.

"You look great, Mom," Jenny told her, watching as she smoothed her hair down for the fiftieth time.

"Are you sure?"

"Yes. Do you want to ask Jackie?"

Her mother paused. "Wouldn't that be a little awkward?"

This is all *a little awkward*, Jenny thought. "I suppose."

Her mother checked her watch, and Jenny couldn't help but notice it was *not* the one she usually wore. She usually wore a small silver one that Jenny's father had gotten her for their last anniversary together. Now she was sporting a sleek gold one. "Oh, he'll be here any second."

Wasn't Jenny supposed to be the one excitedly going on dates and her mother the one helping her get ready? *I mean, I never go on dates, but still.*

"Where are you going, again?" Jenny asked, following her mother from the room.

Jenny's mother was in such a hurry that she was already nearly down the stairs. "Red Lobster!" she called over her shoulder.

"Swanky," Jenny mumbled. Then, a little louder, "That sounds fun, Mom."

"You'll be fine watching Jack and Jessa?" her mother asked, breezing right through the living room and into the kitchen. Jenny had to practically jog to keep up. "Yes, Mom, I can watch two children. I am capable of that."

"Toddlers are hard work," her mother warned.

"I know that. I'll be fine. You just focus on having fun."

Her mother still looked doubtful. "I left money for pizza on the counter, and you have my cell—"

"Mom, this isn't some babysitting movie, okay? This isn't *Sleepover*—nothing is going to happen."

"It's not *Sleepover* I'm worried about, it's *Scream*."

Jenny sighed. "If the call is coming from inside the house, then I will get us *out* of the house."

Jenny's mother rolled her eyes. "I can't deal with your smart-assed remarks right now, Jennifer."

"Sorry, I'll behave."

Her mother grabbed her purse from the barstool and started digging. "I left a little more cash—for emergencies only—in my room. You can call me if you need it, and I'll tell you where it is."

"You could just hand it to me," Jenny pointed out.

"Oh, sure, then I'll have to worry about *Can't Hardly Wait*. No, thank you."

As if I know enough people to invite to a party. Jenny checked the clock above the microwave. "It's ten till," she said.

"I know the time," her mother answered, pulling her planner from her purse and setting it aside. "Why do I keep so much junk in here?"

"Oh, Mom, can I ask you something?" She might as well strike while her mother was happy and distracted.

"Sure, honey."

"A friend of mine asked to hang out after school tomorrow. Can I go?" *Don't ask who. Don't ask who. Don't ask who.*

"A friend?" Her mother paused, thinking. "Is it Kelsey? You haven't hung out with her in a while."

Dammit. "No, um, actually it's a new friend."

Her mother turned to look at her skeptically. "A new friend?"

"His name is Chance."

Her mother's eyes were practically the size of saucers. "*His* name? A boy? You're asking to hang out with a *boy*?"

"Well, yes, he is biologically male." Jenny knew her mother would react this way.

"You never hang out with boys," her mom went on, like an alley cat with a scrap of food. "Is this one special?"

"We're only friends, Mother."

Her mom waved a hand dismissively. "Oh, sure."

"Really. It's not like that. We don't even know each other."

"That's what I used to tell my mom, too, back when I was a teenager."

The doorbell rang then, and Jenny sent up a silent prayer of gratitude. "Go, Mom. Go on your own date." She got up, grabbing her mother by the elbow and shepherding her toward the door. "Be back at a reasonable hour, don't do anything I wouldn't do, and most important: Have fun." *And stop asking me about boys.*

Jenny's mom yanked her arm away, looking down at her daughter. "Don't think that this conversation is over just because Phillip is here. I want to hear all about this boy when I come home."

But the conversation *was* over, and they both knew it. Her mother's mind emptied completely the moment she opened the door and saw Phillip. Jenny hadn't been expecting to meet him. Not so soon, at least. She hadn't even brushed her hair or changed from the clothes she'd worn to school. She'd assumed he'd wait in the car, but there he was in front of her, filling the doorway.

Phillip was there; he was *real*. Of course, Jenny had known he was a real person, but he wasn't quite real to *her* until that moment. That was the moment she saw him for the first time—the moment he became so much more than a concept of a person. He was tall, with broad shoulders and a farmer's tan. He wore a light-blue button-down shirt, with the sleeves pushed up, and dress pants. He had salt-and-pepper hair and a kind face.

He also couldn't take his eyes off Jenny's mother, and Jenny liked what she saw there. Phillip looked at her mother like she hung the moon. Jenny made up her mind right then and there that she *had* to like him, for her mother's sake.

"Hello there," Phillip said, reaching his hand out to Jenny.

Jenny took it. "Hi."

"It's nice to meet you, Jennifer," he said, his voice deep. "I'm Phillip."

"I'm so glad you clarified, dear, or she would've confused you with the dozens of other men I bring home," her mother joked, reaching out to lay a hand on Phillip's arm. Jenny's gaze zeroed in on that hand, on that display of casual contact. How could her mother do that so easily?

Is my mom a better flirt than me? Jenny wondered, before realizing how bizarre that thought was.

"We should probably get going," her mom said.

"Have her back at a reasonable time," Jenny joked to cover up her awkwardness. "Her curfew is midnight."

Phillip laughed, full and loud. "I'll try."

After her mother and Phillip left, Jenny parked herself on the couch, her English book in her lap. She was halfway through reading the introduction to *Mark Twain* when Jack came bounding downstairs, his laptop in his hands.

"Mom says you're not allowed on the computer until after you dust," she told him as he sat next to her on the couch. He ignored her, opening his laptop and browsing away. "Jackie, listen to me. Your fandom debates can wait. The three inches of dust on the bookshelf can't."

"I'll do it later." He barely even looked up from his keyboard, where his fingers were flying away.

"But Mom said—"

"Mom's not here right now," he reminded her. "She's on a date."

"I'm aware of that, but she said—"

Jack looked up at her then, a wicked glint in his eye. "Why aren't *you* on a date, Jenny?"

Jenny froze for a moment, ears turning pink, unsure how to come back from that burn. Finally she spoke. "What about *you*? Have you talked to that girl you like yet? What was her name . . . April Rosenbaum?" She grabbed her phone, opening the Facebook app. "How would you like it if your big sister sent her a message asking her out for you?"

Jack was out of his seat in seconds. "I'll dust!" he cried, running to the supply closet. "You win, I'll dust!"

Jenny tossed her phone back onto the couch, smirking as she returned to her reading.

JENNY WAITED FOR Chance after school. She wasn't sure if she was supposed to meet him at his car or what, so she decided to meet him in the general area *around* his car. Why couldn't people ever give step-by-step instructions? Things would be so much easier then.

Her phone vibrated in her pocket. It was a text from her mother. *Pick up paper towels while you're out.*

Great. As if she wasn't already worried about being boring, now she had to get Chance to run *errands.*

She had started pacing by the time she spotted Chance emerging from the English hall. She was about to call to him when she noticed that he wasn't alone. He was with Samantha Havens, a girl from their grade. Jenny had had a few classes with her their freshman year. Jenny ducked behind a mud-covered truck, almost on reflex. She peeked around, trying to watch them.

". . . I heard that last semester Mrs. Princeton went crazy with favoritism," Samantha was saying. "She actually got down on her knees beside Amy Lyle's desk to tell her that it was an *honor* to read her research paper. Like, in front of the whole class."

"I can tell she plays favorites," Chance replied, fishing his car keys out of his pocket. He looked good in the afternoon sun; it brought out the highlights in his hair. "I can't stand those corny jokes she makes."

Samantha laughed, reaching out to place a hand on Chance's upper arm. Jenny felt something unpleasant run through her at the sight. *Don't touch him,* she wanted to say.

"Oh God, when she read the prologue to *Canterbury Tales* to us in old English. That was ridiculous. I mean, hello, it's American Lit."

"She wanted to show off." Chance shrugged off her hand, turning to unlock his car. "I'm not looking forward to working on that research paper. I mean, what even is an annotated bibliography, and why are we only learning about it now?"

"I'm sure you'll do fine. I'm the one who's going to fail."

Chance turned to look at her, a slight smile at his lips. "You shouldn't sell yourself short, Samantha. I was in your class last year. I remember how you schooled the rest of the class when you recited that speech from *Julius Caesar*. Everyone else was struggling to remember even one line, and you knew them all."

"I wasn't *that* good," Samantha said sheepishly, looking down at her feet.

Chance playfully bumped her shoulder with his. "Oh, c'mon, yes you were. I only memorized the first few lines and then skipped to the end of my speech. You, on the other hand, were amazing."

"Do you want to go out sometime?" Samantha asked bluntly, looking up.

Neither Chance nor Jenny had expected that. "What?" Chance asked, surprised.

"You and me, and my parents' hot tub." Jenny could tell that Samantha was standing so her chest stuck out, but she doubted Chance caught that. "Possibly this weekend?"

"Sure," Chance said, scratching the back of his neck. "That would be fun."

"Awesome!" The girl lit up, even jumping a bit in excitement. "Here's my number." She listed off her digits for Chance to copy into his phone. "We can shoot for Saturday, maybe?"

"Sure, Samantha," Chance responded distractedly. His eyes were already flickering around the parking lot, looking for something.

Looking for you, a voice in the back of Jenny's head whispered.

Samantha trounced off happily, a bit of a skip in her step. Jenny waited until she was out of sight before stepping out from behind the truck.

Wow. Is it always like this? she wondered. Did people just throw themselves at him while he nonchalantly accepted? Was this what dating looked like?

She found that she didn't like it much. She thought of Samantha sitting in the passenger's seat of Chance's car, pulling down the visor and scrubbing away Jenny's lip print so that she could leave her own.

"Jenny!" Chance's voice broke through her thoughts. He had finally spotted her by the muddy truck. "Have you been waiting long?"

"Nope," she told him, trying to act like she hadn't been hiding. "I just got here."

She settled into his car and flipped the visor down, pretending to check her hair, but really checking to see if the lip print was there—it was. She still couldn't believe she had been brazen enough to leave it. There was something so relaxing about Chance's car. It felt safe and familiar, a rarity for her. She could easily envision helping Chance pick it out. It was exactly the kind of car she would've gotten herself: something with character. This car obviously had a history. Jenny could make it up as easily as she did hers with Chance.

"Where are we going?" she asked as he started the engine.

"It's a secret," he said cryptically.

"Like a 'fun surprise party' secret or an 'I'm going to murder you in the middle of the woods and dump your body at a truck stop' secret?"

Chance burst out laughing. "The first one," he assured her.

She eyed him skeptically. "That's exactly what someone who was going to murder me would say."

"I'm not going to murder you, Little Miss Really-Likes-Having-As."

They pulled out of the parking lot, and she looked longingly at the park across the street. She wished they could just go there and play pretend again. She wondered how different things would've been if she had just caught Chance playing Neverland once when they were younger. He had looked so genuine when he told her about that. The sun had lit up his features, making his hair look almost like a halo around his head. He had this look on his face; she couldn't quite make out what it was. She wished that she had something like that to share with him, but she didn't. She had almost made something up, but she felt that right then was the time for truth. Only, she had no truth to share.

"Can we take a detour first?" she asked, remembering her mother's text. She felt odd asking a favor, but it was better to get it over with.

"Where to?"

"My mother wants me to pick up paper towels. I figured we should do it before I forget."

"That's fine," he said, turning toward town. "We can hit Dollar General. There's one kind of on the way."

Jenny found the silence oppressive. Her fingers itched to touch the radio dial and to fill the car with Top 40, but she resisted. It was Chance's car; if he wanted music on, then he'd play it. So they rode in silence. *I bet he's thinking about Samantha. He probably hasn't even noticed the silence. I know I'm overanalyzing the situation, but I can't stop.*

Finally, they pulled up to the familiar Dollar General building, its big yellow sign glowing even in the daylight. Chance followed her out of the car without a word. *Is he still thinking about Samantha?* Jenny wondered, unsure of why she even cared.

The air in the store was cold and stale, like always. The lady working behind the counter eyed them suspiciously as they came in. No one in a bright yellow polyester vest had the right to look that judgmental.

"I think they're back here," Jenny said to fill the silence, pointing toward the back of the store.

Chance nodded, following her.

Does he think I'm lame? Jenny thought desperately. *Why do I even leave my house? This is why I don't hang out with people outside of school!*

"Do you need anything while we're here?" she asked.

"Nah." Chance shook his head.

Jenny pulled a random roll of paper towels off the shelf. She didn't know what to say. She had to do something—anything!

"Oh my God," Chance said. He reached past her, pulling a camouflage print flashlight off the shelf behind her. "Isn't the point of camo to *not* be seen?"

"I don't know what you're talking about," Jenny said jokingly, relieved to have the silence finally broken. "I can't even see what you're holding. It just blends into the background perfectly."

"Oh sure." Chance put the flashlight back on the shelf.

Jenny spotted a package of baby-pink-camo-printed batteries on another shelf and picked them up. "This is the worst idea ever! How will I ever find my batteries when they're camouflaged so perfectly?"

"You're missing the point," Chance told her, taking the package from her hands. He put on a southern accent. "These are camouflaged so those city slickers can't find and take all your batteries."

"Ooh, of course," she said, slapping her hand to her forehead. "How could I have been so dumb?"

They both laughed, and Jenny finally felt at ease. *There's no reason to freak out,* she told herself. *We're going to be fine.* Chance put the batteries back as Jenny rounded the corner, looking for more horrendous camouflaged products.

That's when she saw it. She was looking around for something even dumber than camo batteries—like camo wrapping paper—when her eyes landed on the bargain bin. Not just that, though, but a small black object sitting in it. She reached in, drawing the object out. It was a pirate hat, clearly left over from the *Pirates of the Caribbean* merchandise boom years prior. It was a triangle-shaped thing, and the white skull and crossbones that had once decorated it had faded long ago, leaving only a ghost of the original design.

She thought back to the park, to the swing set, to Neverland. It was perfect. "What do you think?" Jenny turned to face him, placing the thing on her head. "Does it suit me? Tell me, hads't thou ever wanted to be a pirate?"

"I was never the Captain Hook type. I was a Lost Boy, remember?"

"Whatever," Jenny sighed, pulling the hat from her head and tossing it back in the bin. "I guess you're right. Let's go."

They were halfway out the door when Chance stopped her.

"I changed my mind," he said, handing her his keys. "I need to get something after all. I'll be out to the car in a moment."

"Oh, okay," she said. She sat in his car for a few minutes. Maybe he was inside calling that Samantha girl to come get him right now, and Jenny would have to drive his car home.

It was five minutes before Chance reappeared, a small yellow bag in hand.

"What did you get?" Jenny asked curiously.

Chance wordlessly took the object out of the bag and tossed it into her lap. Jenny stared down at it for a moment, then smiled, lifting the pirate hat and placing it on her head.

CHAPTER 6

Chance

Chance didn't intend to buy that stupid pirate hat, he really didn't. It was old and had that weird Dollar General smell to it. But Jenny had looked so adorable staring up at him with it on her head, her expression hopeful. He couldn't shake that image. So he bought her the damn hat.

She wore it the whole drive to the old barn.

The first time Chance had ever seen the barn was permanently etched into his mind. He had been ten, and Levi had just gotten his license. Their parents were having one of their worst fights to date—Chance couldn't even remember what it had been about—and he'd locked himself in his room, afraid. Levi had come home from hanging out with his friends, had taken one look at the situation, and had taken Chance for a drive.

Levi was so much older and so much cooler than Chance. He remembered how excited he had felt just to be included in anything his brother did. Levi had found the barn while dicking around with his friends, he said. It was his secret but he wanted to share it with Chance. Soon Levi took him there every time their parents fought. They logged more time at the barn than they did at home.

Then they stopped. Their parents still fought, but Levi had quit coming home altogether. Then he'd left. The first thing Chance did after he got his license was drive straight to the old barn. That's when he discovered that Levi had still used it—for dates, parties, and sleepovers. He hadn't stopped going, he'd just stopped taking Chance.

Chance hadn't been there since. It seemed tainted—all he could think about was how many nights he'd spent wishing for his brother to come home. But the moment he thought of hanging out with Jenny, he could only picture them in that stupid barn.

It had been his safe place once before. Maybe it could be again.

Only, he wanted to keep it a surprise. Jenny didn't seem like the type who would willingly go hang out at an old barn.

She didn't talk much. He wanted to turn on the radio, but he felt like she would prefer silent drives. She seemed to stare thoughtfully out of the window the whole time. That was all right, though. He could endure silence if it was what she liked.

"We're almost there," he told her as he took a right.

"We're in the middle of nowhere," she told him. "I thought you said you *weren't* going to murder me."

"I'm not going to murder you, Scout's Honor." He held up his right hand.

"I doubt you were ever a Boy Scout."

"True, but it still counts." He could see the barn now, looming on the horizon. He parked, killing the car. "This place is a secret," he told her. "I'm letting you in on it."

She looked out the windshield, less than thrilled. "Thank you for sharing your run-down barn with me."

"It's better up close, I promise."

It was tall, with two doors and a broken wood beam once used as a latch. It had two large windows on the front, and through them Chance could see sunlight streaming in through the holes in the roof.

Jenny got out of the car, slowly approaching the place. "It has . . . charm," she said hesitantly. She pushed the door open, struggling under its weight. "What's its story?"

He followed her inside. "My brother and I found it as kids. I haven't been here in forever, but he used it to have parties and stuff."

She made a face, obviously displeased. "We can do better than that."

It was big. It was open, with a tiny wooden table sitting toward the back, and scattered hay all along the floor. There was a black trunk behind the ladder that led up to the loft. A few of the rafters looked rather shifty, and Chance could hear birds cooing somewhere in the ceiling. The light spilled in in random patches, some of it leaking in through gaps between the wall panels.

Chance watched Jenny wander around, inspecting every inch of the barn. She looked under the small wooden table. She tested her weight on the loft ladder. She looked over everything in her methodical Jenny way. Finally, when she was finished, she ran to the middle of the floor and spread her arms wide, spinning in a circle. "I love it!" she cried. "What do we do here?"

Chance wished more than anything that he could see this place through Jenny's eyes. All he saw were visions of his brother and his friends smoking around the table, playing Cards Against Humanity.

"Hang out, I guess? We go here whenever we need to get away."

He walked up, taking the pirate hat from her. The material was surprisingly rough in his hands. This thing must've sat in that bin for years. "I think we should leave this here," he told her. He placed it on his head because he knew it'd make her smile. "It'll be our thing when we're here."

"Like a tradition." She smiled. "But where will we keep it? We can't just hang it on a loose wall panel."

She had a point. Chance looked around until he spotted the trunk under the loft. "There." He pointed.

It was a black leather thing, with big clunky silver hinges. Chance had no idea where his brother had gotten it. It looked too nice for anything their parents ever bought them. He opened it, surprised to find it wasn't empty. There were a few T-shirts—all Levi's—and about three pairs of lacy underwear—definitely *not* Levi's. There was also a half-empty bottle of Absolut. "Looks like Levi left us a present," Chance said, lifting the bottle. The clear liquid sloshed around noisily.

Jenny eyed the bottle warily. "I've never drank before," she admitted.

"Wait, really?" Chance asked. "You're like, what, seventeen?"

She nodded. "Just turned in July."

"And you've never drank." Chance had had his first drink at twelve. His father had tricked him into drinking some of his beer because his work friends thought it was hilarious. It had been disgusting.

"It never held much interest for me," Jenny explained sheepishly. "It's not like I can knock back shots of tequila while studying for the

ACTs." She thought about it for a moment. "Well, I guess I could, but it wouldn't be very productive."

"Do you want to drink sometime?"

She considered it. "Sure. I mean, it always looks so fun on TV. Besides, my high school career would be a waste if I didn't get wasted at least once."

"I wouldn't say it'd be a complete waste," Chance said. He started to add, "You met me," but stopped himself. *That's dumb. Don't be dumb.* "You don't have to if you don't want to. It's okay not to drink. But we can drink sometime if you do want to. How about Saturday?"

She paused. "I guess that works," she said. She lowered herself to the ground, sitting in the hay. "So this is your spot, huh?" she asked suddenly, fixing him with a serious look.

He sat cross-legged in front of her, absentmindedly putting the pirate hat back on. "What?"

"This place, this barn, it's your spot, right?"

He looked around, taking in the way the light trickled in, casting half the barn into intricate shadows. "I guess it's all right," he said honestly. "It smells like hay."

"Oh wow, how insightful of you, Masters."

"It reminds me of my brother. I don't know how I feel about my brother right now. It's complicated." The words spilled out and he couldn't stop them. "He would use this place whenever he didn't want to be home. I don't want to see it that way."

Jenny cocked her head to the side curiously, almost like a bird. "How do you want to see it?"

"The way you do." He wanted this place to be their fun getaway spot. He wanted to have found it with her—to have discovered its secrets with her. He didn't want to be the kind of person who needed a getaway. He wanted to have that sense of wonder he saw in her eyes sometimes. Jenny was the type of person who looked at this dump and saw potential. Chance wanted that.

She laughed nervously, averting her gaze. "There's nothing special about how I see this place."

"You see it the way Levi did," he told her.

Her eyes snapped back to him. "I remind you of your brother?"

Oh crap. "No, no, that's not what I meant," he hastened to assure her. "He, er, sees everything like it's a story. He sees the wonder in things somehow." Why was he being so candid? *I have to change the subject.* He reached up to run a frustrated hand through his hair, only to end up knocking the hat off instead. *The pirate hat,* he thought, looking down at the thing. He had forgotten all about it. He picked it up suddenly, thrusting it toward Jenny. "Your turn."

"Wh-what?" she stuttered, startled.

He pushed the hat into her hands. "I wore it, and I shared something. Now it's your turn."

She took it, reluctantly putting it on. "My turn?"

"Share Time," he explained, making something up on the spot. "It's what we do here at Our Spot. We take turns wearing the pirate hat and sharing things about ourselves. It's our tradition."

"Our Spot?"

He gestured at the room around them. "We discovered it. It's ours, so it's Our Spot."

"And we come here to share our . . . feelings?"

"Yes." He nodded impatiently. "Now it's your turn."

"Um, well." She chewed her lip uncertainly. Chance couldn't help but notice that she looked kind of hot when she did that. "I have really bad breath in the morning?"

He just looked at her. "Even *I* know that's from *Mean Girls*."

She folded her hands in her lap, looking down at them. "I've never had a boyfriend," she told him, not looking up. "I've never even been on a date."

"Why not?"

"I don't know." She wrung her hands together. "It's never interested me much. It's like a thing that, abstractly, I realize people are doing, but it doesn't seem real to me. I don't know how to explain it."

"Do you feel like you're missing out?"

"Not really?" she answered. She wasn't blushing, though she still couldn't meet his eyes. "Like I said, it seems like an abstract concept to me." She paused, seeming to choose her next words carefully. "How are we going to drink Saturday when you told that Samantha girl you'd hang out that day?"

That was the last thing he expected. "What?" he asked, trying to figure out what she was talking about. What did Samantha have to do with anything? He had forgotten all about that. "How do you know about that?"

She finally looked at him then, her green eyes unreadable. "I was walking up when she asked you. I decided to wait until she was gone to say anything."

Chance felt guilty, and he wasn't sure why. He was single. He was allowed to talk to other girls. But he didn't even *want* to go out with Samantha, especially if it would cause Jenny to make that disappointed face. "I'd forgotten that I'd already made plans with my best friend."

"You'd give up your date for me?" He nodded, leaning even closer.

Her phone went off then, and they both jumped back. She pulled it out, making a face as she checked the screen. "It's my alarm," she told him. "It's getting close to dinnertime."

"Do you need to go back?" He didn't want her to leave. He wanted her to look at him again and maybe bite her lip some more.

"Yeah, my mom always wants us together for dinner. It's family time."

That must be nice, he thought bitterly. "Let's get going, then."

He kept looking back at Their Spot as he left, stealing glances in his rearview mirror. He watched it grow smaller and smaller, the peace he had felt there rapidly fading away. He wanted to capture that feeling— to bottle it up. It could be their place of refuge in a town full of dead ends.

JENNY HAD A nice house. It wasn't a mansion or anything, but it was two stories and white with green shutters and trim—everything a happy family should have.

"Do you want to come in for a second?" Jenny asked excitedly.

"But your parents are home," he protested. Girls didn't typically ask him in when their parents were home.

"My mom is," Jenny corrected offhandedly. She reached out, squeezing his forearm. "Let's go."

He looked down at where their skin met, feeling warm all of a sudden. They hadn't really touched before, had they? At least not skin to skin. "Okay," he found himself agreeing.

Her house looked just as cozy on the inside as it did on the outside. There was a foyer that sported a small end table and a staircase. There was a cute area rug lying in front of the bottom stairs, and a few pictures hung along the stairwell. Chance couldn't help but notice that there wasn't a man in any of those photos. The living room, which Jenny sauntered into the moment she entered, was to the left, with a big armchair right by the entrance. Chance followed her, taking note of the long beige couch and a toy box in the corner of the room.

"This is obviously the living room," Jenny said. "That couch there is where I sit and marathon countless hours of *Buffy the Vampire Slayer*. That end table next to it sports the phone that is never for me. That toy box is what my little sister, Jessa, plays with during the day." Jenny pointed to each object, using a tour-guide voice as she explained everything.

Next, Jenny led him into the kitchen/dining room, which was divided by a counter in the middle. Everything on the kitchen side was sleek and shiny, while the dining room held only a large wooden table. A slender woman sat at the table, an array of what looked like bills in front of her. She had long, curly brown hair like Jenny's, but thinner. She looked up when they entered.

"Oh, hello."

Jenny ignored her. "That counter is where I sit with my laptop and stare wistfully out into the backyard, wishing for the world to end. That table over there is where I occasionally stuff my face. Also, that woman sitting at it gave birth to me."

"Jennifer, what are you doing?" the woman asked. A small smile played at her lips. She couldn't take her eyes off Chance. He was used to this. He was exactly the type of boy parents were wary to have in their daughters' rooms. He wondered if she thought he had ulterior motives.

"I'm giving Chance the tour, Mom," Jenny answered.

Jenny's mother's eyes kept flashing from him to her daughter and back again. "And would Chance like to stay for dinner? We're ordering tacos."

He did want to stay. He almost agreed before he stopped himself. "I can't—" he began, but Jenny cut him off.

"That would be cool," she said, turning to look at Chance hopefully. "I've never had a friend over for dinner before."

That took him aback. *Never?* Even he'd had at least one or two people over, when he was younger. Of course, that was when his parents were still embarrassed to fight in front of other people.

Jenny reached out, grabbing his sleeve. "I can finish giving you the tour while Mom orders the food."

Before he knew what was happening, he was being swept from the room and pulled upstairs. They were only halfway up when Jenny's mother called them back down again. *There it is,* Chance thought. *She's uncomfortable with me.*

"Jennifer," she said, looking amused, as if she couldn't quite believe what was happening. "Can you wake Jessa from her nap while you're up there? Get her washed up for dinner."

Jenny made a face. "Can't Jack do it?" She gestured to Chance. "I obviously have a guest."

Her mother just fixed her with a look.

"Fine," Jenny agreed. "I'll do it, but I'm going to complain the entire time. Loudly, so it'll drift all the way down here and you'll have to listen to it."

Her mother waved her off. "And I will be doing work with my headphones in so I can't hear you."

The upstairs hallway was pale blue with white trim; Chance counted five doors. "That down there is my brother Jack's room," Jenny explained, pointing to a door decorated with Minecraft posters. "He's twelve and he is a nightmare."

"Twelve-year-old boys often are," Chance said, remembering himself at twelve.

The next door had pastel-yellow flowers painted on it and a scribbled drawing of a fairy taped to it. The fairy and most of the page were nothing but dark purple. "This is Jessa's room. Jessa hasn't learned how to color within the lines yet," Jenny said. "She's four."

"That's my mom's room." She pointed to a plain white door. "That one is the bathroom. It's not too bad; there's one downstairs, too, so at least I don't always have to share with Jack."

There was only one room left, with a plain white door just like her mother's. The only bit of decoration on it was an old medal hanging from the door handle. "Fifth-grade Quiz Bowl championship," Jenny supplied at his questioning look. "We used to have a cat, and she'd sneak in my room at night. I started hanging the medal there so I'd hear her come in." Sure enough, it clanked against the door as she pushed it open.

"You have a cat?" Chance asked, looking around.

Jenny's look soured. "We *used* to. Dad took her when he moved. She was technically his, anyway."

Jenny's room was simple, with peach walls and very few posters. There was a white bookshelf in the corner by the window, its shelves sagging under the weight of all the books she had piled on it. She had a white desk with a vanity mirror over it on one side of the room and a twin-sized bed on the other. The bed had a white-painted metal frame that twisted up into an elaborate headboard and footboard, with posts at the corners. The paint was peeling off in places, revealing the metal underneath.

"What do you think?" Jenny asked nervously, gesturing around.

Chance looked from her to the headboard and back again. "You have a princess bed," he said, amused.

"I do not," Jenny said, moving to stand next to him. She gestured to the bed. "If I had a princess bed, then I would have a canopy. Which, trust me, I begged for."

The room was Jenny. The room was nights spent studying and days spent reading. The room was the way she bit her lip and the snort that escaped when she laughed too hard. The room was another little thing, another step he'd taken in getting to know her.

"Jennifer!" her mother called up the stairs. "I don't hear any complaining, and dinner will be here soon! Jessa isn't going to get herself up!"

Jenny moved toward the door. "We should go," she said.

Jessa's room was dark but she wasn't asleep. She sat in the middle of her floor in a fairy costume, scribbling away in her coloring book.

"Jessa, honey, it's time for dinner," Jenny said in a soothing voice, approaching the girl with caution.

The little girl looked at her older sister and stuck out her tongue. "No!"

"Come on, I know you're hungry." Jenny reached for her, but the girl was too quick. She was up and running around her sister before Jenny had time to move. "Come back here. We have to wash your hands."

The little girl ran faster and crashed into Chance, who she hadn't seen in the dark room, and fell backward onto the floor.

Both Jenny and Chance held their breath, waiting for her to cry. But it didn't happen. Instead the little girl looked up at Chance, her eyes the same green as her sister's, and pointed one pudgy finger at his face, yelling, "Pwetty!"

Chance looked down at her, confused. "What is she saying?" he asked Jenny, but Jenny was doubled over laughing as Jessa kept pointing and shouting, "Pwetty!" over and over.

Finally, the little girl thrust both her arms in the air, exclaiming, "Up!"

"What do I do?" Chance asked frantically.

"She wants you to pick her up," Jenny managed between giggles.

"But I don't want to!"

"You don't have a choice in the matter, Chance."

Jenny was still laughing about the incident as they made their way downstairs, Chance carrying Jessa on his hip. She had her chubby arms wrapped around his neck. Jenny's mother was already at the table, a box of tacos in front of her and a brown-haired boy sitting beside her. Both their mouths dropped open at the sight of the three on the stairs.

"But Jessa never likes anybody!" Jenny's mom exclaimed, rushing over to take her daughter from Chance. "I can't believe this," she added as Jessa strained to go back to Chance, once again exclaiming, "Pwetty!"

The place was chaotic and loud, as Jessa perched on her booster seat and Chance took a seat across from Jack. Jenny sat between Chance and her mother. They kept the conversation light, and jokes were shared often. Chance felt odd as he helped himself to a second taco, watching the family around him. He had never had this warmth. He had never sat at the table and eaten with his family. His parents ate in their room or the living room, while they made the kids eat at the table. He didn't know families actually had dinners like this, where parents asked about the kids' day and genuinely seemed to care. They included him, too. Her mother asked him about himself, seeming interested in his answers. Jessa kept getting his attention by throwing handfuls of hamburger meat across the table, and Jack didn't seem to totally hate him.

He wanted this. He wanted this scene—Jenny's mom scrubbing sauce from Jessa's face as Jenny laughed loudly and freely at something her brother had said—etched into his memory always. Maybe he could pull it out and think about it when he faced the coldness back home.

CHAPTER 7

Jenny

J enny had never felt this excited before. She was practically bouncing in her seat as Chance drove them out of town. She watched as the blur of houses out the car window slowly became a blur of fields, all blending together. She reached out to the radio, switching it on. She wanted a soundtrack for this.

"You can change the station, if you want," Chance told her. He had his window down, and the wind was blowing his blond hair everywhere. For a second, Jenny considered reaching out and running her hands through it. She had a feeling it would be soft to the touch and slide smoothly through her fingers.

"This is fine," she told him, turning back toward the window.

She, Jenny Wessler, perfect girl and daughter, was going to drink tonight. Not only that, but she had lied to her mother about going to drink tonight. She had stood in front of her mother, wearing her favorite pink tank top and cutoff shorts, and told her that she was spending the night at Kelsey's. She had walked out the door, smiling wide, pretending to walk to Kelsey's, while really going down the street to meet Chance. She was going to drink, she had lied to her mother, and she was *spending the night with a boy.* It was just Chance, but *still.*

If this was what teenage rebellion felt like, then it felt fucking fantastic.

She wasn't even nervous about spending the night with Chance. Things had been great since she showed him her house. That had marked the turning point for her. She was able to successfully blend their school relationship and her home life. He had stood in her house and met her family, and had become part of her world. She could easily envision him there now, always coming over after school for snacks or *Buffy.* It had been so easy to lock the two worlds together. Why had she been so scared?

If life were a teen movie, then this would be the scene where everything changed. They turned down the narrow road that led to Their Spot, and Jenny could feel her heart hammering in her chest. She could hear the random assortment of beer bottles clanking in the back as the car bobbed and weaved down the road.

"You seem happy," Chance remarked, sounding amused.

"I'm excited!" she told him happily. It was like her nerve endings were all on fire with anticipation. "I guess it seems stupid, but I've never done anything like this before."

"It's cute," he told her, smiling. "I'm glad you're excited."

Chance pulled up to the barn then, big and imposing in the setting sun. It looked just as interesting as it had the first time he showed it to her. Jenny had been wary at first because, y'know, it was a big barn in the middle of nowhere. That had changed when she stepped inside, though. It had *character.* People on TV shows always had strange places they hung out—tree houses, laundromats, hotel lobbies—and Jenny realized that this could be that place for her and Chance. She could have all the quirks she'd always wanted. When she looked at the barn, she saw possibility, and it was amazing.

She hoped that Chance saw it, too.

Chance leaned over his seat, digging in the back. He pulled a beer out of the plastic bag he had put them in, presenting it to her with a flourish. "For you," he said.

She took the thing, the glass cold against her skin. It was already covered in condensation. The bottle felt slippery in her hands. "How did you get this, again?" she asked.

Chance smiled mysteriously. "I have my ways."

She leveled him with a look.

"Fine, Drake's bandmate Nick is old enough. I got him to buy us some."

"Why did we need beer anyway?" she asked, looking down at the bottle cap. Was it a twist top? She didn't want to embarrass herself trying to twist it off if it wasn't. "I thought there was vodka in the barn."

"There is," he told her. "I thought we should go easy this time. We can always hit the hard liquor another time."

He took the bottle from her, popping the top off before handing it back to her. She grabbed it by the neck, but it was so slippery with condensation that it slipped right through her grip and crashed to the floorboard with a hearty *thud*.

"Shit!" Jenny exclaimed as the cold liquid splashed over her Converse, soaking them through. She hastily picked up the bottle, embarrassed. She was pretty sure her face was the color of cherry tomatoes at the moment. "I'm so sorry," she mumbled, shoving the bottle into the cup holder. She drew some napkins out of her purse and began blotting at the spill. She could already see the slightly darker stain setting into his floor mat.

I was doing so well, too, she thought sadly.

Chance, to her surprise, burst out laughing. It wasn't a slight, polite laugh, either, but a big, hearty guffaw. He didn't even look concerned that she had just stained his car. All he did was throw his head back and laugh.

"You don't have to laugh at me," Jenny said defensively. She was still trying to blot out the stain.

"I'm sorry," Chance said, but he kept laughing. "You looked so utterly upset when that beer fell. It was hilarious."

"I'm glad my mistakes amuse you" was her sarcastic reply.

"Jenny," he said, reaching out to pull her up. His hand felt strong wrapped around her upper arm. "I don't care if it stains."

"Really?"

"Look at this car, it's a mess." He looked down at the setting stain. "Besides, doesn't it just give it more character?"

She had a sneaking suspicion that he had used her buzzword on purpose, but she smiled anyway. "I guess" was all she said.

"C'mon," he said. "Let's go."

They had packed as many light sources as they could. Between them, they had two battery-operated lanterns, three flashlights, five touch lights, a bunch of candles, and a bag full of glow-in-the-dark stick-on stars. They each set to work spreading the lights out as much as they could over the floor of the barn, making sure none of the candles touched the scattered hay. The last rays of the sunset poured in through the gaps in the roof, casting an orange-red glow over them as they worked.

Next, they unpacked their sleeping bags. They had packed as many blankets and pillows as they could without seeming suspicious. They built a giant pallet by the wooden table, trying to make it as comfortable as possible. Jenny walked around, throwing handfuls of the glow-in-the-dark stars like a flower girl walking down the aisle.

"You ready to try again?" Chance asked, setting the beer-filled bag onto the table with a *clank*. He pulled out another bottle and opened it for her. She realized in that moment, as he reached out offering her the bottle, that there was no one else she would rather be with. The growing moonlight was spilling in and fell right on him, reflecting off the bottle he held out. She took it from him, her fingers accidentally brushing his.

He watched her expectantly as she took her first sip and seemed amused when she blanched. It was bitter, and she couldn't hide her disgust.

"I thought beer was supposed to be good?" she asked, looking down at the bottle in her hand as if it had slaughtered her family.

"Expensive beer is," he corrected her. "That in your hand is cheap beer. Or, as I affectionately call it, Shit Beer."

"I think I'd rather try the vodka."

"It tastes even worse," he warned her.

"If alcohol is so gross, then why do people even drink?" And yet she took another disgusting sip.

"The more you drink, the better it tastes."

Another sip. "I'm going to have to drink a lot, then."

"Don't overdo it," he told her. "You'll get sick."

She walked over to the trunk as he opened himself a bottle. She took out the pirate hat and put it on. She loved the stupid thing. It made her so happy that Chance embraced it. She turned back to face him, gesturing to the hat. "Guess what time it is?"

"Adventure time?"

"Guess again."

He plopped onto the floor, taking a long swig from his beer. "Share Time?"

She giddily rushed to the pallet, sitting cross-legged in front of him. "Correct." She took another sip.

"You go first," he said.

She bit her lip as she thought of what to say. She didn't want to admit anything too personal right off the bat. They had to ease into that.

"When I was little, I used to get in trouble on purpose so that I was forced to sit out at recess and read in the classroom."

Chance let out a bark of laughter. "That figures," he said, swiping the hat from her head. "Take a drink," he told her. "New rule: Take a drink every time you share."

She did so.

"Hmmm." Chance stroked his chin, pretending to look thoughtful. "My favorite color is blue-green." He took a sip.

"Boooo," Jenny cried, taking the pirate hat back. "That was a lame reveal."

"We never said they had to be deep soul-baring secrets. We're just supposed to share something."

"I still think that's cheating," Jenny huffed. The flickering light from the nearest candle danced over Chance's face, highlighting the sharp planes of his features. Jenny wanted to reach out and trace those angles. She wanted to drag her fingertips along that jawline. The intensity of her want caught her off guard.

"It's your turn," he prompted.

"Um . . . I hate sports. Like, all sports. And any form of exercise. I wish I was the type who could go for morning runs or do Zumba or something, but I have no drive and cardio makes me sneeze."

"It makes you sneeze?"

She nodded, taking another drink. She offered him the hat. "Your turn."

He put it on, looking thoughtful. "I had my first girlfriend at thirteen. She was a redhead named Loralai and she wore skirts over her jeans. It didn't last long."

"She wore skirts over her jeans?"

He nodded solemnly. "I'm talking schoolgirl skirts pulled over ripped jeans. It was not a pretty sight, but the heart wants what the heart wants."

She took the hat back as he took his drink. "I've never had a boyfriend," she said.

Chance shook his head. "No, we already shared that. You can't re-share."

"Can too."

"Cannot. New rule: No re-sharing."

"How come you're the only one who can make up new rules?"

"Because I'm the one who came up with the game, remember? Now, go again."

She looked down at her half-empty bottle, sloshing the liquid around. "I've never been kissed."

He was so silent that she feared he had nodded off in the dim lighting. She looked up, blushing slightly when her eyes met his. He was staring at her, quiet as a mouse. She couldn't read his expression in the candlelight.

She took another drink. "You can laugh now," she told him.

"I'm not going to laugh," he said softly.

"Why not? It's pathetic, right? I'm seventeen and I've never drank and I've never had a boyfriend or been kissed." The funny thing was, she had never felt pathetic until she had seen Samantha ask him out. Ever since then, the feeling had been eating away at the back of her mind.

"It's not pathetic," Chance said. "Everyone moves at their own pace."

"I never felt like I was missing out on anything before," she went on, taking another swig. "Then all of a sudden it's like I finally woke up and realized that people around me are *living*. They're not sitting at home like I always am, doing homework. They're out there with friends and going on dates. Everything still felt like elementary school to me, where you say good-bye to your friends after the final bell and don't see them again until the next morning. Where the boy who sits by you in class is your 'boyfriend' because he passed you a note and sometimes holds your hand, but you don't actually have dates or kiss. It never actually struck me as *real*."

He watched her, not saying a word. She didn't even feel self-conscious as she tipped up the bottle and gulped down the rest of her beer. "Can I have another?"

He gulped the rest of his down, too, getting them both another one. It was his turn with the hat.

"Uh, well, I . . ." He trailed off, looking at her curiously. "My parents fight constantly," he finally blurted out. "I'm talking twenty-four/seven yelling and screaming. My home is hell, Jenny. I can barely even stand to be there."

She hadn't seen this coming. She stared at him in shock as he downed a good portion of his beer. Had she spurred this honesty on with her own outburst? She felt like she owed him her own chunk of personal information in exchange for what he had just given her.

"My father left my mother for a twenty-something-year-old pharmacist," she told him. She, too, took a long drink.

"Jenny, you're not even wearing the hat right now."

She took it from him, placing it haphazardly on her head. "My mother was pregnant when it happened. He left her while she was pregnant."

"Wow," he said. "What an asshole. I mean, I know he's your father, but—"

"No, you're right. He's an asshole." She passed the hat back to Chance.

"I'm afraid my parents are going to turn their anger on me. Levi's been gone a long time and I *know* it's coming," Chance admitted once he had the hat on. "My brother and I weren't close, but at least there were two of us. He hasn't even visited since he left, and the calls stopped a while back."

Back to her. "My mother is starting to date again, and I feel awful about it. Not because she's dating, but because I'm not."

Back to him. "I wish they'd just get divorced. Maybe then we would have a chance to be normal."

Her. "My parents getting divorced was the worst thing I've ever gone through."

Him. "My parents' marriage is the worst thing I've ever gone through."

They both tossed their now-empty bottles aside, opening their thirds. Jenny took the hat once more, her hand shaking slightly as she put it on. She could feel her edges getting fuzzy. Was this what getting drunk was like?

"If things get bad at your house, you can always hang out at mine. You can come over whenever you want. You can stay as long as you want. You don't have to go through things alone, Chance."

"Neither do you," he told her.

She wanted to kiss him. The feeling came from somewhere deep inside her, bubbling to the surface as her eyes traced the shape of his lips in the lantern light. She wanted to kiss Chance Masters, and maybe one day she would, but she knew this wasn't the time. Instead, she lurched forward, throwing her arm around his middle and burying her head in his shoulder.

"We don't have to be alone," she whispered into the fabric of his shirt.

They fell asleep that way, arms around each other, breathing shallow. The candles slowly burned out and the batteries in the lanterns eventually sputtered and died. The one time Jenny woke up during the night, the only light left was that of the glow-in-the-dark stars. She could barely make out the shape of Chance's jaw above her head. She closed her eyes tight and burrowed deeper into his embrace.

She wasn't exactly sure what had changed, but she knew that nothing would be the same after that night.

CHAPTER 8

Chance

Everything had changed. The next morning, Chance woke up completely disoriented for a few seconds, his limbs tangled up with Jenny's.

What happened? Why are we cuddling? Did we—?

Then the memories of the night before came flooding back. He looked over to see her still lying there beside him, her own eyes open as well.

"Good morning," she said in a voice so quiet it didn't even disturb the birds in the rafters.

Dear lord, did he want to kiss her then. There she was lying next to him, her hair fanned out behind her, her perfect little nose almost touching his. He wanted to reach out, cup her face, and bring their lips together. If it was any other girl in any other circumstance, he probably would have. But it wasn't—it was Jenny. Jenny, who had opened up and shared herself with him, too, and it didn't feel right to make a move. So instead he sat up, wishing her good morning as well.

He took her back home and as he watched her sneak into her house, he decided to put the whole thing behind him. But for the entire next week, all he could think about was slamming her against the nearest locker and kissing her soundly, which was pretty distracting—especially during Oral Comm. How was he supposed to listen to Mrs. Tanner when Jenny kept chewing on the top of her pen like that?

He had told her so much about himself. The damn pirate hat must've really been magic or something. He couldn't risk ruining such a good thing by making a move on her. If he did, then he'd be stuck with no one again.

They hadn't been back to the barn since that night, but he was dying to go again. He started going to her house after school most days. There was this pocket of time where her mother was still at work and her siblings were still at the sitter's, when it was just the two of them in her big empty house. God, that drove him crazy.

It was two weeks before Halloween, and midterms were quickly approaching. Chance was falling into the apathy that he typically lived in during the school year.

"Hey." Jenny leaned over and whispered before Oral Comm class. She'd worn her hair down for once, and all he wanted to do was bury his hands in it and drag her lips to his. "Do you want to help me baby-sit after school tomorrow? My mom's got a date."

"I figured I was coming over anyway," he whispered back.

Mrs. Tanner called the class to order then, and Jenny wouldn't speak out of turn in class. They had some kind of "My Plan for the Future" speech coming up. Chance wasn't looking forward to that at all. He didn't know what his future plans were.

AFTER CLASS, CHANCE and Jenny fell into their routine, walking to lunch arm-in-arm.

"She was singing, Chance. Straight up singing happily. It was sickeningly adorable. I've never seen my mother this happy."

"That's good, isn't it?"

"Of course, but it's *weird.* She's acting like a teenager in love."

"What do you know about teenagers in love?"

"I've seen the movies. I know what to expect."

Lunch was the same as always. Emelia talked about something new her niece had done, and Leslie listened. Kelsey sat beside Chance, not really acknowledging him. He got the feeling she didn't like him but he still had no clue why. He'd asked Jenny once, but she had told him it was all in his head and that Kelsey merely seemed abrasive at times. It wasn't that, though. He knew that glare was real.

Drake was late to lunch, rushing in nearly halfway through and throwing himself in the chair next to Jenny.

"Where's the fire?" asked Emelia.

Drake ignored her, pulling out his phone and turning toward Jenny. "Nick just texted me the video of last night's performance. Would you like to see some of it?"

"Sure," Jenny said, scooting closer to him so she could see. "What's this song called?" she asked after a few minutes.

"Untitled," Drake told her. "At least for now. I'm sure I'll find inspiration to name it sometime."

That is so lame, Chance thought bitterly as Drake nonchalantly draped an arm behind Jenny's chair, pulling her closer so she could see better. He could see both Emelia and Leslie craning their necks to watch the video, too. What kind of magic spell did singer/songwriters cast? He cut his eyes away, catching Kelsey wearing a matching look of disgust. At least they agreed on one thing.

After lunch, Chance was waiting for Jenny to pack up, like always, when someone tugged at his elbow.

"Hey, bro, can I talk to you for a sec?" Drake asked.

"I'm supposed to wait for Jenny," Chance said, trying to pull away.

"I know, that's why I want to talk to you." Drake ran a hand through his long sandy-colored hair. He had finally succeeded in getting it to touch his shoulders. Chance knew he had been trying for years.

"About Jenny?" Chance had a sinking feeling in his gut. He could tell he wasn't going to like the direction of this conversation one bit.

"Yeah," Drake said. "She's nice, you know? She always asks about my band and she's actually interested when I show her things. I think she's cute, and I'm planning to ask her to Leslie's Halloween party. I was wondering if, as her best friend and all, you had any pointers?"

Chance was sure his gut had already sunk into the earth's crust and descended into the pits of hell. His gut was probably chilling with Satan right now. "I—I don't know," he said honestly.

Would she? Would Jenny ever give someone like Drake the time of day? She had *told* him that she wasn't interested in those things. *But she's trying to be,* he remembered. It never occurred to him that all this time Jenny had been sitting next to him, she had been sitting next to Drake, too.

"I honestly don't know," he said again. He wanted to warn him off, to tell Drake to back the hell up, but he didn't have a right to do that. Maybe Jenny *did* want to go out with him and wouldn't appreciate

Chance being a territorial asshole and ruining it. She at least had the right to *choose* whether or not she wanted Drake.

"I'm going to ask her," Drake said confidently. "I just thought you would know best."

Chance watched him walk off, head held high. He hated Drake then, and everything he represented. Drake could be the end of the brief friendship of Chance and Jenny. Would their promise that they would go through things together still hold up when she had other options?

"You ready?" Jenny asked, appearing at his elbow. He kept watching Drake.

No, he wasn't ready.

"THIS IS BORING," Chance complained the next day as he buried himself deeper into Jenny's beige couch.

"I asked you. I gave you an option. All you had to say was 'No, Little Miss Really-Likes-Having-As, I don't want to help you babysit,' and you would've been off the hook. But, no, you were all flippant. You don't get to complain now."

Chance fixed her with a stare. "Jenny, I'm booored."

"Ugh!" she exclaimed, flopping down onto the couch beside him. "Well, Jack is old enough to watch himself and all he ever does is play video games anyway. Jessa just sleeps. I don't know what you expect me to do here."

He jutted out his bottom lip in a faux pout. "Entertain me."

Her eyes flittered around, trying to spot something for them to do. "I, uh, dare you to balance those books on your head."

He just stared at her. "What?"

"Come on!" she said, jumping to her feet. "Today is officially the Day of Dares, and I just dared you to do something. Are you going to back out? Are you chicken, Masters?"

He looked from her to the stack of textbooks in question. "I'm not Marty McFly; the chicken thing doesn't work on me."

Now it was her turn to fake a pout. "It'll be fun, Chance. Get off your ass."

"Fine," he grumbled, standing up. He picked up the first book and attempted to balance it on his head. It wobbled precariously but stayed still. He attempted the next one to the same effect. It was the fourth one that ruined everything. It sent his mini book tower careening to the carpet with muffled thuds.

Jenny burst out laughing. "Dude, your head must be weirdly flat under all that hair. I can't even balance two on my head."

"My head is not flat," Chance said defensively. "Besides, it's your turn now. I dare you to . . ." He trailed off, looking around for something. He looked into the kitchen, catching sight of the overgrown backyard through the sliding glass door. "Climb that tree in your backyard."

Jenny looked alarmed. "But I don't go outside. I don't do outside-y things. Besides, we don't cut that grass, not since . . . well, since Dad left."

"That's why it's a dare, Jenny. It gets you to do things you wouldn't normally do."

They went outside, making their way through the high grass to the tree just inside the fence. It wasn't too tall, and it had a few thick, low-hanging branches. Jenny eyed it warily.

"How does one even climb a tree?" she asked.

"You've never done this before?"

"Hello, it's me—I never played outside."

Chance used to climb trees all the time. There was one right in the middle of his front yard. He used to climb it so often when he was younger that his hands had grown calloused. He had liked to climb up and sit there, watching all the houses in the neighborhood. He could see all the normal families shuffling from their cars, their arms full of groceries, or the dads teaching their little girls to ride bikes. He had wished that he could be part of one of the little families he always observed, that one day they'd look up and see him in the tree and tell him to climb down and come to dinner.

"Just grab the lowest branch, brace your foot against the tree, and pull yourself up," he told her.

She did as he said, struggling to pull herself onto the branch. Finally, she made it. "I'm getting you back for this," she warned as she grabbed the next branch, pulling herself up once more.

She plopped herself down on the branch, legs swinging below her. "It's my turn," she told him.

"You're barely even off the ground. That hardly counts."

She picked a walnut off the tree and tossed it at him. "I will throw another one, Chance."

"Fine, what's my dare?"

She pointed to the trampoline on the right side of the yard, by the fence. It looked like an old thing. They had decided that they had spent many summer nights bouncing and laughing, sunbathing and sleeping, but they had never actually gotten on it. Dead leaves curled up on it and the springs squeaked from disuse.

"Get on that."

Chance agreed, grabbing Jenny's hand as he passed, helping her down. "You too," he said, dragging her with him. He hopped up on the edge, releasing her hand to take off his shoes.

Jenny shook her head. "That's a metal death trap. I'm not getting on that. Jackie isn't even allowed on it after last summer."

"And yet you want me on it? Rude." He tossed one shoe to the ground. "How about neither of us jumps? We'll lie out like we used to in our fake past." The other shoe dropped, disappearing into the dying grass.

Finally, she jumped up, kicking off her flats to join him. He crawled toward the middle, then sprawled out on the dead leaves. They were already clinging to his hair like magnets. After a moment, she moved to lie with him.

"How is this a dare, again?" he asked after a moment of silence.

"One wrong move and this whole thing could snap. We could be dead in seconds."

Chance doubted that. "You're being overdramatic, Jenny."

They lay in silence for a while, watching the clouds pass by, until Chance's eyelids felt heavy and he had to fight to keep them open. It had been almost two weeks since he'd had a decent night's sleep, what with his parents and their screaming. Jenny's head still rested on his shoulder, and he could feel her breath on his neck. It was warm, relaxing . . .

IT SEEMED LIKE only seconds had passed when he opened his eyes to find the sun was setting. Jenny's head was on his chest, slowly rising and falling with each breath he took. He wondered if she could hear his heartbeat, slow and steady. Her eyes were shut, her eyelashes fluttering. They both must've dozed off. His hand rested on the small of her back, her warmth radiating through the fabric of her shirt.

He reached up and pushed her hair from her face. He wanted to kiss her.

"Jenny, wake up." He carefully nudged her awake.

She groggily opened her eyes.

"Wha—?"

"We dozed off," he told her.

She sat up, picking dried leaves off her shirt. "Oh, damn. I hope Jack's taking care of Jessa."

He sat up, too, an idea forming. "It's my turn, isn't it?" he asked.

"Huh?" She turned back to look at him, a few leaves still tangled in her brown hair.

"The Day of Dares," he reminded her. "It's my turn to issue a dare."

"Oh, I suppose so."

"I've got a dare for you." He leaned forward, blond hair tumbling into his eyes.

"What kind?"

He laughed at her eagerness. He reached out and grabbed her hands. "I dare you to kiss me."

Her face went blank for a moment, her large eyes blinking rapidly.

"Wait, what?" She blushed. "You're kidding, right?"

"Well, you said you'd never been kissed," he began. A small part of him felt like he was tricking her. He had wanted to kiss her for weeks now. Maybe if he just did it, he'd get it out of his system, and they could go back to how they were supposed to be.

She squirmed, looking down at their clasped hands. "I don't see why we shouldn't. . . . I mean, it *is* a dare."

Color stained her cheeks. She awkwardly shifted her weight.

"Hey"—he smiled—"at least I know what I'm doing."

I sound like a tool. I need to rein it in.

"True," she laughed, relaxing a bit. "I mean, it's just you, it's not like it really counts."

He just smiled, deciding that he deserved that sting. "Yeah, it doesn't count." He pulled her closer, his hands sliding up her arms to her shoulders, just like he had been dreaming about. "You know how this works, right?"

She rolled her eyes. "I'm not stupid, Chance."

"I'm just checking." He laughed, hoping that she couldn't tell how badly his voice shook. "Now, close your eyes."

She did as she was told. His heart beat frantically in his chest. He was glad that she couldn't see his hand shake when he reached up to touch her face; he—Chance—who was never unsteady. He leaned in. He felt awful for trying to get her out of his system but oh, so excited to finally get there. His lips touched hers gently at first, sending electric currents pulsing through his body. After a few seconds, he pushed with more force, opening her mouth with his, moving to deepen the kiss. His hands lowered, finding her waist, and he thought he felt her sigh against his lips.

"Jenny!" a shrill voice called out.

Jenny jerked away as the sliding glass door flew open. Jack stuck his head out, looking annoyed. "Jenny, Jessa is crying! I don't know what to do!"

"Oh shoot," Jenny mumbled. "We've got to take care of Jessa."

Chance watched her find her shoes and get off the trampoline, brushing off everything that had just happened. It was over. That meant she was out of his system now, right?

Except she wasn't. He was still thinking about kissing her—about holding her, about laying her down on the trampoline and kissing her thoroughly again.

CHAPTER 9

Jenny

Jenny had never had much interest in kissing. Sure, it looked fun on TV and, yeah, the best parts of books were when the official couple *finally* kissed, but she'd never actually wanted it in reality. She wasn't one of those people who sat around daydreaming about her first kiss, hoping it would be with the high school quarterback in a sunlit garden the afternoon of the big game or something like that. She figured if it happened, it happened and if it didn't, well then, it didn't.

That had been before. Before Chance kissed her. Before he awoke something inside her and opened her eyes to all that she was missing. She had wanted something to happen between them ever since the night at Their Spot. Then yesterday was the Trampoline Incident on the Day of Dares. It was all she could think about during first block the next day.

She had spent all night obsessing over it. She wanted to kiss him.

Again. She wanted to feel those emotions coursing through her veins. If this was what dating was like, then sign her up.

Maybe, just maybe, she could have that with Chance? She had been there, had felt the way he kissed her. There was no way he wasn't at least interested in something, right? She was the first person out of her class the moment the bell rang, bobbing and weaving her way down the crowded hall toward Oral Comm. Finally, she spotted him. He was just a few feet away, getting something out of his locker.

There were only a few steps between them when a girl slipped through. Jenny faltered. She hung back, ducking behind a burly boy who was shoving books into his locker. She busied herself, pulling out a notebook and pretending to be engrossed in it.

"Hello, Chance," the girl said dreamily. "I've been looking for you."

"You have?" Chance asked distractedly. Or at least Jenny *thought* he sounded distracted. She refused to look up from her notes, afraid of being caught eavesdropping.

The girl giggled. "Yes, silly. I was wondering if you were going to Leslie's Halloween party."

"I usually do," Chance told her. Jenny heard his locker door slam. "It's always pretty fun."

"Sooo . . ." The girl drew out the word. "Maybe I'll see you there?"

Jenny saw them walking away from the corner of her eye and— dear Lord, they were walking right in front of her. She scooted closer to the burly locker boy, who looked alarmed but said nothing as she buried herself even deeper in her notes.

Chance stopped, causing a few passersby to swerve around him angrily. He turned back to the girl, looking surprised. "You want to go out again?"

"Well, yeah, you're Chance Masters. Who wouldn't want to go out with you?"

True, Jenny thought.

"I don't know. . . ." Chance shuffled from one foot to the other, not looking at the girl. "I don't really *do* relationships, you know?" he told her. "I'm not the dating kind."

Jenny pushed herself from the locker, shoving her notebook back into her bag. She felt like crying, and she wasn't exactly sure why. Chance hadn't rejected her, at least not directly. It still hurt all the same. She rushed down the hall, her face hot, fighting tears.

Jenny burst into the nearest girls' bathroom, looking at herself in the mirror over the sink. She looked sad and pathetic. She slumped against the sink in front of her, her hands gripping the cool porcelain to keep herself steady. She felt so stupid. She had actually been considering going after Chance. The boy every girl in school hooked up with. She had fooled herself into thinking that stupid dare meant something. She had thought she was different. She knew now that he didn't see anything in her and probably never would.

The door opened, startling her. She didn't want anyone to see her looking so pathetic.

Luckily, it was only Kelsey. She took one look at Jenny and said, "Okay, who do I need to beat up?"

Jenny laughed. "It's nothing, really."

"It's not nothing. You look like your cat just died."

"I'm just . . . disappointed, I guess. I don't know." Jenny turned away from her reflection, focusing on Kelsey's instead. "It's Chance—"

"Say no more," Kelsey said. "I warned you about him, Wessler. I told you he wasn't safe."

"No, it's not like that. . . ." She trailed off. That wasn't exactly true, though. It *was* like that . . . just not for him. "I mean, not really. He was upfront about things only being for fun and I got carried away thinking that maybe they meant something they didn't."

Kelsey leaned against the sink next to Jenny. "Something happened between you two?"

"Kind of," Jenny said. "I mean, we kissed, but it was only a dare."

"He kissed you on a dare?"

Jenny shook her head. "I kissed him."

"Who dared you?"

"He did. And I got it in my head that it meant something."

"You don't think it did?"

"I just overheard him turn down a girl because he doesn't 'do relationships,'" Jenny said. "I don't know why I'm surprised; he is Chance Masters, after all. I just need to collect myself."

Kelsey placed a hand on her shoulder. "It's okay to be disappointed, you know. Even if he has a reputation, it's understandable that it still hurts."

The bell rang.

"Crap, we're late!" Jenny exclaimed. She picked up her backpack. *This is* not *my day*, she thought bitterly.

"Look at you, Wessler, getting me in trouble," Kelsey joked. "You're ruining my spotless record."

"I'm just being stupid, aren't I?" Jenny asked distractedly.

Kelsey shook her head. "Of course not. Your feelings are valid. You're allowed to want more, and you're allowed to be upset that things aren't happening that way. You should take some time away from him to figure yourself out."

She knew Kelsey was right. She'd never move past this thing for Chance if things continued the way they were. She was *not* going to be the girl pining after her playboy best friend as he dated his way through the school, praying for him to one day turn around and notice her. She was *not* living that cliché.

She made a promise to herself that day to be his friend only and nothing more. It wasn't in the cards, and she had to let it go. He was in the friendship box, now and forever, and that was where he had to stay.

Squaring her shoulders and holding her head high, Jenny left the bathroom and marched straight to second block.

CHAPTER 10

Chance

Chance couldn't believe he beat Jenny to class. He looked around, waiting for her to burst through the door any second. He had meant to find her before, to talk to her about everything that had happened, but he'd gotten distracted by some girl. *God, of all the days for a random girl to throw herself at me.* He had tried his best not to let his annoyance show on his face, but inside he had been seething. He didn't have time for all that. He had wanted to find Jenny.

Now he would just have to talk to her after class. He had it all planned out. He was going to pull her aside before lunch and ask her if she wanted to try going out sometime. Or he was just going to go ahead and kiss her again. He still wasn't exactly sure which.

He smiled at her as she ducked into class, but her eyes cut away. She didn't even look at him as she sat down beside him. She steadfastly stared forward the entire class, not even sparing him a glance.

Was she angry? Did this mean that she *wasn't* cool with the kiss? Had he misread everything?

He couldn't focus in class; his nerves were shot. *I'll talk to her after class. I will straight up ask her if things are all right.* All thoughts of kissing her flew away. He had to focus on making sure they were even still friends. The bell finally rang after what felt like three hours. Chance nearly leapt from his seat in his haste, but Jenny was already at the door with Kelsey.

"Jenny," he said. She didn't even look over. "About yesterday—"

"That?" she said a little too loudly, causing Kelsey to pause, turning back curiously. "It meant nothing, I know that. I'm glad we're close enough to not let something as silly as a dare get between us." Then she was speeding away from him, shouldering her bag, practically running away with Kelsey hot on her heels.

Chance stood there, watching after her, the classroom emptying around him. *I ruined everything*, he realized. He had been afraid of it, but he went and did it anyway. *I never should have kissed her.*

He was surprised to find Jenny and Kelsey still at their table at lunch. He half expected them to eat somewhere else. He took his seat beside her, but she still hardly looked at him. Instead, she was engrossed in a conversation with Drake about his band again.

"I think we really have a chance, but then again I'm in the band," Drake was saying.

"True," Jenny told him. "You may be a bit biased."

"Only a bit," Drake agreed with a laugh. He reached out then, his fingers sweeping Jenny's hair out of her eyes. Chance bristled as she blushed.

Panic overtook him—had Drake asked her out yet? Had she said *yes*? Why wouldn't she look at Chance?

When the bell rang signaling the end of lunch, Chance reached out to grab Jenny's arm, her name on his lips, but Drake got there first.

"Jenny, can I talk to you?" the taller boy asked, his hair tumbling into his face as he looked down at her.

"Sure."

The two stepped away, leaving Chance at the table, his stomach sick. *Drake is asking her out right now. I never even had a chance.* He was so busy worrying that it took him a bit to realize that Kelsey was also still at the table, glaring at him.

"What exactly is going on with you?" she asked when he noticed her.

He shrugged. "I honestly have no clue."

"What about what's going on over there?" She pointed to where Drake and Jenny stood. Jenny's face was bright red as she stammered something to Drake, who laughed.

"I think it's obvious what's going on over there," he said, each word feeling like a slap to the face.

Kelsey pursed her lips, looking from the new couple to Chance. "Funny, I thought it'd be you. But I guess not."

Me too. "No, it's not like that with us."

Kelsey rolled her eyes. "Of course not. I'm just warning you. I'm president of, like, every club. People listen to me, and they fear me. It's quite nice."

"I highly doubt anyone fears you," Chance said, finally turning away from Drake and Jenny. He grabbed his backpack, slinging it over his shoulder.

"They do, I assure you. I made a freshman council member cry the other day because they ordered the wrong color streamers for the fall dance. I'm ruthless. This whole mess is throwing me off." She vaguely gestured from Chance to Drake. "It came out of nowhere. I mean, how many more best friends is she hiding? What else don't I know about her?"

Chance watched Jenny and Drake walk off together, Drake carrying Jenny's messenger bag.

"I'm wondering the same thing," he said.

HE COULD BARELY even process what had happened.

He wasn't sure where he'd messed up or why Jenny was being weird and . . . and . . . *My life is shit.* He needed someone to talk to. He had his phone out, finger poised over Jenny's name, when he froze. She had been so standoffish with him at school. She agreed to go out with Drake. Would she even want to hear from him right now?

How could a day that started out so wonderful end so badly? He walked into the barn, phone still in his hand.

He could always call Levi, he realized. He could explain about their parents getting worse and ask Levi to come visit sometime soon. It had been *years*, after all. He had to come home eventually. What was he even doing with his life nowadays, anyway?

Maybe Chance could even explain about Jenny. After all, his brother had an even worse reputation than Chance did. He had to at least know something about this kind of situation. He dialed his brother's number and waited, listening to the phone ring.

And ring. And ring. And ring.

Frustrated, he hung up and tried again. Still no answer. Same thing with the third and fourth tries, too.

"Fuck it," Chance said quietly, the sound echoing in the empty barn. He wanted his brother to answer his fucking phone. He didn't want to be so alone. He sank to the ground, wrapping himself in the blankets he and Jenny had left there. He didn't even care that a few of them were sticky with spilt beer.

He lay there for hours, stewing in his anger and despair. He kept replaying the damned day again and again, his phone still in his hand. *Why won't Levi call me back?*

The more he thought about it, the more he realized that Levi was the smart one. He wasn't the one lying in a barn, wrapped like a burrito in a beer-stained blanket and suffocating on the scent of straw. No, he was far away. Far away from their parents and Chance and everything else that had brought him pain.

Levi was lucky. Levi had escaped. He had abandoned Chance.

CHAPTER 11

Jenny

Jenny Wessler had a date.

It had happened so suddenly. She'd gone from the heartbreak of realizing things would never work with Chance to being asked out by Drake Sellers in a matter of hours. She hadn't seen it coming at all, but she tended to be oblivious to those types of things. Her pulse hadn't quickened and her heart hadn't skipped a beat, but she'd smiled and said yes all the same. She hadn't even pointed out that the way Drake took her bags was a little overconfident. He was talented and cute. He was tall, he was nice, and he liked her. That was enough. There were plenty of girls who would kill to be in her shoes, and even accepting a date was a big step for her socially, so why not?

After all, Chance wasn't an option. Yeah, she had a crush on him, but she couldn't hold on to an unrequited crush forever. He didn't do romantic love, so she should let him go and embrace the next thing that came along.

That next thing just so happened to be Drake.

The only problem was that she didn't have a costume for the party, but she knew the exact person to help her out there.

IT WAS TWO days before Halloween when Jenny found herself walking down the History hall after school, looking into every classroom she passed. She knew the Student Advisory Board met somewhere on this floor, she just had to find it. She knew she was in the right place when she heard voices coming from the Psychology classroom. She waited patiently outside for the meeting to end before barging in.

Kelsey was at the front of the classroom, her backpack on top of the teacher's desk as she packed away her stuff.

"Kelsey." Jenny tried to get her friend's attention. "Kelsey, I need you."

Kelsey didn't even miss a beat. Her hand flew to her chest with a dramatic flourish. "Oh, Jennifer, this is so sudden, but I'm sure we can make it work!"

Jenny shot her an annoyed look. "Not like *that*, Kelse. I need your help picking out a Halloween costume."

Kelsey dropped her hand, her face full of mock disappointment. "And you got my hopes up and everything."

Jenny crossed the room, shoving her hands into her front pockets. "I'm going to Leslie's Halloween party."

"So I've heard."

"You've heard?" But she hadn't told anyone, and she couldn't picture Drake texting Kelsey.

Kelsey nodded, her blond curls bouncing as she did so. "I saw him ask you out. The whole school knows. You know what kind of legendary dream boy Drake is."

Jenny blanched. "Yay, even more pressure." She hadn't realized that agreeing to go with Drake was going to be such a big ordeal.

Kelsey studied her friend, her face full of concern. "Are you going to be all right? I know parties aren't really your style. . . ."

"I'll be fine," Jenny hastened to assure her. "I mean, I'm slightly terrified, but I'm also kind of excited to go to a real high school party like in the movies."

Kelsey shouldered her backpack and shoved her hands into the pockets of her oversized Razorbacks hoodie. "Jenny, real life is nothing like the movies. But, yes, I will take you costume shopping. I never see you anymore, not since Masters became your ride to school."

AN HOUR LATER, they found themselves rummaging through the racks of a popup Halloween store, unhappy with everything they found.

"So," Kelsey said as she pulled a costume from the rack. "Do you want to be a sexy nurse or a sexy butterfly? Ohh," she said, pointing to a costume on display. "What about a sexy crayon?"

Jenny grimaced. It had been like this at every place they'd gone: The store didn't carry adult costumes, all the costumes had been picked over, or it was like shopping at a lingerie store.

"You know I really don't mind all the sexy costumes," Kelsey went on, still flipping through the rack. "For most girls, Halloween is the only time they can dress sexily, so more power to them. But, like, don't make it the only option."

Jenny wasn't having any luck with the rack she was searching through, either. "Maybe I can go as a nun."

"Oh!" Kelsey exclaimed, pulling another costume from the rack. "You could be a *sexy* nun!"

"Oh, yes, my dream costume, with equal amounts sex appeal and blasphemy."

Jenny hated this store, with the Halloween decorations that shrieked when people walked past. It smelled like the inside of a cheap rubber mask, and children were running around everywhere, screaming and playing with fake swords and axes.

"Maybe I'm not meant to find a costume. Maybe it's a sign that I shouldn't go."

This was supposed to be easy, wasn't it? People in shows or books always found the perfect costume right off the bat, one that hugged them in all the right places and was unique to them, and would turn every head. Why wasn't it like that? "We should give up. I should just wear every piece of black I own and call myself a witch."

Kelsey paused, her mouth slightly parted in thought. "You know," she said at last, "that's not a bad idea. I mean, not *all* the black you own, but a simple black dress and a witch hat."

"It'd be better than this." Jenny held up a sexy hot-dog costume.

"No, no," Kelsey was saying, scrutinizing the costume. "I think the hot dog might be a winner."

"No." Jenny tried to keep a straight face, but she couldn't.

They found the perfect witch dress at Forever 21, a high-low number with long willowy sleeves, the darkness of it making Jenny's pale skin pop.

"Do you want me to go to the party, too?" Kelsey asked as she drove Jenny back home. "Keep in mind that I don't want to, but I'll be there if you need me."

"You're always so charming, Kelse," Jenny told her, looking down at the bag in her lap. "And, no, I'll have Drake."

Kelsey glanced over at her, unsure. "Okay," she said at last. "If you say you'll be okay, then I believe you."

The more Jenny thought about the party, the more unnerved she became. She was only comfortable when she thought of it in terms of clichéd high school experiences. As long as she viewed it through that lens, she was fine, because she knew what to expect. *It's going to be exactly like in the movies*, she told herself.

SHE FELT LIKE throwing up as she sat in her living room, watching the seconds until Drake was supposed to come pick her up tick by. She nearly talked herself out of it a thousand times. And, God, her palms wouldn't stop sweating. What if Drake got there and grabbed her hand and was disgusted by how clammy it was? That thought made her sweat even *more*.

Why did I think I could do this?

Then her phone was buzzing and Drake was there to get her. *It's too late to back out now*, she told herself.

She grabbed her purse, donned her witch's hat, and caught sight of her sleek dress in the foyer mirror. She paused as she looked herself over, fingering the smooth material of her dress. She hardly recognized herself. Who was this girl in the mirror, and where had Jenny Wessler gone?

She had always admired the girls on TV who got dressed up and went on dates—the type who thrived on social interaction and always said the right thing at the right time. That had always seemed so unobtainable for her, and yet here she was going for it. For the first time, happiness seemed like it might be a real tangible possibility for her, not just an abstract concept.

I can do this. It's no big deal, and I can do this.

Drake was standing outside his car, propped against it like Jake Ryan in *Sixteen Candles*. He wore a long gray coat and red scarf: the perfect Bender. It was as if he knew exactly the way to make her comfortable. He opened the door for her, beckoning her forward with a flourish.

"Are you ready?" he asked, his grayish-blue eyes lingering on her exposed legs.

He drove a car that was as spotless inside as it was outside. There were no rips in the upholstery or stains on the floorboard. He ruled the radio, plugging in his phone and refusing to leave the driveway until he found the perfect song. It would take some getting used to, Jenny figured, but she could do it. Besides, it seemed very Drake. He gave off the wild rock star image, but he definitely came from privilege and liked things just so. He was organized under the purposeful disorganization, the type of boy who would spend hours making sure his hair was the right level of elegantly disheveled.

Being next to him in the car was a lot like sitting next to him at lunch. It was only as she came to terms with this that she realized just how much attention Drake had been paying her. He always looked right at her, talking directly to her and only her. There was something exciting about his eyes. She felt like they could see right through her if she gave them the chance.

"Don't worry, okay?" Drake told her after she admitted it was her first party. "These things are supposed to be fun, so just enjoy yourself."

"Will there be booze?" she asked.

He nodded, his hair brushing the collar of his coat. "I won't be drinking, though, because I've got to drive you home."

She didn't want to drink, either, not without Chance. *Chance.* There was a pang in her chest. *I wonder what he's doing now. . . .*

"—couldn't get another band to replace The Bleeding Axe Wounds, so Leslie will probably play one of her Spotify playlists loaded with songs from the nineties. Which, okay, might suck, but we don't have to dance if you don't want to."

"Wait, what?" Jenny asked, tearing her mind away from Chance.

Drake gave her a smile before turning onto a street loaded with cars. "It's okay to be nervous. I'm not going to leave your side all night, I promise."

Jenny had to admit that the closer they got to the party—she could see the house and its over-the-top Halloween decorations now—the less anxious and more excited she became. She could feel the bass from the stereo all the way outside, pulsing through the sidewalk and the soles of her feet as Drake helped her from the car. *It's just like a movie*, she told herself as he led her up the walk. *It's just like a movie.*

And it was. Drake opened the door, ushering her in, and she almost collided with a mass of bodies. There were many more people than she had expected, and Leslie had brought out a ridiculous amount of black lights to set the Halloween mood. There were skimpily dressed angels grinding against rowdy werewolves. A Hogwarts student in a black bathrobe was doing shots with a toilet-papered mummy. Deadpool ran around yelling random things and taking people's drinks, being chased by a very angry-looking Sailor Moon. Jenny stuck close to Drake, grabbing his coat more out of necessity than desire, though she'd be lying if she said having to plaster herself to Drake's side was the worst thing ever.

"No, no, the second *Pirates of the Caribbean* was the best," he told her later as they sat on Leslie's couch, watching a guy in a Captain Jack Sparrow costume unsuccessfully trying to hit on a man painted up like a zombie. "It has that scene with the cannibals. That shit was hilarious."

"No, I'm telling you, the third one was better." Jenny laughed. She had to shout to be heard over the music. "Elizabeth became king of the pirates—what's better than that?"

"It was confusing," Drake told her. "Everyone kept betraying one another."

"That's what pirates do!"

"Can't they at least do it so I can follow?"

The music changed then, the whiny singer replaced by a dreary voice saying, "It's astounding . . . time is fleeting . . ."

"Wait!" Jenny asked, excited. "Is this 'The Time Warp'?"

Drake grinned at her enthusiasm. "I believe so."

The people in the living room were standing in rows now, doing as the song told them: a jump to the left, a step to the right. The crowd moved as one, laughter blending with the music.

But Drake wasn't watching them; he was watching Jenny, taking note of her expression. "Do you want to do it?"

"What?"

He stood, pulling her to her feet as well. "Come on." He dragged her to the group. "Let's dance."

Her first instinct was to sit back down, but Drake looked so hopeful and it was dark, after all, and everyone else was dancing, too. It wasn't too nerve-wracking if no one could see her among the crowd.

"Okay, okay . . ." And then she was dancing, too, hands on her hips and knees in tight.

Drake kept getting it backward and bumping into her, but he never stopped moving and neither did she. She looked up at him, at his profile highlighted in the black lights, his long, crooked nose and sharp chin. The small smile he made every time he misstepped. There was something endearing in the way he looked over to make sure she was smiling, too.

I could do this, she realized as the song ended and the crowd thinned. She stood there, in the middle of Leslie Vandercamp's dark living room, looking up at Drake. *It would be so easy to just let this happen.* And so she did. She grabbed Drake by the hand and led him back to the couch, listening as he told her about how his band practiced on Thursdays at his house and would she like to come sometime?

At the end of the night, after way too many candied apples, he drove her home before midnight, just like her mother had demanded. Their conversation was pleasant, and he made her laugh a few times. He smelled overwhelmingly of Axe body spray; it flooded his car, and Jenny supposed that she liked that. She liked his long hair and his sharp collarbones.

"So, this is it," he said, parking in front of her house.

She looked out at her house, a few of the lights still on. Her mom's car was in the driveway for once, which meant she was back from taking Jack and Jessa trick-or-treating. Jenny knew that her mother was seated in the living room, ready to pounce and hear all about her date.

"Jenny?" Drake asked, waving a hand in front of her face.

She snapped out of her thoughts, slightly startled.

"Oh! I'm so sorry. I had a good time at the party. It was fun." And, surprisingly enough, it *had* been.

"I thought so, too." He grinned, lazily slinging his arm around her shoulders and giving them a squeeze. His hand felt a little too warm on her skin, but she didn't shrug it off.

"We should do it again sometime," she told him. She meant it. She could see herself easily falling in with Drake, becoming the girl at his side. He was rubbing small circles on her shoulder, and she guessed that felt kind of nice.

When he shifted toward her, leaning in ever so slowly, muttering, "I think so, too," she knew what was happening and felt powerless to stop it. She wasn't even sure if she wanted to stop it. Drake was moving in, and it was now or never.

So Jenny chose now, the road less traveled. She chose Drake. She chose to lean forward and press her lips to his. There weren't any fireworks. It wasn't the Best Kiss Ever. The earth didn't tilt on its axis, and the stars didn't shine any brighter in the sky. She knew, because she'd opened her eyes halfway through. She couldn't help it. But it wasn't bad. It was clumsy and awkward, but she still grabbed the back of his neck and pulled him closer.

After kissing Chance on the trampoline, she thought kissing must be world-stopping. This was different, but different wasn't bad. She clung to him, her hands sliding from his neck and tangling in his hair, her eyes closing again. He responded in kind, tightening his hold on her.

"I'll see you soon," Drake promised breathlessly.

Jenny waited on the porch, watching Drake drive off. She checked her reflection in the living room window, running her fingers through her now-messy hair. She didn't want her mom to know she'd just been making out in the car.

CHAPTER 12

Chance

Chance's phone came to life, lighting up the inside of his car. He glanced at it, catching sight of Jenny's contact photo—her sticking her tongue out at him. He reached over, putting the call on speaker.

"How was your date?" he said by way of greeting.

"It was . . . all right." Her voice filled the car. He could almost imagine she was there with him.

He chuckled. "Did you have fun at your first party?"

"To be honest, it was all kind of a blur," she told him. "Drake seemed nice, like he does at lunch, and we talked a lot."

"That's good," Chance said distractedly as he took a turn. It was so hard to see on these back country roads at night.

"You can at least *act* like you're interested," Jenny said. "I know you go on dates all the time, but it's kind of a new experience for me."

He was silent for a moment. "I am interested, Jenny. It's just—"

"Are you driving?" she interrupted, her tone softening.

"Late-night Walmart run." That was half true—he *had* gone to the store; it just wasn't where he was headed now. "It's late, okay? I'm tired. But I'm glad you called to tell me about your date."

She was silent. He was afraid she'd ask more questions, but she didn't.

"I think I like him," she said at last.

"You do?" Chance asked, his voice quiet in the dark.

"He seems nice and different. I need a little different. I think we're dating now."

"More than one date typically means dating," Chance informed her.

They lapsed into silence and he was afraid that she'd fallen asleep on him.

"What have you been doing?" she asked, and for a split second he thought he'd been found out.

She doesn't know, he reminded himself.

"Thinking, mostly," he said as he pulled up outside the old barn. He killed the car, sitting in silence.

"About what?"

He paused. "Infomercials."

"Infomercials?"

"Yeah," he said. "I've never understood how incompetent people always are during infomercials."

Jenny laughed. "Me neither. People are always like, 'Oh no, I can't lift this jug of milk and now I've knocked out an entire row of cabinets!'"

They kept going on about the increasing incompetence of TV salespeople, the rhythmic sound of Jenny's voice almost like a lullaby. It must've been somewhere around two o'clock when their words dried up and her breathing slowed, the phones still pressed to their ears. He kept dozing in and out of consciousness, the sounds of Jenny's breathing lulling him to sleep. Finally, he hung up, pulling himself from the car. He pulled the new pack of batteries he'd bought for the lantern from his pocket and headed inside.

SO HE WAS sleeping in the barn. It wasn't supposed to happen. He had told himself that he'd find somewhere else to go when things at home calmed down, but they didn't calm down. Jenny was finally talking to him as if everything was normal and none of the awkwardness had ever happened. He was thankful. They could put that whole kissing mess behind them and go back to being just friends. He didn't ask about Drake, and she didn't offer to tell. Not after that first date.

He went to Jenny's after school, but even that had a time limit. It would get around eleven o'clock and Chance would read all the little social cues for him to go home, and his heart would sink. Jenny's mother would impatiently walk by her open bedroom door, Jack and Jessa already in bed. Jenny would stretch on her bed, letting out the cutest of yawns.

He never wanted to go. All that was waiting for him at home was nothing. His parents hadn't even tried to contact him about where he'd been. He'd pop in right after his father left for work, sneak to his room for some clothes, and be out again before his mother heard him.

I'm only going to stay at the barn one night, he'd told himself. He'd thought it was true, too. The glow-in-the-dark stars were so faint now; he could barely make out where they were. The pallet wasn't exactly comfortable, covered in hay and beer, but he could deal. It wasn't a luxurious king-sized bed, but he could pretend it was. Then one night faded into two and two into three, and the next thing he knew it was mid-November.

He knew Jenny wouldn't like it, so he kept it from her. It wasn't her business anyway, right? He could handle this all on his own. He had a duffel bag packed with clothes, and he still managed to take showers by slipping in and out of the house when his parents weren't home. Besides, he was at Jenny's until nearly midnight every night, so in reality he was only spending, what, five or six hours tops at the barn? That was totally manageable.

Chance didn't need any help. It was nothing to worry about. At least that's what he told himself.

That next Monday when he woke up, back stiff from sleeping on the hardwood floor, he decided to pack up the blankets to be washed. He figured he could stop by a twenty-four-hour laundromat before heading to the barn that night. He thought nothing of throwing the blankets into the trunk of his car. In fact, it was so far from his mind that he didn't even remember they were there that afternoon, when he took Jenny grocery shopping.

They were loading everything into the backseat of his car, chatting idly. It was like playing Tetris, getting everything to fit without falling over or squishing something else. Chance didn't notice when Jenny grabbed his lanyard and slipped the keys from his front pocket. It wasn't until he heard her unlocking the trunk that he remembered the blankets and started to panic.

"What are you doing?" he asked, almost dropping his bag of chips.

"I'm putting the bottled water in the trunk," she said, opening it. She stopped for a second before looking at him, her face confused. "Why are the blankets from Our Spot in here?"

He tossed his stuff into the backseat, rushing to stop her. "I brought them home to clean the other day. They were covered in beer and dirt. It's nothing." He tried to push her aside, to throw the water in and be done with it.

"When the other day?" she asked, confused. "You were with me every day."

"Last night, after I left your place," he told her, shoving the blankets aside and tossing the bottles in. He was just about to slam the trunk when she reached out and stopped him.

"At midnight? You're telling me you drove out there at midnight to pick up some blankets?"

"Yes."

Her gaze shot back to him, boring holes right through him. "Chance! Are you sleeping there?"

"No," he lied.

She leveled him with a look.

"Fine," he said at last, letting go of the trunk lid. "I've been sleeping there for the past week or so. It nothing, Jens. Things have gotten . . . tense at home. My parents said some things to each other, and then they both said some things to me. . . . It's not a big deal, really."

That was the wrong thing to say, though, because her green eyes got wide, filled to the brim with worry and something he couldn't quite identify. She shook her head and sputtered, searching for words. Finally, she said, "Why didn't you tell me?"

He felt as if he was being pulled to the ground, weighed down with all these expectations he never had before. "I didn't want you to worry about me."

Her fist snaked out, making contact with his arm. He flinched, instinctively reaching up to rub the spot where she'd punched him. For a tiny girl, she packed quite the punch.

"Ow! What the hell?"

As she glared up at him, he realized what that other emotion had been: anger. Jenny was mad at him. "If you don't tell me when something's bothering you, then I'm always going to worry, you nimrod." She turned away from him, pacing in a small circle, her hands at her temples. It was what she did when she was trying to concentrate, and even now Chance found it adorable. At last her arms dropped to her side and she turned to face him, expression serious. "Come stay at my house."

He blinked at her. "What?"

"Stay with me," she repeated. "I told you that you didn't have to go through this alone, and I meant it. Stay with me, Chance. Stay at my house. You can't sleep in that barn."

"*You* slept there," he pointed out. They had both stayed there, buzzed on Shit Beer. "How is that any different?"

"Because I wasn't alone. We stayed there together," she explained, exasperated. Her nose scrunched up the way it always did when she was angry or frustrated, and he couldn't help but find it cute. "You know what? If you're sleeping there, then so am I."

"Oh come on, that's ridiculous."

"No, what's ridiculous is that you tried to hide this from me." She put her hands on her hips, like a mother in an old cartoon. Chance half expected her to start tapping her foot impatiently.

"Because it's not a big deal," he tried to tell her, frustrated.

"Do you not trust me with this?" she asked, looking up at him. He didn't understand why she looked so distraught. "I have to ask before you spill anything. I have to hear things in hallways. I have to find blankets buried in your trunk to get you to admit anything. Do you not trust me?"

Hear things in hallways? "Of course I trust you, Jenny. I don't even know where this is coming from."

Was this about the dare? She was the one who blew that off, not him. She was the one who made it clear that they were just friends. She was the one who said that kiss was nothing, who walked away like nothing had happened. He was only following her cue to leave it alone. Besides, she was with Drake now.

She was still looking up at him expectantly.

"It's difficult, okay? I guess I'm not used to having someone care about me, so I keep things to myself. I'll stay at your place tonight."

She had won, but neither of them treated it like a victory. She was texting the entire ride home, her phone letting out angry *dings* every few minutes. He hadn't wanted to be a burden, and now here he was, transforming into a charity case.

Jack was waiting in the living room when they got there, a wicked grin on his face. "I'll keep quiet," he said when the door opened. "But it's going to cost you so much, Jenny. I'm talking free rein of the house and your allowance for months."

"Fine," Jenny said, unconcerned. "You can have whatever you want. You can do whatever you want. Just don't tell. Promise me, Jack, that you will not tell." Jenny held out her pinkie.

"It's not like she'll notice, anyway," Jack said, linking his pinkie with his sister's. "She's too preoccupied with Phillip to notice anything anymore."

Chance had a bad feeling about this. "Jenny," he said as her brother walked away, "I was fine staying at the barn."

"No." Jenny shook her head. "Let me take care of you, all right? If we get caught, then I'll deal with it, but I am *not* letting you go back to that barn, Chance. It's not right."

"I can't stay here without your mom knowing."

Jenny laughed at that. "I'm sure this won't be your first time sneaking into a girl's house for a sleepover."

She had him there.

They decided that he would stay for dinner and then leave afterward only to park up the street and sneak back in. As far as plans went, it was shoddy at best, but it was all they had. There were about a thousand ways it could fail, and he was dreading every one of them. If he was caught, there'd be no way her mother would let him come over anymore. He could lose one of his only safe havens.

Before dinner, Jenny suggested something to keep his mind off the plan. "Trampoline time," she told him, grabbing him by the arm and dragging him outside.

"I thought it was dangerous?" But he was amused by her determination.

"I live for danger. It's my middle name." She pulled him through the long grass, the setting sun casting half the backyard into shadow. She all but tossed him onto the trampoline. "Besides, it should be fine."

He let out a bark of laughter. "That doesn't sound like you."

"Desperate times and desperate measures and all that." She hopped onto the trampoline, reaching down to pull him to his feet as well.

They both stood up, cautiously, taking a few steps toward the middle. The mat beneath their feet gave each step a bounce, and then suddenly Chance was rocking back on the heels of his feet—testing it. First just rocking back and forth, and then bouncing lightly, until finally they were both jumping—full-out, arms-flailing, in-the-air jumping. Up, down, up, down. Chance fell and he rose, his heart in his throat.

They were laughing, jumping together, trying not to elbow each other in the face. It was wonderful. It was exhilarating. They reached out, grasping hands to keep from falling over. The last thing he wanted was to accidentally trample her. Her hair flew all around her, getting tangled as they jumped. Her hands were small in his, but they felt *right*. Everything at home—everything with Levi and his parents and shit—it all felt wrong and weird. But *this*, this right here—holding Jenny Wessler's hands and watching her smile—felt right. This was where he belonged. This was—

The mat stretched taut as they landed, a spring to their right shooting off and hitting the wooden fence that surrounded the yard. The noise echoed like cannon fire around them, silencing everything. Chance's foot slipped from underneath him, sending him careening to the mat, dragging Jenny along with him. She crashed on top of him, their foreheads knocking together painfully.

He could feel her weight on him, pressing him down into the trampoline. They both stared at each other, centimeters apart. Chance couldn't help but remember what had happened the last time they were on the trampoline. From the blush on Jenny's face, he figured she was thinking about it, too.

Jenny burst out laughing, the sound unbelievably loud in the silence. She rose up to her knees, rolling off Chance. She looked from him to the missing spring, laughing hysterically. He couldn't help but laugh, too, the sound spilling out of him unexpectedly. They both collapsed into a giggle fit, rolling into each other, their sides brushing.

"That was ridiculous," Jenny wheezed.

"It was terrifying," Chance corrected.

Jenny's mother emerged from the house then, looking concerned. "Get off that trampoline!" she ordered. "It's dangerous!"

Jenny and Chance only laughed harder.

IT WAS AROUND ten when he snuck back in. Jenny's mother had gone to bed already, claiming she had to leave for work early the next morning. Chance stood outside Jenny's house, hoping that none of the neighbors had watched him drive down the street and walk back up. He texted her, letting her know he was back.

Jenny was at the door quick as a flash, pulling him back in. She held a finger to her lips, signaling him to be silent as they snuck up the stairs. He could hear the sound of a running box fan from within her mother's room as they tiptoed past it. He saw that Jenny had removed the Quiz Bowl medal from her own door, so as not to make any noise.

"We did it!" Jenny whispered as she shut the door behind them. "We actually did it. I actually snuck a boy into my room. And he's going to spend the night. Oh my God, it's like an episode of *Pretty Little Liars* or something."

He couldn't help but chuckle at her enthusiasm, though he was still worried about being caught. "I'll sleep on the floor," he told her, taking off his jacket and setting it on her desk chair.

"My mom sometimes wakes me up in the morning," she told him, shaking her head. "If you're on the floor, then you won't have time to hide when she knocks."

"Then where am I sleeping?"

Both pairs of eyes fell on the bed at the exact same time, and suddenly Chance felt very uncomfortable. Oh no, he couldn't do this. He was trying to be platonic, for God's sake. He couldn't curl up with her on a twin-size bed. "Jenny, I don't know about this."

"It's the only way," she told him, although she was blushing furiously. "You'll have to sleep against the wall so that I can throw my blankets over you if Mom knocks."

This really isn't a good idea. How am I supposed to move on when she's sleeping beside me?

"Seriously—"

"I'm not letting you go back home, Chance. And if you sleep in the barn, then so do I." She sounded braver than she looked.

"Fine." He gave in, sitting on the bed and taking off his shoes. "If it makes you feel better, I'll do it."

Jenny sat down next to him. "Good."

CHAPTER 13

Jenny

rake slid into the chair next to Jenny, slipping his arm around her shoulders. She started at the contact, pulled from her daydream. She hadn't even noticed that the band had stopped playing. They'd been practicing for hours in Nick's garage, and she had tuned out long ago.

Not that it wasn't fun watching Drake sing—it totally was. It was a clichéd teen experience for a reason, after all. Jenny was more than excited to play the role of the dutiful girlfriend looking up at her boyfriend from the crowd. She was less excited to sit for hours on an old stain-covered sofa in Nick's garage and watch The Bleeding Axe Wounds argue over which songs to practice.

"What did you think?" Drake asked. "That song is pretty new; we've only played it a handful of times. " He picked up the worn spiral notebook he kept all of his notes in. He showed Jenny the page on which he'd scribbled the lyrics to his newest song, "The Push and the

Pull." She took the notebook, glancing over the lyrics. He had marked them out so many times that he'd ripped through the page in spots.

"Well, you really like to rhyme *skin* with *sin*," she observed. "Also, *lips* and *hips*."

"That's what I always tell him!" Nick chimed in, causing the other band members to laugh.

Drake glared at his best friend before turning back to Jenny. "It's a stylistic choice," he told her. "It's kind of my thing."

She looked it over again. "It's just that you've done it ten times that I've read, and it isn't even part of the chorus."

The drummer let out a bark of laughter, causing Drake to glare even harder. "I'll keep that in mind," he said through clenched teeth. He took the notebook back, flipping to another page. "What about this one?"

His fingers brushed hers as he handed the lyric book back, and she instinctively moved away from the contact. She still wasn't used to the casual way he touched her. *This is how couples are*, she reminded herself. She looked down to a doodle-heavy page. Drake was a margin person. He loved doodling and scribbling in the margins. She skimmed over the lyrics to a song called "Good Mourning"—*dear God*—when her eyes slid to the bottom corner of the page. There, in the margin, Drake had doodled her name with tiny hearts.

Her head jerked up, looking at him in confusion. What was this? Were they in third grade? She felt *weird* looking at the doodle, as if it was an invasion of privacy. She had never considered Drake thinking of her often, especially if she wasn't there. It just never occurred to her that his head would be so filled with her that he'd doodle her name in his songbook.

"Well?" he asked, gesturing to the song. "What do you think?"

"The title is a bit . . ." She trailed off as his face fell the tiniest bit. *Oh. He doesn't want me to tell him the truth. He just wants me to tell him I like it.* ". . . perfect," she finished. "I like it a lot. I can't wait to hear it."

"Perfect!" Drake exclaimed, jumping to his feet. "You hear that, guys? Start up 'Good Mourning'!" He grabbed his guitar from its perch by the drums.

The band launched into a slow song, and Jenny soon found her eyes sliding from Drake back to the notebook in her lap. She traced her fingers over the well-worn pages, feeling the indents of the pen marks. Her gaze fell back onto her name and the little hearts. She imagined Drake absentmindedly writing it while trying to think of the next thrilling line in "Good Mourning" (originally titled "Mourning Death" according to one margin note).

Then her mind kept going. *I wonder if Chance doodles like this.* Did he write the names of the girls he liked with little hearts? Did he have a notebook somewhere filled with conquests? Did he ever write *her* name? *What is he doing now, anyway?* She never knew how he spent his time when he wasn't with her. *He's probably out with a girl*, she realized. She knew that Chance went on dates, but she never heard about them. At least not from him, but she'd heard the gossip plenty of times. She remembered Chance brushing off that girl in the hall. *And to think, in another reality that could've been me.*

The band finished then, the sudden silence jarring. Jenny recovered quickly, clapping enthusiastically. She chastised herself: *I need to focus on what's in front of me.*

"So—" Drake beamed down at her. "What did you think?"

A lot of things. "I loved it." She grinned. "It's great."

CHAPTER 14

Chance

The new happy couple was inseparable. It was a subtle switch, but Jenny began sitting with Drake, complete with hand-holding and his arm around her shoulder, rather than sitting with Chance. The difference was in the way she leaned into Drake, creating a minute amount of space between her and Chance, where their arms used to brush. Chance was sure he was the only one who noticed the slight shift, and he hated it.

He wanted to be happy for her. She was his best friend, and Drake was her first boyfriend. Part of him was jealous—jealous of the way Drake's hand lingered on the small of her back as he guided her down the hall, of the way her gaze lingered on Drake as he walked away and of that wistful smile playing at her lips. Chance tried to choke that part of him down, but it was hard.

The only saving grace seemed to be that Drake wasn't ever invited to Jenny's house. Chance and Jenny still had their quiet afternoons and clandestine sleepovers—though they were regulated to when things were particularly bad at Chance's house. He didn't think Drake knew about them, but he didn't want to bring it up. Sure, some nights she went to Drake's band practice and he had to go home, where his parents were always bickering about something or other. And she was out with Drake most weekends. But Chance was still the only one invited to her house. He knew he shouldn't, but he took pride in that little victory.

"Jenny, do you want to go to my show tomorrow night?" Drake asked a week after they'd become Facebook official. The weather had turned cold and he had traded his loose, short-sleeved V-necks for long-sleeved ones layered over tank tops.

Jenny, to his left, looking adorable in a striped sweater, was too busy focusing on her AP US History reading to hear him.

"Jenny," Drake said again, sounding annoyed. "I asked you a question."

Chance nudged her. "Wessler, your boyfriend asked you a question."

Jenny's head shot up. She looked between Chance and Drake. "What?"

"Your boyfriend is trying to talk to you." Chance gestured to Drake, who was looking at them both worriedly.

She turned to Drake. "I'm so sorry. I heard there's going to be a quiz next block, and I didn't have time to get this reading done last night!"

"It's all right; it's cute when you concentrate." Drake slipped an arm around her shoulders. "Would you like to go to my show tomorrow night? We're playing at that coffee shop downtown. You know, the one that still thinks cyber cafés are cool."

"The one with those neon Macs and inflatable furniture?"

"Yeah, that one. The Cyber Bean or whatever. They're doing a showcase on local bands this week, and the band for tomorrow night backed out, so we got their slot. You wanna come?"

Jenny's eyes lit up excitedly. "I haven't seen you play a concert yet. Of course I'd like to go!"

Chance felt weird witnessing this moment—like a Peeping Tom looking in on something private that he wasn't supposed to see. And that, honestly, he didn't *want* to see. He pretended to read his book—*Native Son* by Richard Wright—but it was hard to do so when Drake and Jenny were excitedly making plans less than two feet across from him.

He was jealous, and the jealousy only made him feel guilty. It was a horrid cycle. He had no right to be jealous and he knew it. Jenny could do whatever she wanted. Chance knew all that and yet, sitting there surreptitiously watching them over the top of his book, he burned with jealousy.

"Am I going to ride with the band, or do I need to find my own way?" Jenny asked her boyfriend.

Drake thought about it for a moment. "I don't think there'll be room in the van for another person, what with the equipment."

"Okay, no problem. Chance can take me," she said, as if that solved everything. Both boys looked at her as if she'd sprouted a second head and started speaking German.

"Chance is coming?" Drake asked, not sounding too pleased with the idea.

Jenny looked at him as if he were an idiot. "Yeah. Obviously. You wouldn't just make plans in front of him without inviting him, would you? That's rude."

She has a point, Chance thought, *but that doesn't mean I want to go.* On one hand, it was better than sitting around at his house or going to Their Spot. On the other hand, he didn't want to go to Drake's show. He had seen The Bleeding Axe Wounds live many times, and none of them were good. Also, the last thing he wanted to do was spend more time around the Happy Couple.

"I don't mind," Chance said, meaning he didn't mind being excluded.

"See, he doesn't mind taking me," Jenny said, gesturing to Chance. "It's settled, then. Chance will take me to your show tomorrow night."

Drake shot Chance a glare, but agreed. Chance sank his head into his hand, biting back a frustrated groan. *Tomorrow night is going to suck*, he thought bitterly.

CHANCE PULLED UP to Jenny's house around seven the next night, his music blaring. He had briefly considered bringing a date of his own, but decided against it. He wasn't the double-date type. He was halfway up the drive when Jenny came sprinting from the house.

"Chance, let's go!"

He stopped in his tracks, eyes on her. She stood before him, brown hair completely straight for once and falling about mid-back. She wore a denim miniskirt over black tights patterned with little golden stars and half-moons. Her shirt was maroon with long sleeves; the color suited her pale complexion.

"I would've knocked on the door," he said when he was able to speak again, still unable to take his eyes off her.

"Then my mother would've assaulted you with questions about Drake," she said. "What do you think?" She turned around so he could see her entire outfit.

The tights complemented her shapely legs and the skirt showed off her hips. "It looks very nice," he said lamely.

"Kelsey helped me," she went on, walking past him to his car. "I went to her house after school."

That explained why she'd wanted Kelsey to take her home that afternoon. Chance rushed to the car before her, opening her door. He wasn't sure what possessed him to do it, but it felt right.

The Cyber Bean was just as lame as he remembered it being. It was downtown, between a bakery and what used to be RadioShack. It was trying to cash in on that early 2000s nostalgia, but Chance didn't see the point. That wasn't that long ago, after all. But people flocked to it "ironically." The door even had a beaded curtain that little girls used to hang up over their doors. It had "modern" egg-shaped chairs and old neon-colored Macs at tiny round plastic white tables, which he assumed were supposed to look cool.

The worst was the type of people who came: people in metallic clothing and clear backpacks, who had crimped hair and tattoo choker necklaces, people who still wore Jelly shoes and holographic jewelry. Chance hadn't enjoyed his childhood the first time; why would he want to relive it through this place?

"I love this place," Jenny said gleefully, looking around wide-eyed. "It's so *Lizzie McGuire*."

Maybe that type of nostalgia is a girl thing? Chance shoved his hands in his pockets, slowly making his way to one of the small tables and uncomfortable egg chairs. *It's like a froyo place in here.*

Jenny pulled out her phone. "Drake says they'll be doing sound check soon."

Chance had almost forgotten about Drake. "Do you want to go backstage and see him before they start?"

"Nah." Jenny shook her head. "He says that seeing me before the show might throw him off. He needs to have a level head to go onstage."

Jenny noticed a flyer advertising Drake's band on the table next to theirs. She snatched it up and folded it into her purse. "You've seen them live? How are they?"

Horrible. "They're all right."

"Kelsey says that they're whiny garbage," Jenny said, glancing back at the stage. "I'm sure that's not true. Drake seems really passionate about his art. It's all he ever talks about."

"Really?"

Jenny nodded. "He's always like, 'Babe, listen to this song I wrote,' or 'Babe, I'm going to write the best song about you.' It's a little annoying, but he's cute when he's excited."

So are puppies, Chance thought bitterly.

"Remember when we tried to start a band?" Jenny said suddenly, turning back to Chance. She leaned forward over the table, talking fast. "I started piano lessons because Kelsey's mom made her take them, and you and I came up with the brilliant idea that we could be some kind of alternative band."

"Of course," Chance said, picking up where she left off. "You would play the piano and I would play guitar, as soon as I learned how to play one. Or had access to one."

"We picked out a name—"

"Friends Are Formalities."

"Naturally, we had to keep up with all those new emo bands. We were going to be circus themed."

"Our Panic! At the Disco phase had a strong hold on us at the time," Chance said solemnly.

"We even made a MySpace for it. That was the pop-punk thing to do."

Chance couldn't help but laugh at that. "We even convinced some people that we were a real band."

"Not just 'some people,' Masters. I remember a little blond boy running around in guyliner."

"Why do you always put me in eyeliner in our stories?" Chance asked, remembering the eyeliner scar story they told when they first met.

"Clearly I have a fetish." Jenny shrugged. "You can take the girl out of the emo, but you can't take the emo out of the girl."

Chance loved this. He loved making up stories with Jenny. He loved the adrenaline rush that came with spitting out the first response he could think of when Jenny volleyed a story at him. He loved seeing her eyes light up as they hand-painted their own past.

It was at that moment that the band came onstage. Drake staggered up to the mike, saying a few words into it, startling Jenny. She turned around to look at her boyfriend, waving to catch his attention. He saw her and nodded once, giving her a wink.

Just like that, their story was finished.

Chance wondered if Jenny ever got like that with Drake—if she ever got caught up in her stories and if she ever showed him that excited, thoughtful face she always wore with Chance. He knew he'd make himself sick wondering about the intimate details of their relationship, but he couldn't help it.

"Good evening, everybody!" Drake yelled into the mic, causing the twenty or so people in the audience to howl. "We are The Bleeding Axe Wounds!"

"Woo!" Jenny exclaimed, jumping to her feet. She reached over and grabbed Chance's wrist, dragging him up, too. "Let's get closer."

They weaved through the crowd until they were almost on the stage themselves. Chance averted his gaze, pretending not to notice the way Jenny was staring up at her boyfriend. In doing so, he noticed the way the two girls next to them were also staring up at Jenny's boyfriend. He also noticed the way her boyfriend was kind of staring back at them.

"This is so exciting," Jenny hissed in Chance's ear, bouncing up and down on the balls of her feet. "I can't believe I'm at my boyfriend's concert. This definitely has to be a teenage experience."

She already had her phone out, taking pictures of everything around her, not even noticing the way Drake was now smiling directly at her. When the band finally did start up, she started filming the whole thing, watching it through her phone screen. She was itching to dance—Chance could tell by the way she kept bouncing with the beat. Finally, he reached out and snagged her phone.

"What the hell?" she said, reaching to take it back.

He held it out of her reach. "Dance with me."

"What?"

"I can tell you want to dance, so let's dance." He slipped her phone into his pocket.

He grabbed her hands and spun her around, her straight hair fanning out around her as he did so.

She laughed, her hands resting on his chest. "Fine," she said, smiling. "We can dance."

They danced to every song Drake played. Neither of them could actually dance, and the moves they busted were awkward and hilarious, but they kept their eyes on each other the whole time and the smiles never left their faces.

By the end of the set, they were sweaty and panting, collapsing into each other. He wrapped his arm around her waist as he led her toward the bar. She threw herself onto the nearest barstool, the biggest grin on her face. Chance looked at her, his own heart pounding in his chest, and felt like he was home.

She pushed her sweaty bangs from her forehead and stuck her tongue out at him. "Stop looking at me. I know I'm gross right now."

"You are not," Chance said, sliding onto the stool next to her.

"I should go fix my hair before I go backstage for Drake," she said, reluctantly getting up. "I'll be right back."

Chance felt like he'd been dropped from a plane. He'd forgotten about Drake, weirdly enough, even though they had been dancing to his music. The world had shrunk down to just him and Jenny and the way they danced together. He had forgotten that they weren't there together—they were there for her boyfriend.

Something vibrated in his pocket, and for a moment he thought Levi might finally be calling, but there was nothing there when he checked his phone. Something vibrated again. He was confused, staring down at the phone in his hand, before he remembered that he had taken Jenny's phone. He dug it out of his pocket. Her mother was calling her.

He looked around, trying to find her. He doubted she was still in the bathroom. Chance made his way toward the restrooms just in time to see Jenny rush away backstage. He pushed himself through the crowd to catch up with her, ducking backstage as well. People rushed past him, taking equipment from the stage. Nick—Drake's bassist—nodded at Chance as he passed.

The phone kept ringing in his hand, but he couldn't find Jenny anywhere.

"Hey!" He turned back and called to Nick.

Nick turned around, his curly brown hair in his eyes. "What?"

"Where's Sellers?"

Nick pointed behind Chance. "Room on your right, bro."

Chance set off, disappearing down the corridor behind the curtains. Sure enough, there was a big black door on his right, standing ajar. He put his hand on it, pushing slightly. He'd just hand Jenny her phone, congratulate Drake on his show, and then be on his way. He looked up from the still-buzzing phone and nearly dropped it in shock.

The room was mostly bare—the only things in it were a small coffee table, a black leather sofa, and a small vanity with a mirror. Jenny and Drake sat on the couch, tangled in each other. Drake had Jenny pinned against the arm of the couch, his body half covering hers. His hands were in her hair and their faces were smashed together.

Chance backed out of the room, hiding behind the wall outside it. He felt sick. He kept seeing Drake's hands all over Jenny, pawing at her. He kept seeing her arms around his neck, her hands pulling at his hair. He wanted to run. He wanted to burst in there and pull them apart.

No, he told himself. Jenny had made her choice and it obviously wasn't him. He couldn't chase off any boys she liked or force her to like him just because he had feelings for her. That was dumb, and Chance knew better.

He decided then and there, standing outside the dressing room his best friend was getting felt up in, that he'd just have to learn to live with his feelings. She was happy and he was miserable, but that was the way it was and he couldn't change it.

So he squared his shoulders and went back out to the dance floor, to find a girl sitting alone to chat up. He was going to move on the best he could.

CHAPTER 15

Jenny

Jenny sat at the lunch table, flipping through her history notes, ignoring the loud buzz of students around her. Drake was at her side, arm around her once again. They'd only grown closer in the week since his concert. Chance's seat to her left was empty, however. He had been suspiciously absent from Oral Comm. Jenny was trying to hide her growing sense of worry.

"Did you hear about Chance and Leslie?" Emelia asked excitedly, plopping into the seat next to Drake.

"What?" Jenny asked. As far as she was concerned, Leslie and Chance barely even interacted.

"I heard second block," Drake said, his eyes shining mischievously.

Jenny glared at them, annoyed. It got on her last nerve when people withheld information. "What happened?" she asked again.

Drake looked down at her, grinning wickedly. "Let's just say the librarian ran into our two friends in various stages of undress in the hallway."

Jenny's eyes went wide. *What? Chance and Leslie*—together? In the hallway? Her mind was flooded with images of the two pulling off into some stolen corner, feeling each other up, and her stomach churned. "Is it true?"

Emelia nodded. "At least three people saw them in the office afterward."

That's why he wasn't in class. She knew, of course, that Chance went on dates. He was Chance Masters, after all, and the number of dates had increased a lot over the past week—at least three that she knew about. But she'd never had evidence of them thrown in her face before. She knew the stab of jealousy ripping through her chest wasn't right, but she couldn't stop it. He didn't want a relationship with her— he had made that abundantly clear—but hearing about how he got with someone else still hurt. He hadn't even *told* her that Leslie was one of the girls he was going out with.

"That's such classic Chance," Drake was saying, his arm tight around Jenny's shoulders.

I can't be jealous, she told herself. *It's not fair to Drake.* How could she be envious of Leslie's rushed hookup with Chance when she was in a full-blown relationship? So okay, the conversation between them wasn't stellar and they didn't have much in common, but Drake liked Jenny so Jenny *had* to like Drake . . . right? It was her mission. She wanted a boyfriend, and she would make herself like him. Jenny Wessler never backed down once she set her mind to something.

A rush of whispers broke out in the cafeteria, culminating into a background hum. Jenny looked around to see Chance enter the room and stalk toward their table, openly glaring at anyone who dared cat-call or wolf whistle.

Jenny couldn't read his expression as he sat down, couldn't tell if he was embarrassed or annoyed. She reached up to where her hair was pulled back at the nape of her neck, twisting the ends around her fingers. "Well," she said after a beat, "I heard that you've been busy."

He didn't even look at her. "I'm sure the rumors of my promiscuity have been vastly exaggerated."

Drake let out a snort. "So the librarian *didn't* catch you going down on Leslie by the computer desk?"

Chance made a face. "They never clean the computer stations."

Emelia leaned forward, eyes on Chance. "We know you were caught making out by the locker during first block."

Jenny glared at him. "You skipped class?"

"You sound like the principal," he said.

She ignored him. "How much trouble are you in?"

"Detention after school for a few days. It's nothing to worry about."

Her green eyes went wide. "How can you not be worried? Hardly anyone gets detention anymore. We're too old for that."

"I assure you that there are tons of people in detention. They're just not the people you hang around with. Speaking of which, I see Kelsey heading over now." He pointed toward the entrance.

"Masters, I heard you got caught going at it in the field house with a student teacher. True or false?" Kelsey said, bringing her tray down onto the table with a *clack*.

Jenny saw Chance's jaw twitch, a sure sign he was annoyed by all the attention.

"True," Jenny answered for him, turning it into another one of their games. "All the rumors are true. Haven't you heard?" She looked at him for a moment before turning back to Kelsey. "He *is* Chance Masters, after all."

"SO WHAT REALLY happened with Leslie?" she asked as they sat on her couch after detention. She had been itching to ask ever since she heard, but knew better than to do so in front of the others.

Chance shrugged, not meeting her eyes. "I ran into her when I was late to class. She was taking a note to the office and we were talking. I don't know, it just kind of happened."

Jenny looked incredulous. "What do you mean, 'it just kind of happened'? Suddenly neither of you could bear it, so you jumped each other in the hallway?"

Chance gestured to himself. "Have you met me?"

She shoved him playfully. "Chance! Be serious!"

"I'm trying," he told her. "But you're kind of hot when you're annoyed."

She grabbed the pillow behind her and hit him with it. "Inappropriate!" she yelled, but she was laughing.

"Okay, okay," he said when he finally stopped laughing. "Honestly, it was nothing. It just happened and now it's over. Anyway, I have another date tonight."

Another date? She hoped her displeasure didn't show on her face. "Seriously, what is that, the fourth this week?"

Chance shrugged. "You're not the only one who can go out."

He was only teasing, but the words stung just the same. It wasn't fair of her to judge him. "I hope she's nice," she said. "Are you excited about Christmas break?"

Chance lounged back onto the couch. "Not particularly. At least school gives me a valid excuse not to be home."

Jenny winced. She hadn't meant to bring up anything painful. "Are things getting worse?"

Chance shook his head, not taking his eyes off the TV. "They don't really pay me much attention. It's . . . eerily calm, which means that everything is probably really bad or about to be. They would do this when I was younger, too—have long periods of peace. I always thought that meant the fighting was over, but not Levi. No, Levi knew better. He knew that no fights meant a huge one was on its way."

Jenny chewed her bottom lip worriedly. "Maybe not this time," she said. "Maybe it's finally over."

Chance leveled her with a look. "We both know that's not true."

CHRISTMAS EVE WAS stressful for many reasons, the main one being that Phillip had been invited to join them for dinner. It would be his first holiday with the entire family, and a big milestone in his relationship with Jenny's mother. Jenny ran around the house, making sure all their Christmas decorations were perfect, not even a piece of tinsel out of place. She wanted to make sure everything was flawless for dinner that night.

Her mother insisted that it was only a normal evening, but Jenny didn't buy that. If Phillip was invited, then Phillip was most likely sticking around. But what if something happened, and then he left like her father had? Everything had to be perfect.

"Jennifer, go get dressed and leave the poor village alone," her mother told her as she went to straighten the ceramic light-up village on their coffee table for the fifteenth time.

"The fake snow doesn't look right," Jenny said, reaching out for the fluffy cotton.

"You're the only one that cares," Jack told her from his seat on the couch, craning his neck to see the TV behind her. He was ready for dinner, wearing a dress shirt and slacks. He looked like he was going to a school dance.

"Please go get ready, Jennifer. I already have enough to do making sure Jessa doesn't get spaghetti on her nice new dress. I can't wrestle with two daughters right now. I have to get ready myself, you know."

Jenny relented, vowing to fix the fake snow after she was dressed. She had had Kelsey help her pick out her outfit days ago: a knee-length, deep-green velvet dress with three-quarter sleeves. It was very *Clueless*, which she adored. She coupled it with a pair of black tights and flats. She wore her hair down, falling in loose ringlets down her back. She looked herself over in the mirror over her vanity, twisting around to look at her back. *I really need a haircut*, she thought.

The doorbell rang, shattering her spell. She tore her gaze away from the girl in the mirror, rushing out her bedroom door. She heard voices floating up the stairs as she came down, catching a glimpse of her mother leading Phillip into the living room.

"Hello there, Jennifer," Phillip called up to her.

"Hello, Phillip," she said as she made her way downstairs.

Her mother smiled. "Oh, honey, you look great."

Phillip was already deep in conversation with Jack, the two of them moving together toward the dining room. Her mother hung back, waiting for Jenny to meet her by the front door. "It is okay that he's here, right?" she asked, eyes on her two men. "I know you were stressed, and it didn't occur to me that you might not want him here."

Jenny didn't want to make her mother worry. "No, Mom, it's fine. That's not why I was stressed."

Relief flooded her mother's features. "Oh, thank goodness. Then why all the worrying?"

"You two are getting serious, aren't you?"

Her mother stared down at her, the hint of a blush staining her cheeks. "I will admit that I'm thinking of keeping him around, if that's okay with you?"

Jenny looked over at Phillip, who was gesturing enthusiastically as he told Jack about what had happened at the last game he coached. Jack was beaming up at him.

"He's nice, but if he chews with his mouth open, he's got to go."

"Fair enough." Her mother nodded solemnly.

Phillip didn't chew with his mouth open. In fact, he was the perfect gentleman at dinner. It was a little infuriating, really. After months of him sporadically hanging around and being Mr. Perfect, Jenny wanted there to be at least *something* wrong with him.

"You should have seen your mother the other day," Phillip was saying, waving his fork around as he spoke. "I've never seen her as angry as she was when that person took her parking spot."

"That's because they drove past multiple spots to deliberately take the one I wanted," her mother defended.

Phillip shook his head. "Or maybe they didn't see those other spots."

"No, they definitely had it out for me."

The doorbell rang, silencing their banter.

Jenny made her way to the front door, not bothering to look through the peephole before answering. It was below freezing outside—if someone was out there in the icy cold, then they had a good reason to be. The last person she expected to see was Chance.

He stood on the doorstep, shivering violently, his duffel bag slung over one shoulder. He wore no coat, just his black hoodie with the hood up. His nose was pink and so were his bare hands. Had he *walked* there? His eyes looked watery, sunken into his head with dark circles framing them. He tried to stutter out a few words, but couldn't manage.

She reached out instinctively, dragging him inside and slamming the door behind him. Her heartbeat was erratic in her chest as she led him to the couch.

"Mom!" she called out, worry blossoming inside her. *"Mom!"*

Her mom ran into the room quickly, alarmed by her daughter's tone. "What is it—" She broke off when she saw Chance, now huddled on the couch, shivering so hard his teeth chattered. "Oh my God, Chance!" She rushed to the boy, feeling the sides of his face. "He's like ice. Jennifer, go grab the extra blankets from the linen closet. Jack!" she called out. "Make some tea or cocoa—just make something hot!"

Jenny passed Phillip on her way out of the living room. He looked as confused as Jenny felt. "What's going on?" he asked as he walked into the room.

"Jennifer's friend is here," her mom told him. "He must've walked here."

Jenny reentered the room, blankets in hand. "Here, Mom." She handed them over, never taking her eyes off her best friend. *He looks so cold. What the hell happened?* The one night she hadn't thought to check up on him—the one night she had forgotten about Chance, and it was the night he seemed to have needed her the most.

"Mom," Jenny said quietly. She pulled her mother aside. She had to say something, to explain. That familiar crease was forming on her mother's forehead, and Jenny knew she needed answers. "Chance has been having some issues at home."

"Issues." Her mother's brow furrowed even more. "Is this something I should be concerned about?"

Jenny shook her head, glancing over at Chance. "His parents fight a lot, that's all."

Her mother looked over at him, too. "Go talk to him," she said. "Figure out what happened."

Jenny flew to the couch, reaching out and wrapping her arms around him, burying her face in his neck. His skin was still cold. She didn't know what had happened, but she knew it had to have been bad for Chance to walk all the way to her house.

Chance finally moved, wrapping his arms around her as well. "I'm sorry you're going through this," she whispered.

He let out a weak, humorless laugh. "S-sorry I ru-ruined your dinner," he said through chattering teeth.

Jenny's mother seemed to realize that they needed privacy. "I'll make you a plate of food," she said. She paused before adding, "Phillip, will you help me in the kitchen?"

Phillip was a good man. He easily picked up on her subtle "let me explain things to you in private" hint and followed her out of the room.

Jenny glared at Jack until he left the room, too. Jessa wandered over to the couch, pointing at Chance with one spaghetti-stained hand.

"Pwetty!"

Jenny tried to steer her back toward the kitchen. "Not now, Jessa."

Jessa didn't budge. "Pwetty is sad."

Chance let out a bark of laughter, reaching out to ruffle Jessa's curls. The girl shivered at his cold hands.

"Pwetty is cold!"

Jenny scooted closer to him, pulling Jessa onto her lap. "What happened, Chance?"

Chance looked over at her, the tips of his nose and ears still pink. "Well, Jenny, my dad left."

CHAPTER 16

Chance

W hat do you mean he left?" Jenny asked, giving voice to the very same question Chance had asked his mother earlier that day.

"He's gone, Jenny. He moved out, all his stuff gone, Mom deserted and crying in her room." Chance let out an unamused laugh. "It's funny, you know, because I don't think she has any right to be upset about it. They fought constantly, but now she's playing the victim."

Jenny looked up at him, wide-eyed. "Chance, start at the beginning. What happened?"

Honestly, he felt numb to the whole thing. It was even funny in an I-Can't-Believe-I-Didn't-See-This-Coming kind of way. "I went to pick up some last-minute things. We were running low on milk, so Mom sent me to the store. Dad was still asleep. His car was gone when I came back and so was everything else. Mom was crying in their room." He recalled what it was like to walk into their bare room and see his mother on the floor, propped against the bed and cocooned in blankets, her bony arms and sunken face the only parts of her exposed. She had glared at him.

But I'm not going to think about that right now.

"He just left?" Jenny asked, batting away Jessa's hand as she tried to pull on Jenny's hair. "Without a word? What did your mom say?"

What had his mother said? That it was his fault. She had told him that his father had left because of Chance, not because of her.

"I don't want to think about it," Chance said. Some things he had to keep to himself. "I couldn't stay there anymore, Jenny. Then my car wouldn't start, and I didn't know what to do, so I just walked here."

"You can always come here, you know that," Jenny told him earnestly.

"I don't want to go back there tonight, Jenny." His mother didn't want him back, either. "I can't do it."

He couldn't even remember the last time he'd seen his father. It had to have been one of the times he was rushing in or out, either going to Jenny's or the barn, but he couldn't remember. He didn't even know the last thing he'd said to him.

Jenny pursed her lips. "Wait here a moment," she said, putting Jessa down. "I'll be right back." She jumped to her feet, rushing into the kitchen. He heard muffled voices talking frantically.

"I think she's asking if I can stay," he told Jessa, who was sitting to his left, looking up at him curiously. He didn't want her to tell her mother some sob story to get her permission, but he didn't want to leave and sneak back in, either. He couldn't go home, and it was too cold to stay in the barn. He didn't know how Levi had survived winter nights in that place.

Levi. He hadn't thought to tell Levi. His brother would know how to handle this, what Chance should do. He pried his phone from his pocket, his fingers working on autopilot. The phone rang and rang, but there was no answer. Finally, the voice mail picked up.

"Hey, you've reached Levi Masters. I'm not here right now, so please leave a—"

Chance hung up and tried again.

"Hey, you've reached Levi Mast—"

Again. More ringing.

"Hey, you've reached Levi—"

Chance hung up, tossing his phone onto the couch. He felt like throwing something, but doubted it would win him points with Jenny's mother. Besides, he didn't want to scare Jessa, who was now picking up his phone to play with.

Jenny reentered the room then, a plate of food in her hands. "Mom says you can sleep on the couch tonight." She sat down between him and Jessa.

Chance could spend the rest of the evening locked in his mind, waiting for Levi and the call that would never come, or he could push it all aside and try to move on. So he chose to move on, at least for now.

"Do you want to watch *Buffy*?" she asked as he took the plate from her.

"Nah, I'm not really in the TV-watching mood." He took a bite of spaghetti, chewing before he spoke again. "To be honest, I don't want to think about any of this at all. I want to *do* something to take my mind off it right now, not stare at a screen."

"Oh really?" Jenny said, picking up the throw pillow behind her and placing it in her lap.

"Yeah," Chance said. "So distract me with your wit. Blow me away with this dazzling intellect I've heard so much about."

"Put me on the spot, why don't you," Jenny mumbled, her face scrunched up adorably as she tried to think of something to say.

"Don't hurt yourself," Chance teased.

Jenny hit him with the pillow she was holding. "I'm trying to think, Chance!"

"Oh yeah?" Chance wrestled the pillow away from her and hit her back.

She grabbed the other throw pillow off the couch, jumping to her feet. "Do you wanna go, Masters?" She couldn't stop laughing. "Do you wanna go right now?"

He set his plate aside, jumping to his feet, too, pillow in hand. He spread his arms out to his sides tauntingly. "Bring it on, Little Miss Really-Likes-Having-As."

And so she did.

HE WAS REPLAYING the night's events for the thousandth time when he heard quiet, precise footsteps on the stairs. They started out slow at first, as if the person was tiptoeing, before growing quicker as they ran the rest of the way.

"Chance?" Jenny stage-whispered, appearing in the doorway. Chance could barely make her out in the flashing Christmas lights. "Are you up?"

"No," he told her, pulling his blankets over his head.

"Bullshit." Her footsteps drew closer, and then the blankets were yanked off him. Jenny stood above him, clad in a pair of flannel sleep pants with purple Bat-symbols on them and a black tank top. Her hair was pulled back in a high ponytail. "No one sleeps the night before Christmas."

He tried to take his blankets back. "Forgive me for not being too excited about this particular Christmas."

She relented, only to pull him upright and plop herself onto the couch next to him. "It's better than the year we broke my mother's favorite toy train," she said.

He looked at her in the dim light, grateful she was there. Somehow she knew that a fake story was just what he needed. "I think you mean the year *you* broke the train, Wessler."

"I distinctly remember it breaking when *you* tried to take it away from me."

"Because it was my year to set it up."

"Excuse you, it was *my* year."

"That's not how I remember it."

"That's the thing with fake pasts: Everyone remembers it differently," she said, bumping his shoulder with hers.

They grew quiet then, taking solace in each other's company.

"I hate your parents," she said suddenly, her voice unusually loud in the quiet. "I know it's ridiculous and unreasonable, but I *hate* them. I've never met them but I hate them."

"I'm not too fond of them myself," he told her. He doubted she could see his expression in the dark, so she couldn't possibly read how much her outburst meant to him. He suspected it was the single kindest thing anyone had ever said to him. Or at least the most thoughtful. "I admire parents who earn their children's respect. There are so many parents who demand respect just because they gave birth to you but do nothing at all to earn it. There are so many parents who treat their children like shit. . . ." He thought of his parents dragging him into their fights.

He could sense Jenny studying him in the dark, from his narrowed eyes to his balled-up fists.

"I get the feeling you're not speaking abstractly here."

"I'm not going to be that kind of selfish parent," he told her, his voice strong with conviction. "I mean, if I become a parent at all."

"Of course you're not," she said, as if it were the most obvious thing in the world. "And I'm not going to abandon my family. We're not going to be them." She paused a moment before adding, "Though we might be every nineties movie cliché right now. Quick, say something antiestablishment."

"Screw the man."

"Yeah!" Jenny exclaimed, laughing. "How punk rock of you."

"You know me."

Her laugh died on her lips as their eyes met. "Yeah," she said slowly, "I do."

He could see the reflection of the Christmas lights in her eyes. They were set on chase and running circles around her irises. The red, blue, and green hues lit up her entire left side, leaving the right side of her face in shadow. He leaned forward, reaching up to brush aside some hair that had escaped from her high ponytail.

Her breath hitched as his fingertips grazed her temple, and he suddenly found it *very* hard to breathe. He leaned in, his hand slowly making its way down the side of her face to cup the back of her head.

"Chance . . ." Her voice was barely a whisper. "I—"

Footsteps thundered down the stairs, approaching quickly. They hardly had time to break apart before they were cast in bright light, blinking away the spots in their vision.

Jack stood in the doorway for just a second, his bedhead making him look only slightly more disheveled than usual, before throwing himself onto the couch between the two of them.

"So," he said, looking from his sister to Chance, "I take it you guys are too excited to sleep, too?"

CHAPTER 17

Jenny

The first snow was the day after Christmas. Jenny and Chance sat in the living room, watching season six of *Buffy the Vampire Slayer*, a bowl of Chex Mix between them.

"I don't get why it continued after season five," Chance said honestly, reaching into the bowl. He was sitting cross-legged, a throw blanket draped over him. He gestured to the TV. "It had the perfect ending, and then it moved to UPN and got depressing."

Jenny looked horrified. "Season six is my favorite," she defended. "It's realistic. The demons aren't from hell; they're from the real world. Besides, it has the musical episode."

"I will give it that: 'Once More with Feeling' is an exemplary episode." He relaxed against the sofa, brown eyes fixed on the TV.

Her mother had taken Jessa to Phillip's to meet his family, but she'd left Jenny and Jack behind to stay with Chance. Chance hadn't mentioned what had happened at home. He was ignoring it, and although she didn't like it, Jenny figured that was for the best.

They were halfway through the episode where Buffy turns invisible when Jack came running downstairs, his footsteps echoing throughout the house. He flew past the living room in a blur of wool scarves and a giant parka, and was out the front door in a flash. Jenny and Chance started, staring after him curiously.

Jenny jumped up to follow. She was supposed to be watching him; he was grounded for saying a certain four-letter word at dinner the night before. She couldn't let him run off somewhere.

Jack had left the door wide open and was already halfway through the front yard, twirling around in the snow, his arms out wide and head tilted upward. Wait—snow? Jenny looked up, seeing fluffy flakes flittering from the sky, lightly landing on the ground and piling up. It was actually snowing! They never got snow this early in the year, not in the South. It was actually snowing in December!

Jenny ran back into the living room, as excited as Jessa had been that morning, rushing to the couch and grabbing Chance by the arm, pulling him up.

"Chance! It's snowing!"

He looked at her dubiously. "Are you sure it's not freezing rain?"

"It's not, I promise! C'mon, look!"

She dragged him from the couch and shoved him toward the front door.

Chance stood in the doorway, looking out into the yard. There was already a considerable dusting covering the grass and the cars, melting only when it touched asphalt. There was no telling how long it'd actually been snowing—neither of them had bothered to check until now. They watched as Jack continued to run around the yard, yelling ecstatically. Other people had begun to emerge from their houses to enjoy the snow as well.

Jenny rushed upstairs to change into warmer clothes, calling behind her, "Let's go outside!"

"I don't have anything but my hoodie!" Chance called up to her.

Fifteen minutes later, the pair stood outside, Jenny in her heaviest green peacoat with a knit gray scarf, hat, and gloves; Chance in his raggedy black hoodie and one of Jenny's old white knit scarves, a green hat, and magenta gloves. He looked at Jenny bitterly.

"I look ridiculous."

She reached out, dusting some snow off his shoulder. "You look adorable."

Snowflakes were sticking to the tips of his hair; he reached up to brush some out of his eyes. "Wanna build a snowman?"

"I'd love to."

They ran around the yard like children, snow twirling to the ground all around them. It was building up fast, new flakes replacing the ones they stole for their snowman. Chance set to work on the base while Jenny crafted the torso and Jack the head. As the snowfall grew heavier, Jenny rolled the snow along the ground, picking up fresh layers on her snow torso. She looked up from her task, taking a moment to watch Chance work.

His nose was already pink from the cold and his hoodie was soaked through. He worked carefully, rolling the large snowball around the ground in orderly lines, trying to make the base as even as possible. His bangs hung in his eyes as he looked down, and she longed to push them back into his hat. Her fingers practically ached for it.

The cold air bit at her face and her gloves were cold and damp, but she didn't care. To her, right there, that moment was perfect. She stooped down, scooping up some snow in her hands. She molded it into the perfect snowball. She weighed it in her hand, waiting for the opportune moment. The second Chance was lost in his task, she launched, volleying the snowball straight into the back of his head.

He spun around, sputtering. "What the hell?"

He looked so ridiculous standing there in the magenta gloves, with snow dripping from the back of his head, expression adorably confused. Jenny couldn't help but laugh. She kept laughing while Chance processed what had happened, not noticing when he crouched down to make a snowball of his own. In fact, she kept laughing up until the moment said snowball hit her in the chest.

Now it was Chance's turn to laugh. "I can't believe you didn't try to dodge that!" he said, howling with laughter. "You look so shocked."

She looked down at the snow clinging to the front of her peacoat. "Oh, it is *on* now. This means war."

He spread his arms tauntingly. "I'm ready."

She ducked behind her partial snowman, scooping up more snow. Adrenaline filled her as she tossed the next one, hitting him in the leg. A snowball sailed over her head, hitting the tree that separated her yard from the neighbors'.

"You gotta be better than that, Chance!" she called, emerging from her crouch to throw another.

He had anticipated her move, waiting until the moment she exposed herself to throw his next two, both hitting her in the abdomen. The cold seeped through the fabric of her coat, but she hardly noticed. She launched another one, missing Chance by inches.

Chance took cover behind Jenny's mom's car, which sat in the driveway completely blanketed with snow. Jenny ran up to the car, tossing her next snowball over it. "You can't hide behind a car," she told him. "That's not fair."

Chance ran around the back of the car then, grabbing her by the waist and tackling her to the ground. They landed side by side, the fall knocking the breath out of her.

"Cheating!" Jenny wheezed when she could finally speak again. She turned her head, the snow sticking to her clothes like a second skin, and glared at her best friend. "That is definitely cheating."

Chance's hat had fallen off in the tussle and his damp hair stuck to the sides of his face. He smiled brilliantly.

"There are no rules in a snowball fight, Wessler."

Her pulse quickened, and she remembered another night where they had lain like this, on the barn floor. Looking back, she had barely known him then. Now he was essential to her being. She couldn't picture this moment with anyone but Chance. No one else could fit so perfectly beside her. She thought of Christmas morning, sitting on the couch and leaning toward him. . . .

I love him, she realized, reaching out to squeeze his hand. *He's my best friend and I love him.*

"Chance, I—"

A snowball sailed through the air, connecting with the side of her head. She sat up, sputtering, barely catching sight of Jack as he ran around the corner of the house, laughing victoriously.

"Good one, Jack!" Chance called, jumping to his feet. He scooped up some snow, running into the backyard after her brother.

Jenny sat there, the snow soaking through her jeans. Her heart was thundering in her chest. The cold wasn't the only reason her face was turning red. Guilt washed over her as she heard Chance's and Jack's laughs echoing from the backyard. She wasn't allowed to feel anything for Chance, not anymore. She had a boyfriend, for goodness' sake! A boyfriend she hadn't even called since Christmas Eve.

She got to her feet, heading back inside to find her phone. She had to call him, to take her mind off Chance lying in the snow next to her. It wasn't fair to Drake for her to think of Chance that way. Drake liked her so much. He was a good guy.

She found her phone upstairs on her bed. She sat down, dialing Drake's number.

"Hey," she said when he answered.

"Hey to you, too." He laughed. "Have you been out in the snow yet?"

She let out a shaky laugh. "Yeah, a little bit."

"Do you want to play in the snow together?" he asked. "The roads aren't bad, so I could swing by and pick you up."

"You could just hang out here, if you want. Mom is at Phillip's, so it won't be a problem."

"Oh, so I'm only allowed when your mother's not home?"

"What are you talking about?"

"This is the first time you've invited me over," he said, as if it were obvious.

Jenny opened her mouth to respond, but stopped. *Oh my god, he's right.* She had never invited him over. It had never even *occurred* to her to ask him over before. They hung out at band practices and gigs and school, and she never thought to do anything more than that.

"I'll be over in thirty," Drake said, breaking the silence. "See you then."

I'm a bad girlfriend. Jenny lowered the phone from her ear, looking at it. The guilt from before crept over her again, tenfold. *I've been a bad girlfriend and I haven't even* realized *it. How do other people do this?*

"**YOU DON'T HAVE** to leave," Jenny told Chance. "We can all hang out."

They stood in the kitchen, melted snow dripping off them. Jack had taken the news that Drake was coming over quite well, just shrugging and asking if he could go to a friend's to play video games.

"You're grounded," Jenny had pointed out.

"I won't tell Mom you had your boyfriend over," he'd countered.

"Deal."

They'd shaken on it.

Chance shook his head, though, water droplets cascading to the floor. "I should let you two have some time alone." He took the towel that Jenny offered, rubbing it through his hair. "Besides, I think it's time I check on Mom. We've both had some time to calm down."

"Are you sure?" she asked. She hated to chase him out of the house.

"Yeah, it's fine." He handed the towel back to her. "I can't hide out here forever; we both know that."

She followed him to the foyer. "You can come straight back here if you need to."

"I know." He paused by the door to smile down at her. "Don't look so worried," he said, reaching out to ruffle her hair like he had Jessa's. "I can take care of myself. Tell your mother thanks for letting me stay."

"Chance—"

"Wessler, it's all right. Your boyfriend is coming over; it's not my place to keep you from that. And, to be honest, I don't feel like being around a happy couple right now. So focus on him, okay?"

He was right. She needed to clear her head of him—sitting across from her in the dark, leaning ever closer—altogether.

"All right. I'll call you later to see how you're doing."

He had barely cleared the driveway when the doorbell rang, causing her to break out in a light sweat. *This is it. Drake's here.*

Drake looked good. His hair was damp from the snow and Jenny could smell the faint scent of his Axe body wash wafting off him. He was so much taller than her—taller than Chance, even. He stormed past her, heading straight for the living room. She could feel the anger radiating off him in waves, but she wasn't sure why.

"Is everything okay?" she asked, closing the door behind him.

He ignored her question. "Did I just pass Chance leaving your house?"

"Yes," she answered. "He's going home."

Drake looked down at her, his jaw twitching. "He comes over here?"

She nodded dumbly. "He's my best friend."

"I assumed when you called me it was because you wanted— never mind." Drake stopped, shaking his head. "I'm being dumb. Of course he's your best friend, I know that." He stopped to look around. "So this is your house, huh? Give me the tour."

She eyed him warily. She was almost positive that he was still irritated. "Well, that's the living room." She pointed toward said room. "The dining room-slash-kitchen is in there."

Drake was still looking down at her. "What about your room?"

"My room?"

"Yeah, can I see your room?"

Heat flooded her face. Was he asking what she thought he was asking? "It's upstairs. We can take a look, if you want."

It was different than showing Chance her room. She was worried that Drake would judge her, would look around at her girly decor and scoff. She never feared that Chance would judge her, but it felt like Drake was looking at everything under a magnifying glass, ready to pounce on anything he could.

He didn't ask about the medal on the door or mock the princess bed frame. He threw himself down on the bed, feet dangling off the end. He looked good, stretched out there, his shirt riding up and his skinny jeans riding low. "This is it?" he asked.

Jenny looked down at him. "You're not even looking at it."

"I'm looking at you." But he sat up, looking around. "It's nice. I like the bookshelf. What's that?" He got up, crossing the room and picking up a shirt that had been dropped under her desk. "Are you secretly a slob who throws her dirty laundry on the—" He broke off. He'd been absentmindedly holding the shirt out to get a look at it, but now he stared at it, frozen.

Jenny took a good look at it, too. It was forest green and short sleeved, with a faded logo of some sports team on the front. It was Chance's favorite shirt—he wore it all the time. Not because he cared about the team or whatever, but because the mascot on it was making the dumbest face he'd ever seen.

Jenny reached for it instinctively, and something about her expression must have given it all away. Drake balled up the shirt in his hand.

"What is this doing here?" he asked, glaring down at her. "What is Masters's shirt doing here, in your room?"

Jenny was trying to figure out the same thing. He must've left it one morning when he changed out of the clothes he'd slept in. He always did that while she was checking to make sure the coast was clear to sneak him downstairs.

"He must've left it."

That only enraged Drake more. "What was he doing in your room without a shirt on?"

"Changing," she answered.

"Why was he *changing* in your room?" He tossed the shirt at her.

Chance's family issues weren't her secret to tell, but she had to do something.

"Things are tense at his house, okay? Sometimes he stays here to avoid going home." But that was the wrong thing to say.

"He *sleeps* here?!" Drake looked around her room with disgust. "Chance Masters is sleeping with *my* girlfriend?!"

"No!" She rushed forward, placing a hand on his shoulder. "It's not like that, I promise!"

He looked down at her incredulously. "He's *Chance Masters*, Jenny. I *know* what it's like."

"He needed a place to stay!"

But he wasn't even listening. "I was so happy when you invited me over. I thought we were finally getting somewhere, but I should've known he was here first. Is there anywhere Chance hasn't been first?" He shot a pointed look at her bed.

She couldn't believe he was even *implying* that. "Drake, no!" She felt her temper rising and had to bite it back. She needed to calm down. She needed to get out her planner and make a color-coded list of pros and cons of the situation. She needed to *fix* this. *I messed up monumentally. I've messed up this relationship so badly.*

"Drake," she began, "I'm sorry. He's my best friend and he needed me. I was trying to do what's right. Chance *needed* me."

Drake rolled his gray eyes at that. "Of course he did."

Jenny bristled at his tone. "He did, Drake."

"You could've told me, Jenny. I'm your damn boyfriend. You could've come to me and I could've given him a place to stay. But you didn't—you invited him into your bed instead."

"I told you it's not like that! Once again, he's my best friend! Besides, I can invite whomever I want over to *my* house! I don't have to justify having him over to you!"

"I would've done anything you asked me to. But, no, you didn't ask me for help. Did you even think of me? You're always with him, Jenny. It's always him." Drake ran a hand through his hair, tugging on it out of frustration. "I mean, he sleeps over here. You're always together. I get here and he's leaving. Is it wrong of me to think there's something going on?"

His accusation brought Jenny up short. She knew that Drake was a bit jealous of her best friend, but she had no idea that he suspected something was going on between her and Chance. Did he honestly believe that? Did Drake think she'd do that to him?

"How could you think that?" she asked, unsure whether she was more angry or stunned. She reached out, grabbing the sides of his face and twisting him to look at her. "It's you I want. You're the one that I'm with. Like you said, you're my damn boyfriend. I wouldn't be with you if I didn't want to be, Drake."

He looked at her in disbelief. "You sure as hell don't show it half the time."

That really stung. She felt like she'd been struck—how could he think she didn't show it? She was always trying her hardest to show how much he meant to her.

"How could you say that?" she asked, her voice trembling.

"You give me nothing, Jenny," he said. He reached up, pulling her hands away from his face.

Does not compute. She acted like a girlfriend was supposed to act. Every emotion she could feel she poured into him. Relationships weren't supposed to be this hard, right? Unless—unless he didn't mean emotionally. On every teen drama Jenny had devoured over the years, all the major arguments had been solved physically. The main couple would have a falling out—one consumed with jealousy and the other with guilt—and they'd push their relationship to the next level to prove themselves. Maybe sometimes words weren't enough. But actions? Actions speak louder than words every time.

"That's not true," she said. Then she rose to her tiptoes and kissed him.

He was surprised at first, leaning away from the kiss, but after a moment he gave into it, backing her up until the backs of her knees hit the bed, then he slowly lowered her down. His hands slithered up her body, tangling in her hair. He deepened the kiss, slowly reclining her back onto the bed until half of his body covered hers.

His lips moved to her neck, allowing her a moment to breathe. Her skin tingled everywhere his lips touched. She pulled his mouth back up to hers.

They had never gotten past second base before. They had always run out of time, or stopped because she wasn't ready yet. Well, she was ready now. If he was ready (and, oh yes, she knew he was ready), then so was she.

It wasn't like she was saving her virginity for a special occasion. She wasn't Cher in *Clueless*, saving herself for Luke Perry. Like with kissing, the thought of sex had never really interested her much. It was something some people did and others didn't. It meant something to some people, and it meant very little to others. Jenny liked to think she fell somewhere in between. It was just something she was deciding to do.

She pulled Drake's shirt over his head, laughing at the way the static caused his hair to stand up. She leaned up to meet his kiss, smiling against his lips. She couldn't feel an ounce of his previous anger, but she could feel his heart beating against her chest.

Drake reached down, hooking a finger into the waistband of her jeans. "Do you want to?" he whispered huskily in her ear.

"I want to," she sighed as Drake lowered his head to kiss her neck once more.

CHAPTER 18

Chance

*C*hance wanted a freaking drink. He wanted to be world-spinning drunk. His father had left, his mother was barely talking to him, his best friend had been so busy with her boyfriend that he hadn't seen her since Christmas, and the cup in his hand was almost empty.

He hadn't even wanted to come to Leslie's stupid New Year's Eve party, but he knew it wasn't healthy to hang around his house anymore. He wanted out and he wanted free booze, so there he was.

People in *Happy New Year* hats and giant plastic glasses chatted away happily, but Chance couldn't muster up any excitement. He had a sinking feeling that the new year was going to be even worse than the current one.

That feeling was basically confirmed when he spotted Drake setting aside his guitar and making his way through Leslie's living room. Chance tried to slip into the hall unnoticed, but no such luck. Drake was making a beeline straight for him.

Chance chugged what was left of his mixed drink, putting on a fake smile. "Sellers," he said by way of greeting. "You guys sound good tonight."

"Have you seen Jenny?"

"No, I haven't."

"That's right, I haven't seen you around lately, Masters." Drake smirked, taking a drink from his own cup. "I've been hanging at Jenny's every day, but I haven't run into you."

Chance wanted to punch that self-satisfied smirk right off Drake's smug little face. But he was determined not to let Drake get to him.

"Didn't want to cut into her boyfriend time," he muttered.

"I appreciate that," Drake went on, "because things are going great for us. *Really* great, actually. Spectacularly great. However great you're thinking right now, it's going even better."

There was something about Drake's tone that made Chance pause, unconsciously crushing the Solo cup still gripped in his hand.

"So, you're going to have to *keep* hanging back, got it, Masters?"

Chance's eyes narrowed as he turned to face Drake directly. "I don't know what you're trying to say here, Drake, but we're both important to Jenny. As long as she needs me, I'm not going anywhere. You got a problem?"

Drake laughed. "Oh no, I'm so scared of you right now. I already told you that things are going great. Super great, Masters. In fact, I don't see that she needs you at all."

Chance's hand balled into a fist at his side, his fingernails leaving half-moon imprints in his palm. He was going to punch something—the wall, Drake, that stupid band kid walking past talking way too loudly about *Supernatural*, whatever got in his way first.

"You don't know what you're talking about," Chance said through clenched teeth. *Jenny would hate me for punching her boyfriend*, he reminded himself. *She loves Drake and she hates violence.*

Drake laughed again, an annoying throaty sound, before walking off.

He thought about what Drake had told him and his stomach churned. If Jenny had decided to—to—*I can't even think it*—then that was *her* decision and definitely wasn't something Drake should be brandishing like a weapon, as if to prove that he'd "won" her. But that was the Drake he had always known—the one he wished Jenny could see.

The music started up again, Drake back at the microphone. Chance saw Jenny in front of him, staring dreamily up at her boyfriend. *If she had heard him just now*, he thought bitterly.

Chance went to the kitchen in search of another drink. He felt out of place, like he didn't belong anywhere. He felt *off.*

The crowd was too thick in the kitchen. Leslie sat on the counter, weighed down by her usual dozen necklaces.

"Hey," she said when he approached. "Weren't you just in here getting a drink?"

"I finished it." He reached past her, going for one of the cheaper-looking bottles.

"That's, what, your third drink since you got here?"

"Are you the drink monitor?" he asked, pulling a two-liter of soda toward him.

"Actually, yes," she said. "I procured the liquor, so I monitor the liquor."

"I'll chip in next time." He poured the soda in a cup before adding booze.

"Regardless, you should slow down. I don't need you running around sloppy drunk."

"Well, Leslie, it's not really your job to take care of me."

She rolled her eyes. "Whatever. Just, please, do not puke on my carpet."

"I'll aim for the tile, Scout's Honor."

He weaved through the crowd and out the door, heading toward the stairs. Everyone looked so carefree, running through Leslie's house, laughing and drinking. It was like he was five years old, sitting in the tree in his front yard, spying on his neighbors like he used to. Would anyone realize how alone he felt and ask him to join them?

"What are you doing on the sidelines, Masters?" came a voice from a step above him.

Chance turned around to find Kelsey standing above him. "What's it look like I'm doing, Molar? I'm enjoying the party."

Kelsey snorted in disbelief. "If you're enjoying the party, then so am I." She stepped down, sitting on the step next to him. "So what's your damage?"

Chance glanced toward the living room, catching a glimpse of Drake and Jenny.

Kelsey followed his gaze. "Ah," she said knowingly.

"What about you?" he asked her.

She shrugged. "I didn't want to be the only one without plans for the night, so I figured why not go to a party. Then I got here and remembered why I hate parties."

Chance took another sip, eyes still on Jenny dancing in the crowd. "You've known Jenny a long time, right?"

Kelsey looked at him curiously. "Not as long as you have, though."

Of course, the fake past. "Do you think she's happy with Drake?"

Kelsey looked away, watching the people around them. "I honestly don't know. I thought I knew her, but lately that's been up for debate."

He tore his gaze away from his best friend to look at Kelsey. "What?"

She wouldn't meet his eyes. "Tell me, do you guys laugh at me? This whole time, all these years that Jenny and I have known each other, was I a joke to the two of you?"

"Where is this coming from?" Chance asked.

Kelsey took a sip of her own drink. "I've considered Jenny my best friend since middle school. I don't have many friends, but I always had Jenny. She was shy and distant, but she was my best friend. I told her everything. I thought she told me everything, too, but she didn't tell me about *you*. All these years and she never mentioned you. So I can't help but wonder if I even knew her at all, or if I was some kind of joke."

Chance had never once considered Kelsey or her previous role in Jenny's life. It had never occurred to him that by claiming the spot of Jenny's best friend he was taking it away from someone else.

"We've never laughed at you, Kelsey." Then he added, "Why don't you try to talk to Jenny about this?"

She shook her head. "She's been doing so well, opening up to people and stuff. I mean, look at her, dancing at a party. I don't want to be the petty one on the sidelines of her personal growth, going, 'What about me?' She *has* been hanging out with me more, which should be enough, but I can't help freaking about the fact she didn't tell me about you."

He wanted to tell her the truth. He wanted her to know that there wasn't anything wrong with her, that he and Jenny were just liars playing a lying game that Kelsey had gotten caught up in, but he couldn't. It wasn't his secret to tell.

"There's nothing wrong with you," he told Kelsey. "You need to talk to Jenny about this. I promise she can explain everything."

She downed the rest of her drink before pointing a finger at him threateningly.

"You can't tell anyone I got all soft with you. I can't intimidate people into doing what I want if they know I got all mushy with you."

"I wouldn't dream of it." Chance laughed. "Cross my heart and hope to die."

"Good." She smiled then, and it lit up her whole face. "I guess I should offer you some advice for your Jenny predicament, too?"

"*My* Jenny predicament?"

She looked at him knowingly. "You *know.*"

There was no use in denying it. "I'm working on it," he told her.

"I know. I heard all about Leslie in the hallway. Your situation might suck, but it doesn't have to. I mean, why are you sitting here on the steps? It's New Year's Eve, so make the best of it. See Glenda Hargrove over there?" She pointed to a tall dancing girl with long blond hair cascading down her back. "Go dance with her. Have fun."

Have fun? He looked to the living room, searching for Jenny once more.

"I don't know," he said.

Kelsey scoffed, "Are you or are you not Chance fucking Masters?"

"I am," he said confidently, rising to his feet.

"Then go!" Kelsey nudged him forward, laughing.

Chance made his way down the remaining steps, past the living room and the brunette dancing in there. Glenda was getting closer, the body heat from the dense crowd already making Chance sweat.

"Hey," he said to Glenda once he was close enough to be heard over the roaring music. She was tall enough that he didn't have to look down to talk to her.

She smiled at him, bringing his attention to the adorable smattering of freckles across her nose.

"Hey."

"Do you want to dance?" He was already reaching for her hand.

Her arms snaked up his chest to wrap around his neck. "I'd love to."

Chance kept dancing and he kept flirting. After Glenda, he danced with a girl named Miranda. Then he spent some time in the kitchen, helping a girl named Kate operate the keg. He felt looser and less stressed with every dance and with every girl. He didn't catch himself looking for Jenny or waiting for his phone to ring. He lost himself in the music and laughter around him, not even pausing when he caught Drake shooting him a glare from behind his microphone.

Chance only smiled back, pulling the girl he was with closer still.

CHAPTER 19

Jenny

Parties are better in theory than in reality, Jenny thought as she stood in the foyer of Leslie's house for the second time, craning her neck to look past another group of her classmates. She realized that TV had been very wrong about high school parties—in reality, if you've been to one, then you've been to them all. This was her second and she was already thinking it was one too many.

People were dancing in the living room to the left, grinding against each other. Drake's band was set up by the doors that led to the backyard. He was already wailing away at his latest song. The kitchen, where the drinks were, was to the right.

She hated the stench of weed, cigarette smoke, and vomit that hung in the air, clinging to her like a second skin as she forced her way into the crowd. She eyed the red Solo cups that littered every available surface. She hated everything about parties when she didn't have someone to use as a buffer.

This wasn't like Halloween. At Halloween she'd had Drake, but he had decided that his band *had* to play this time and, of course, she had to come support him. She wanted to go find Chance, but she knew that wasn't a good idea. Drake had finally calmed down about the two of them, and she didn't want to cause any more animosity.

She spent a few songs in the living room, pretending like she wasn't freaking out about the mass of people dancing too close to her. She smiled at Drake every time he looked out at the audience. When she couldn't take it anymore, she escaped, slipping from the mass of gyrating bodies and out into the hall.

She made her way to the kitchen, spotting a lot of familiar faces. She even passed Emelia and associates hiding out in an alcove under the stairs. There were more people in the kitchen, and Leslie was sitting next to a plethora of drinks on the counter.

"Hey," she said to Leslie as she approached, her mind flashing to what Leslie and Chance had been caught doing a few weeks earlier. "What's up?"

"I'm the booze monitor," Leslie told her, taking a sip from her cup. She gestured to the bottles next to her. "Take whatever you want."

Jenny stood at the counter, staring at her choices. She grabbed the Hawaiian Punch and then looked for something that might go well with that. *Is Heaven Hill a good vodka?* She reached for the bottle.

Leslie's hand shot out, taking the bottle from her. "You're going to poison yourself," she said, hopping down from the counter. "Let me make you something."

"Is that not good?" she asked.

Leslie shook her head. "It's cheap, but it's trash. Don't touch McCormick, either; it's like drinking rubbing alcohol."

She watched as Leslie picked up a bottle and looked at it. "Doesn't it all taste like rubbing alcohol?"

Leslie shrugged. "Basically. I don't mess with mixed drinks; they only prolong the pain. I find shots are a better and quicker alternative. Do you wanna do shots?"

Jenny wanted to say no, to take a nasty mixed drink and slink back into the living room, but where was the fun in that? *Always take the road less traveled*, she reminded herself.

"Let's do it," she said.

"I'll do a few with you." Leslie smiled and pulled over the coconut rum, pouring them both shots.

On the count of three, they downed them. The liquid was even worse in its pure form. It burned the whole way down. Jenny had to keep from gagging.

"Woo!" she exclaimed, slamming her cup down. "Coconut-flavored anything is *awful*."

Leslie had handled hers like a pro, not even flinching. Tyler—one of the many football players and already three sheets to the wind—came ambling up to them.

"Are you guys doing shots?" he asked the redhead.

"Yeah, want one?"

"Yes!" he exclaimed, pumping one meaty paw into the air.

"If you start chanting, I won't pour you one."

Tyler lowered his arm.

Leslie poured them another round of shots and on the count of three, they all downed the liquid. Jenny was starting to feel a bit fuzzy around the edges and declined the next round, deciding to switch back to mixed drinks. *Maybe I can handle the crowd more*, she thought, taking the cup Leslie offered her just as she heard Drake's voice call out, "The band would like to take a short break!"

The living room was as packed as it had been when she left, sweaty bodies everywhere. A few people had set up beer pong on the coffee table by the couch. Jenny watched them, fascinated. She had never really understood the game.

"You wanna play?" a voice asked in her ear, causing her to jump. She spun around, frantic, ready to punch some perv away, when she saw it was just Drake. His long hair was stuck to his forehead with sweat and he was wearing gray skinny jeans with a black tank top. He looked good.

"I don't know how," she told him truthfully. It infuriated her how little reaction her body had to him, even after everything they'd been doing lately. She wanted her heart to leap out of her chest and her tongue to twist itself into knots.

"You're telling me Jenny Wessler doesn't know how to do something?" Drake shook his head in disbelief.

"Why don't you show me, then?" she said flirtatiously.

"I would if I had the time. The band is back on in five."

"You sound good tonight," she told him. *Isn't that what girlfriends are supposed to say?*

"I know," Drake said. "I'm playing some new stuff that I wrote recently." He gave her a squeeze.

Drake went back to his band and Jenny went back to watching him. There was something so electric about the way he moved behind a microphone. He was passionate about it.

Over the course of a few songs, she noticed people staring transfixed at Drake. They looked at Drake the same way girls looked at Chance.

More people kept pushing themselves into the room, some dancing and some just standing. Drake had the whole crowd eating out of his hand, and from the glint in his eye, he knew it. Jenny looked down at her long-since-finished drink and decided she needed a new one.

Leslie wasn't in the kitchen anymore, the booze left unmonitored. A group circled the counter, all taking shots. She weaseled her way in, snagging a glass in the next round. One shot. Two shots. Three shots. They were pouring their fourth when she ducked out.

The room was spinning around her and she imagined the clear liquid sloshing in her the way it did in the bottle she picked up. She shakily poured herself another drink, mixing in some generic soda she found. It tasted awful, but she found it hard to care about that anymore.

She parked herself on the bottom step, sipping her drink and watching the party unfold. People came and went in large groups. A couple made out against the banister beside her, the boy's hand slowly creeping up under the girl's skirt. Drunken girls stumbled by like trains, linked by clasped hands as they tried not to lose each other in the crowd. Her drink was nearing empty, and she wondered why she was sitting out.

She stumbled a bit when she stood, her head spinning. Using the wall for support, she propelled herself into the living room. She stood in the arch of the doorway, her eyes scanning for the person she wanted to see. Her head was spinning, and she was sure she felt a hand on her waist. The music was too damn loud; it was driving her crazy. She pushed past people, stumbling. *If they would just give me space*, she thought. A guy she vaguely recognized from her freshman English class—*Jesse? David? Michael?*—danced up to her, dry humping the air she was quickly trying to vacate.

The world was tipping up at the sides and her cup wasn't in her hand anymore and she just wanted everything to *stop*. The music grew louder and she cursed the band. People danced tighter around her and she felt the bile rising at the back of her throat. She had to get out of there, but how? *Chance. I have to find Chance.* He was the only person who could help her. She broke through the throng of people around her, frantically searching. *I need my best friend.*

Chance would stop the spinning and the groping. Chance would hold her close. Chance would take her home.

He was on the couch; a beautiful girl had her mile-long legs draped across his lap, his hand absentmindedly stroking her calves as she spoke. *Bingo.* Jenny stumbled through the crowd, not sure whether someone she passed grabbed her ass or accidentally brushed against her. *Whatever.* She stumbled up to Chance, drawing his attention from the girl on his lap.

"You need to come with me now," she slurred, taking his drink from his hand and taking a sip. She spat it back. "This is the worst thing I've had all night."

He apologetically pushed the girl's legs off him, standing to put an arm around Jenny's waist, taking his drink back. "I could've warned you."

She clung to his shirt for support, the room rocking. He looked so ridiculously good standing there in his black T-shirt, blond hair tussled. She wanted to dance, to feel his body pressed against hers—moving along with her. She pulled on the hem of his shirt, trying to drag him toward the grinding teens. She lost her footing, almost falling.

She felt disconnected to her legs, as if her limbs were not her own. Chance's hands steadied her, but she still felt like she was falling. She kept seeing her vision fall into place again and again—never settling and never stopping.

"Whoa," Chance said into her hair, trying to keep her steady. "Hold on, I got you." He kept repeating it as he led her through the crowd, like a soothing mantra, again and again. "I got you. I got you. I got you."

And she knew he always would.

CHAPTER 20
Chance

Drunk Jenny was very kittenlike, Chance decided. She clung to him as he stumbled around in the dark barn, trying to relight all the candles she kept blowing out when his back was turned. The glow-in-the-dark stars that littered the floor were finally dead. The blankets he'd brought when he was sleeping there were still folded up in the trunk where he'd left them.

Jenny trailed after him, wrapping her arms around his waist and burying her face into his back every time he stood still. She had puked outside when they got there but had calmed down since.

Chance never thought of himself as the hold-your-hair-while-you-puke kind of guy, but it was turning out that there was very little Jenny could do to drive him away. He couldn't leave his best friend to fend for herself. She had never been this drunk before. She needed him.

He pulled her arms from his middle for the fifth time, turning to lead her to the pallet he had made. She stumbled along, still trying to put her arms around him as she walked.

"Shhh," he said, lowering her to the blankets.

She whined in protest when he let her go, reaching out for him.

"Stay," she told him.

She looked so beautiful lying there, the flickering lights from the candles making the shadows dance around her. Her arms were still outstretched for him, open. Her eyes were wide and her full lips parted slightly, as if she were about to say something.

Don't try to romanticize this, Chance told himself. *She might be about to puke again.*

Chance stretched out beside her. He could feel her warmth along the entire right side of his body. She wrapped herself around him within seconds, her arms around his chest and face buried into the crook of his neck.

"You smell good," she mumbled into his skin, her breath hot on his neck. "Like sandalwood. I like it. It's not all chemically like Axe."

"Thanks," he said awkwardly, shifting them into a more comfortable position. He put his arm around her, drawing her in closer. His eye flickered up to the ceiling. "Look," he said, pointing up with his left hand. "You can see a few stars through the holes."

Out there, in the middle of nowhere, there were way more stars than in the city. Chance even thought he could make out the handle of the Big Dipper . . . or possibly the Little Dipper. Chance wasn't big on astronomy.

"Pretty," Jenny cooed, looking up. "Space is pretty. All those galaxies and nebulas and here we are, just two little specks on a floating rock in the vast fields of space."

Chance laughed. "Are you sure you're drunk? Or are we at the pensive philosopher level of hammered now?"

"We're so little." She giggled, wide eyes still locked on the stars.

"Speak for yourself."

She snorted. "Perv. We're nothing, y'know? We get these simple little lives among bunches of people—"

"Ah yes, there are only bunches of people on Earth."

"—and they're all we get but we spend them all making the wrong decisions and then get jobs we hate and then we pay bills and die," she finished, as if he hadn't spoken. "And some people's one life is spent being homeless or abused and it's not their fault but it's the only life they get and they can't ever go back and live another one. They'll never know what it's like to have some other kind of life. None of us will."

"Okay, that's enough," Chance said. He could feel her heart hammering against his side. He was sure his own was racing, too. He didn't want to think about this stuff. He never wanted to think about this stuff. The future was off-limits to him. He'd rather van Gogh it and cut off his own ear than think about the future. "We're done with philosophy hour, Jens."

"I saw you with those girls," she said calmly as she snuggled into his side again.

He didn't know why he felt ashamed—like a kid caught in a lie—but he did. His first instinct was to defend himself, but he bit it back. "I figured."

She lazily nodded. "Mm-hm. I want you to know it's okay."

His breath hitched. "It's okay?"

"If hooking up with someone makes you happy, then I'm happy, too."

"I'm not serious with any of them," he felt compelled to assure her. "We were just hanging out."

She snorted again. "I know that."

He took offense. "What is that supposed to mean?"

"You don't *get* serious with anyone," she said sleepily, nuzzling into his shirt.

Where did that come from?

"Who told you that?" he asked, still looking at the ceiling.

"You . . . said . . ."

"What?" he asked. After a moment of silence, he turned to look at her. Her eyes were closed, her breathing even. She had fallen asleep on him.

Where did she hear that I don't get serious? he wondered, almost laughing to himself. It was funny, in a not-funny way. He wanted to laugh at the cruelty of the situation. Here he was, looking down at the most serious relationship he'd ever had in his life, and she didn't believe he was serious about anyone.

A buzzing noise filled the room, making him jump. It rattled against the floorboards, loud and angry. He looked around, trying to find the cause.

We're going to get murdered, he thought. *Jason has come for us.*

It wasn't until the sound died and started up again that he realized it must be Jenny's phone. Jenny was still out of it, a bit of drool running from the corner of her mouth. The phone kept buzzing again and again.

I can't answer her phone. For one, it's in her pants pocket! But . . . wait . . . what if it's her mom? She might be calling to check in.

Chance carefully pulled the phone from her pocket just as it stopped vibrating. It started up again almost immediately. It wasn't her mother. It was Drake.

Chance stared down at the phone in his hand, Jenny's contact photo of Drake—taken one day at lunch, him smiling down at her—staring back at him. He wasn't sure if he should answer it. He wasn't too keen on speaking to Drake, not after their conversation earlier. *He might be worried about her,* he considered. *He might want to know that she's safe.*

The phone went blank before starting up again. It was clear that Drake was going to keep calling until he got an answer. Chance detangled himself completely from Jenny, moving to stand by the ladder to the loft. He thought about stepping outside, but he didn't want a wild raccoon or something to sneak past him and make a nest in Jenny's hair, or worse.

"Hello?" he answered.

Drake was silent, most likely stunned to hear a guy answer the phone.

"This is Chance," Chance clarified.

"Yeah, I can tell" was Drake's reply. His voice was quiet—angry. "I was worried about Jenny, but obviously I shouldn't be; she went home with *you.*" He spit the last word like it was something foul he couldn't bear to have touching his tongue.

"She was drunk," Chance tried to explain, looking over at Jenny curled asleep on the floor. "She needed to get out of there. You were busy—"

"And you couldn't help but graciously swoop in and take our little lush home," Drake filled in bitterly. "You couldn't wait to play the damn hero."

"You were busy," Chance repeated. Hearing Drake call Jenny a lush got his blood boiling. "I tried to signal you, but you were too busy looking at that blue-haired girl with the low-cut top."

"I was doing my *job*, Masters. You just wanted to take advantage of my girlfriend."

"Your girlfriend happens to be my best friend," Chance pointed out. "She needed me and I was there. You weren't. End of story, Sellers."

"Look, I'm happy she's safe," Drake said, his tone softening a tiny bit. There were sounds of whooping in the background. "The band got done and I couldn't find her and Leslie said she was too drunk to function, so I got worried. I just fucking *hate* that you were the one to take care of her."

"I wouldn't let anything happen to her. You should at least know that much." Chance deflated, too, his anger leaving him. God, he was so tired.

"I can't do this right now." Drake hung up.

Chance looked down at Jenny. She looked so young curled up in the blankets, her hair fanned out behind her. The lights were dying slowly, wax dripping down the sides of the candles as they threatened to burn out.

He picked up the one nearest him, looking at the way the flame was reflected in the melted wax. He wondered if he was going to be one of those people Jenny had talked about—one of the ones who wasted their wholes lives and could never get out or restart. Was he going to be like his parents? His brother? He looked down at Jenny again, her chest slowly rising and falling.

Chance blew out the candle.

* * *

THE SUNLIGHT SPILLED in through the cracks in the ceiling and right into Chance's eyes. He rolled over, throwing his arm over his face. His back hurt—hell, his *everything* hurt. He didn't want to get up yet.

Something moved beside him. The warmth that had been at his side disappeared, replaced with bitter cold. He wanted to reach out for it, to grab the body the warmth belonged to and *drag* her back beside him.

"Chance," a voice called as hands shook him. "Chance, get up. I know you're awake."

"Am not," he mumbled, throwing his other arm over his face as well.

"Stop being a baby and get up," Jenny ordered, but her voice sounded weak. "How did we get here?"

Chance finally dropped his arms and opened his eyes. Jenny sat above him, elbows on her knees and head in her hands. Her hair was a mess, bits of straw poking out everywhere.

"Hungover?" he asked her.

She slowly raised her head, glaring at him with bleary eyes. "How'd you guess?"

"'Cause you look like shit." He sat up, reaching out to place a hand on her back. "Your first hangover. We should take a picture to commemorate the moment."

"Eat me," she said bitterly. "I feel like my head is going to split open and then throw up."

"That's a beautiful image."

"Everything is shaky and weird. It's like I'm here but I'm not *really* here and how did we even get *here* in the first place?" She halfheart-edly gestured to their surroundings.

Chance dropped his hand. "You were really blitzed. You had to get out of there and I didn't know where else to take you."

"Last I remember I was sitting on Leslie's stairs," she told him. "I was waiting for Drake to get through playing—" She broke off with a gasp. "Drake! Where is he? Does he know where I am?" She winced at the loudness of her own voice. She looked a washed-out mess, her complexion all pale and shallow. "Where's my phone?"

He pointed to the table.

Jenny gripped his shoulder, trying to rise on unsteady legs. She bumbled to her feet, standing for a full five seconds before slapping her hand over her mouth and tottering backward.

Chance recognized the signs: Jenny was going to hurl.

He sprang to his feet, wrapping a steadying arm around her waist to hold her upright.

"Can you make it outside?"

She nodded again.

Chance led her outside, taking it one slow step at a time. He wanted to toss her over his shoulders and run her out, but he doubted that'd be good for her stomach. She ran behind the barn door as soon as they stepped through it, already dry heaving. Chance held her hair as she retched. He had to look away as much as possible.

He led her back inside when she was done, sitting her down care-fully on the floor. Her hair was plastered to her forehead now, sweat-ing regardless of the cold. "I'm so sorry," she croaked, her voice hoarse. She clutched at her stomach, doubling over. "If I move, everything gets weird—"

"You might still be drunk," he told her, reaching out to push her hair from her face. She felt clammy to the touch. "How much did you even have?"

Jenny shrugged. "Too much."

"Obviously." This was the first time he'd woken up next to someone who was hungover without having a hangover himself. "We'll have to get you some water and maybe some toast. Greasy food can help, too."

Jenny tried to shake her head. "God, no, greasy food sounds horrible right now. I feel like my brain is just rattling around my skull."

They sat in silence as she tried to compose herself, Chance stroking Jenny's hair methodically. After a while she lay back down, staring up at the ceiling.

"The sun is so bright," she told him. "How do people deal with this?"

Chance lay down beside her. "I was too young to drive when I got my first hangover, so I was at the mercy of someone else to take me home. We were halfway there when he got a call from work—he was supposed to be at a staff meeting and didn't have time to drop me off first. I had to sit in a hot car for nearly an hour, feeling like I was dying. When he finally did get around to taking me home, we ended up driving next to the loudest train ever created. I threw up three times when I got home."

Jenny blanched. "Please tell me this is fake history."

Chance shook his head sadly. "Nope, real past here."

"I am so sorry that happened to you. Why did you even drink again?"

Chance thought about it. He had sworn off drinking after every bad hangover, but never stuck with it.

"It's fun, I guess. I like escaping for a while."

Jenny brought her arms over her face, blocking out the sun as Chance had earlier. "I need my phone," she said reluctantly. "I have to see if Drake called."

Chance's insides squirmed. "He did. Multiple times." He decided to be up front about it, like ripping off a Band-Aid. "I eventually answered so he'd stop freaking out."

He was glad he couldn't see her face, but he could tell from her tone that she wasn't pleased. "Please tell me you didn't."

"He was worried, Jens." Chance got up, picking her phone up off the table. He placed in on her stomach. "He called like twenty times and was obviously not going to stop. I let him know that you were all right, that's all."

Jenny let out a loud groan, picking up her phone. Chance could see her face now—see the hard set of her mouth and the annoyance in her watery eyes.

"Oh my God, you weren't kidding. I have like fifty messages here." She scanned the texts, her frown deepening with each line she read, her body shuddering slightly. "He's so pissed," she whispered.

He hated that Drake got under her skin like this. "It'll be fine. It'll all blow over," he hastened to assure her. "I mean, hey, it's a new year, right?"

She paused, finally looking up from her phone. "Oh my God," she said, turning to face him. "Chance, I missed the New Year. I was blind drunk and I missed the New Year. It's the first time I even had someone to kiss, and I missed it. They say that the way you bring in the year is a reflection of how you'll spend it. Chance, I don't want to spend the year drunk off my ass."

Chance rested a calming hand on her shoulder. "Jenny, you're not going to spend the year drunk off your ass, and you didn't miss the New Year. You definitely noticed it."

"I did?"

"Oh yeah." He nodded. "We were nearly here when you noticed that the clock on my dash said it was midnight. You proceeded to attempt to roll down the broken passenger's window and scream, 'Happy New Year!' at the top of your lungs for several minutes while blowing plenty of kisses at some very startled cows."

Jenny buried her face in her hands, struggling to hide her blushing cheeks. "Please tell me I didn't."

"Oh no, you did." He regretted that he'd been too busy driving to film it.

"Tell no one," she said sternly, still hiding her face.

He acted offended, placing a hand on his chest. "I would *never.*"

It took another thirty or so minutes for her to be able to stand without throwing up. When that was possible, Chance helped her into the car. They were silent the whole drive back. Jenny claimed her head hurt too much for them to play any music, but that didn't seem to stop her from attempting to call Drake a few times. She'd dial his number, hands shaking, and hang up in a huff when he didn't answer.

He hated that Drake had become this big strain—not only on Jenny, but on their friendship as well. He knew what was coming. Drake and Jenny meant the ending of Chance and Jenny. Her boyfriend was going to ask her to stop hanging out with him, and that would be it. Chance knew it was coming. He had seen it the moment she started dating Drake.

He looked over at her, sitting in the passenger's seat with her forehead pressed to the window.

"Don't worry about it," he told her. He didn't have to clarify for her to understand.

"Have you met me? Worrying is my primary character trait."

"Worry about it tomorrow. Today, let's just enjoy the New Year. Let's go watch *Buffy* or something."

His days with Jenny were most likely numbered, he knew that, but that wasn't going to stop him from spending as much time with her as he could while he was still able. They were going to sit on her couch, buried in blankets, and spend the day laughing and eating popcorn. They were going to revel in their friendship and get as much happiness as they could from it before it was all yanked away. He wanted one day—one good day to remember, before she stopped letting him come around.

He saw her smile reflected in the window.

"I'd like that," she said.

CHAPTER 21

Jenny

Everyone at school knew what had happened New Year's Eve. Or at least, they thought they did.

Jenny heard the whispers as soon as she entered the cafeteria the next morning. People stared as she passed, a few people laughing. She heard the same few words float through the air, following her like a swarm of angry hornets:

"She practically mauled Chance on the couch."

"They left together...."

"I heard she's been cheating...."

"... Chance Masters ..."

"... should've known."

Then she heard the most hurtful word of all, casually tossed into the fray:

"Slut."

Jenny felt the tears she'd been holding back threatening to fall. She had to get out of there, quick. She couldn't give anyone the satisfaction of seeing her cry. But where to go? People were every-where. She couldn't escape and hide out in the bathroom all day.

She had tried to get ahold of Drake all night, but her texts had gone unanswered. She knew he wouldn't respond, of course—Drake knew the silent treatment was the worst punishment—and it just added to the pile of things that made her head pound and her body ache. But she knew that he was going to have to talk to her at some point. Sure, he must've been angry about her running off with Chance, but she knew he'd believe her when she told him it was nothing. After all, it *was* nothing. So she composed herself and ignored the whis-pers, even though they set her nerves into overdrive. She and Drake would be fine.

Chance wasn't at school, which made everything worse. She had waited for him before school, but he never showed so she had to get a ride from her mother. She tried to call, but there was no answer. She knew he wouldn't just abandon her without a good reason. After everything, he wouldn't leave her to face all the rumors alone.

And, God, there were so many rumors.

They were flying faster by lunch. The latest Jenny heard was that she had been dating them both. Jenny had managed to sit through two classes of whispers and stares, her anxiety through the roof, but she couldn't walk through a crowded cafeteria, where it was more than just the spotlight effect making her think every eye was follow-ing her. Jenny couldn't step foot in the cafeteria. She wanted to—it would be the perfect time to talk to Drake, but she couldn't do that to herself. She felt like she was getting close to sensory overload as it was. She ate in the library instead, in the back where no one could see her, nose buried in her history textbook. She didn't have time to think about the whispers when she was too busy learning about the American Revolution.

After school—and after building up her nerve—she scoured the parking lot, searching for the tall boy in his classic V-neck and skinny jeans. She finally spotted him heading toward his car.

"Drake!" she called out, rushing to his side. He glared back at her, speeding up his pace. "Drake, please, just talk to me!"

"I don't think so," he said, refusing to look at her. "There's really nothing you can say, Jenny."

"You haven't heard a thing I've said!" she exclaimed, her frustration getting the best of her. "I don't know what you want from me."

He wheeled around to face her, anger flashing in his gray-blue eyes. "I wanted *you*, Jenny! But you wanted Chance!"

"This again? Drake, I *told* you we're just friends."

"Y'see, that's the worst part of all of this. I *believed* you when you told me that. I honestly did, and look at what a fool I've been. The egg is definitely on my face now. After New Year's, I see everything so clearly. I see *you* so clearly."

She stared up at him, confused. "What does that even mean?"

"You've been with *him* this whole time!" he roared, spreading his arms wide. People were staring now. "I sat around believing you were, as you put it, 'just friends,' while you were with him behind my back this *whole time*. You went to *him*, Jenny, not me. I was your boyfriend!"

They had an audience now. People ranging from freshmen to seniors were gathered around, silently watching The Public Humiliation of Jenny Wessler.

"Drake—"

"You told me he slept over *in your bed*, and I still believed you when you said nothing was going on. Am I some blip on the radar of the great love story that is Jenny and Chance? I was just some petty revenge or something, wasn't I? Some weird pawn in whatever game the two of you were playing. Did he sleep around on you, too? Were you just getting back at him?"

Jenny could only stare at him. Where was he getting this from?

"I will not be a momentary complication in your Epic Love, Jenny. Fuck that!"

"Drake, wait!" She reached out, snagging the hem of his shirt. "Chance and I have never been together. I'm with you, you know that."

"Fuck you, Jenny. And fuck Chance, too. Everyone knows you're already fucking each other."

It was like a slap in the face. Hell, it was like someone had dug their fingernails into her face and scraped. How could he say these horrible things to her?

"How can you talk to me like that?" *You love me.* How was everything falling apart so fast? It wasn't supposed to be like this. "It's not like that. I promise."

"You promise? As if that means something to me? I loved you, Jenny. I gave you my fucking heart on a platter and you spit on it."

Drake was walking away and people were still staring and she felt like she was crashing and burning and dying all at once.

"That's enough!" a voice called out. Kelsey forced her way past the group, shooting death glares at everyone. She rushed to Jenny's side, wrapping her bony arms around her friend, letting Jenny lean on her for support. "You should all be ashamed of yourselves!" she yelled, trying to walk Jenny to her car. "Go home and get your fix watching *One Tree Hill* reruns or something! Get out of my way!"

Kelsey fought the crowd to her car, supporting Jenny the whole time. Jenny felt like she was shutting down. This wasn't how this was supposed to go. First relationships weren't supposed to end in public humiliation. Drake loved her; he wasn't supposed to hurt her. She could still feel everyone's eyes on her, even after they were long gone.

CHAPTER 22

Chance

*C*hance knew something was wrong when he woke up. It wasn't the lack of yelling. He had gotten used to that. It had been calm ever since his father left. No, it was a feeling in his gut that made him shakily climb from bed the day after New Year's. Something felt *different*. Things didn't feel peaceful, they felt dead.

Something was really, *really* wrong.

He stumbled across his room, getting lost in piles of laundry almost knee high. He used his doorknob as an anchor, pulling himself free from the mess and launching himself into the hall. He felt drenched in sweat, soaked all the way through his clothes. How was that possible when it was so damn cold inside his house?

Chance's feeling of dread intensified as he hobbled into the kitchen. Something was *off*. It took him a moment to realize that the only thing he could hear was the sound of his own blood pumping. Everything else was silence.

He looked around the room, trying to figure out what was wrong. But everything was the same. Nothing had been moved. Everything was exactly as it had been the last time he'd been in there, so why was he so worried?

Chance stumbled over a stack of books behind the couch. He clung to the counter like a child clings to the railing at the skating rink to keep his balance.

"Mom?" he called out, his voice weak. There was no answer.

Chance crossed the living room, his pulse quickening as he got closer to his mother's room.

"Mom?" he called again, not sure if the walls were closing in or if he was wobbling to the side. Everything felt like it was spinning, and all he could think about was that episode of *Buffy* where she found her mother dead.

He reached his mother's closed bedroom door, his heart in his throat. For the second time in weeks he was afraid to open it—afraid of what he would find. He could taste bile rising at the back of his throat as he pushed open the door.

The room was empty.

Oh sure, there was still a bed, a dresser, a window seat, and even a wicker wastebasket by the door, but there was nothing in or on those things. No clothes, no possessions, and definitely no sign of his mother.

She was gone.

Chance took in the bare room, his tired eyes searching for any sign of her. Maybe she was hiding? Maybe she'd gone out for a walk . . . and taken all her stuff with her. He felt his legs give out from under him.

He barely had time to catch himself as he plummeted to the ground. He got to his knees, still desperately searching for a sign—for anything—to give him hope. But there was nothing. The room was bare.

It was nearly thirty minutes before he composed himself enough to get up off the floor of his parents' bedroom, before he could find the strength to stand. He left the room, closing the door behind him.

One thought kept racing through his head: *Where is she?* He had to find his mother. She could be lost somewhere, wondering around. She might hurt herself, for God's sake! She might already *be* hurt! He grabbed the house phone from its jack on the kitchen counter, ready to start making desperate calls, when he finally looked at the fridge.

There, on purple stationery, stuck up with his mother's favorite *Gone with the Wind* magnet, was the answer to all his questions. She had left him a note with a couple of twenties folded in it.

Chance, the note read in his mother's elegant loopy script, *I've gone to stay at your aunt LaLaina's for a mental vacation. Take care. I'll be back sometime. Don't worry.*

From, Mom.

That was it. With only two lines, she had abandoned him just like everyone else. Levi was gone. His father was gone. Jenny was leaving. And now his mother, too. Everyone had fled; they couldn't leave him fast enough. He crumpled the note in his hand, feeling as though he might barf. He felt the tears coming, felt the sadness crashing over him like a wave, threatening to pull him down. Chance sank down onto the kitchen floor, the coldness of the tile seeping in through his jeans. He looked at the house phone, still clutched in his hand. He had to pull it together. He had school—he couldn't break down now. He continued staring at the phone, fighting back tears.

He still had one call to make.

"Hey, you've reached Levi Masters. I'm not here right now, so please leave a message at the sound of the beep or whatever it is on this stupid smartphone."

"They're gone," he said. He knew that it was obvious he was crying. His voice was thick with tears, his nose already runny. "They're gone, Levi, and I don't know what to do. It's like when they went AWOL before your graduation, only worse. They're not together now. They're both gone, and the house is so empty. Please just don't—don't leave me here."

Chance hung up, already ashamed of his emotional plea. *I need to be stronger than this, Goddammit!*

So his mother had bailed; was it really such a surprise? What reason did she have to stick around, anyway? *I'm not going to school today*, he decided. He recalled his thoughts about how he had wanted only one more normal day with Jenny before things changed.

I'll give myself one day, he thought. *One day to grieve and to wallow, and then tomorrow I'll figure out how to deal.*

Chance marched straight to his room, closing the door behind him. He turned on his stereo, desperately trying to drown out the silence. Standing there in the middle of his messy room, he realized how totally alone he really was. Despite his reputation, he had no friends except for Jenny, and she was too busy with Drake for him now. His world was so small. He had no one to call, no one to talk this out with.

He decided to clean his room, since he didn't have anything better to do.

A little more than two hours and three full trash bags later, Chance surveyed his work. He could see the floor for the first time since they had moved there. His room had beige carpet; who knew? It was amazing what a bit of cleaning could accomplish. His clothes were either in the closet or the drawers, and his bed was made for once. It was all in complete order.

And yet he still felt like a total wreck.

From his room, he moved to the bathroom, scrubbing the counter and cleaning the mirror. He found some Scrubbing Bubbles under the sink and set to work cleaning the bathtub. He didn't know if he was crying again or if the fumes were making his eyes water. His knees ached from kneeling on the hard linoleum, but he didn't care.

From there he moved to the kitchen, methodically cleaning and reorganizing every cabinet. Their kitchen had no system—no rules, like "all canned veggies go in one cabinet" or "cereal goes on top of the fridge." No, they just threw things wherever there was room. His parents never cared enough to create a system.

He was just finishing up when he caught sight of the clock in the living room. *Is it really three already?* He couldn't believe he'd spent the whole day cleaning. Tiredness washed over him, and he braced himself against the counter. *I can't slow down. If I slow down, then my thoughts can catch up.* But he'd already cleaned everything he could. *Except me*, he thought. *I could definitely use a shower.*

He was halfway through washing his hair when he heard his phone go off. *It's probably Jenny, asking why I wasn't in school.* His phone went off again. And again. He heard it vibrate so much it careened off the sink counter, landing on the floor with a *clack*. Who needed to get hold of him *that* badly?

Chance cut off the water, wrapping a towel around his waist before stepping from the shower to pick up his phone.

It wasn't Jenny. In fact, it wasn't any of his saved contacts.

This is Kelsey. Leslie gave me your number.
Go to Jenny's ASAP. She NEEDS you.
Bro, this is NOT a drill.
I am legitimately worried for her.

He stared down at her messages. Jenny *needed* him? But she had Drake. Surely this was something a boyfriend should take care of? *Unless*... He remembered his phone conversation with Drake on New Year's.

Is Drake out of the picture? Is that the emergency? He'd assumed they would've made up at school.

He dialed Jenny's number, but she didn't pick up. He tried once more just to be safe, but still no luck.

If she's not picking up, then she doesn't need me right now, he decided. He couldn't keep his mind off her, though. What had happened? Was she all right?

It was then that he heard a noise from the kitchen. He froze, phone in hand, straining to hear more. He heard someone mutter a curse under their breath, the voice clearly masculine.

Dad? he thought. He couldn't help but hope that one of his parents had come home, that someone had come to save him. He stumbled down the hall blindly, rushing to see who it was. His phone vibrated in his hand, another message from Kelsey:

She says she wants to be alone, but idk if I buy it.

A tall man stood in the living room, his back to Chance. He wore a rough brown jacket, the sleeves so long they covered his hands. His blond hair stuck out in every direction, much longer than the last time Chance had seen him. He had an overnight bag at his feet and was looking around the room.

Chance froze, hardly believing what he was seeing. Finally, after what felt like hours, he found his voice.

"Levi?"

Levi turned around, grinning wide. "Hello, little brother." He paused, eyes sweeping over Chance. "Is this a bad time?"

Chance stood there, unable to come up with something to say. Water dripped from the tips of his hair, and his thoughts were still on Jenny. The sight of Levi standing in the living room was so bizarre that he couldn't even *process* the information. When was the last time he'd even *seen* his brother?

"Chance?" Levi took a step toward him, which snapped Chance out of it.

"I don't . . ." He trailed off, looking back down at his phone. "I don't have time for this. I have to go." He tried to rush past his brother, but Levi grabbed his arm.

"Chance, don't you think you need clothes first?"

Shit.

Chance looked down at his towel. "Right," he mumbled, turning back toward his room. Levi followed him, still talking, even when Chance closed the door in his face.

"I got your message . . . obviously," Levi's muffled voice said as Chance searched his room for clothes. *It's funny how I can't find anything the moment I clean my room.* "I didn't realize things had gotten this bad. When you said Dad left at Christmas, I actually thought things were going to be all right."

So Levi *had* gotten his previous messages and just never bothered to respond. Chance dressed quickly, trying to call Jenny again. Still no answer.

"I got in the car and headed over as soon as I got off work."

He grabbed his shoes, slipping them on without undoing the laces. *Where are my keys?* He looked in his bedside drawer before remembering he'd hung them up by the front door.

"I've decided to use my vacation time, so I'll be staying awhile. We have to figure out what we're going to do. If neither of them comes back, then—"

Chance opened the door, pushing past Levi. Levi broke off midsentence, watching him go.

"Chance, you have to talk to me."

Finally, he broke. "I will, all right? Just not now. My friend needs me and I'm going to be there for her. I don't want to talk about this—about Mom or you or what you're going to do with me. Not now, okay? I just want *one* day. Can you give me that?"

Levi looked at him for a second, and Chance saw pity in his eyes.

"Fine," Levi said at last. "We'll talk about it tomorrow."

"HEY." JACK ANSWERED the door, ushering Chance inside.

"Where's Jenny?" Chance asked, glancing into the living room. From the looks of it, Jack had been playing video games on the couch—discarded plates and food wrappers were everywhere.

Jack shrugged. "Her room, I think. She's been up there since she got home. Is something wrong? She usually would've yelled at me for setting up camp in the living room."

"Everything's fine," Chance told him before rushing upstairs.

Jenny's door was closed, muffled music spilling out. Chance knocked once: no answer. He knocked again, but no luck. Finally, he twisted the knob, pushing it open slightly. Jenny sat at her desk, back to the door, open books covering every surface. She stared at her laptop, and every few seconds she'd type something and then erase it all.

Chance crossed the room, reaching out in front of her and closing her computer. She jerked back, startled, and whipped her head around to look at him.

"Chance!" she yelled. "What the hell did you do? Are you aware of how much time I've put into that?"

"About five minutes of you typing and backspacing everything."

She crossed her arms, glaring at him. "How'd you even get in?"

"Jack," he said. "Kelsey told me something happened." He moved to take his place on her bed. He lay back, his hands behind his head. "You weren't answering your phone."

"Some people would take that as a hint." But she wasn't angry. "Feet off or shoes off, you choose."

"Gosh, Jenny, live a little." He obediently kicked off his shoes and gestured for her to lie next to him. "I'm here to make you feel better, but I can't do that until you tell me what happened."

"You should be happy I'm not royally pissed at you for interrupting me right now. I was in the middle of working on my research paper," she said, resting on the pillow.

"Jenny, papers aren't due for another two months."

"Still, I have all the justified motive in the world to hurl snow globes at your head."

"And risk disfiguring my beautiful face?" he said in mock horror. "You wouldn't dare."

"Oh, really?" She laughed. "Give me a reason not to, pretty boy."

Chance sat up and rubbed his chin, his eyebrows drawn in feigned concentration. Finally, he called out, "Aha!" in an overly enthusiastic manner, a grin covering half his face. "You love me too much."

"Two minutes. You had two minutes of serious thought and that's all you could come up with?" She laughed. "Remind me again how you got into the smart classes?"

"Was I wrong?" he asked, lying back down. He playfully nudged her arm with his hand for a response. "Huh? Was I? You do love me, right?"

Her expression remained deadpan until he began to tickle her, causing her to struggle for both breath and control.

"Stop!" she laughed.

"Say it, then." He continued tickling. "Say it!"

"Fine, I—" Jenny began, but a knock on the wall next to the bed interrupted her.

"I don't know what you guys are doing, but by the sounds, I can guess. Please, for the love of my innocence, stop!" Jack called from their mom's room.

"Stop listening through the wall, creeper!" Jenny called back, still laughing. She took Chance's momentary distracted state to seek revenge, going for the one place he was ticklish: his feet. "Lucky for me you decided shoes instead of feet." She began tickling.

"No! Sto—" He broke off, laughing. "If—I—end up—kicking you in—the—face, its your own fault!" he managed to get out between laughs.

"That's it!" Jack called though the wall. "I'm going back downstairs! Just tell me when he leaves!"

"It's not what you think!" Jenny called, but she broke off, gasping, once Chance regained his breath and began tickling her again. Now it was a full-scale tickle fight.

"Truce!" they both yelled when breathing became impossible.

"Tell no one," Jenny wheezed. "The last thing we need is people talking about you, me, and a tickle fight that took place on a bed." She looked over at the boy lying next to her. Her hair was coming down from its bun, lazily sexy.

"Jenny, people say a lot worse stuff about us than tickle fights in bed," he said unthinkingly. For a moment there, he'd forgotten everything: that Jenny was upset, that his mother was gone, even that Levi was waiting at home.

The atmosphere changed, all traces of laughter disappearing from Jenny's face.

"I know. Trust me." She sat up and rested her chin on her knees.

"Are you ready to talk about it?" he asked, sitting up, too.

She heaved a heavy sigh and told him everything. Chance sat, listening, growing angrier by the second.

What the hell? I knew Drake was a jerk, but to do this? I should've been there. Then, an even worse thought: *I wouldn't have been able to help. I would've made things worse. My being here is what caused this whole situation to begin with.*

This is partially my fault.

"I can't believe it happened in the school parking lot," Jenny said, more to herself than to him. "I could've handled it one-on-one, or even through a text, but not publicly. He *humiliated* me."

Chance wanted to comfort her, but it didn't feel like the right time to wrap her in a hug. He went to pat her on the back but missed and ended up getting her shoulder, knocking her into the wall.

"What the hell?" she laughed, straightening up.

"I meant to get your back, obviously." He bit his bottom lip. "I missed."

"With that much force behind it?" She pushed him playfully. "Did you think I was choking or something?"

"It was an awkward fumble, never mind." *I can't even comfort her correctly.* "What are you going to do?"

She got up and began pacing the room.

"Where to start?" She moved to run her hand through her messy brown hair but paused, seeming to remember it was up in a bun. Her hand dropped to her side. "I mean, what *can* I do? I'm the villain here, Chance."

"You are not the villain," he assured her. "There are no villains here. Breakups happen. Drake will get over it, and everyone will forget this whole thing. He's just being dramatic."

"He said that I was incapable of feeling love. He yelled it, too, so everyone was staring. I started crying—really crying, not those polite pretty tears I cry when I see sad movies, but big ugly sobs. No one is going to forget that, Chance. Not anytime soon."

She stopped then, tears falling down her face. Not the polite pretty kind, either.

"It'll be okay. . . . I'm here for you." Chance got up to wrap his arms around his crying best friend. He didn't even think about it this time, working solely on instinct. "I'll admit that me being here is what got you into this mess in the first place, but I'm not going anywhere. You're better than that scene-boy-wannabe and you know it—besides, his band sucks."

"They *are* terrible." She sniffed into his shirt.

"You weren't right for each other," Chance went on. "You seemed like you were going through the motions of what you *thought* a relationship should be." He gave her another squeeze before changing the subject. "How about we go bowling? You love bowling."

"You're talking to me like I'm five." She rubbed the tears from her eyes, but more came cascading down. "Plus, do I look like I'm ready to go out? I'm crying ugly tears here."

"I see that. You've also got snot running all down your face, but I've seen you worse than this. Remember your eighth birthday party, when you . . . Okay, I've got nothing but you know what I'm going for: Insert witty fake story about our past here."

"I don't know. Being seen with you so soon after all his allegations wouldn't be very . . . I mean it would be like proving him right. And I *really* do not want to see anyone. Can't we just go to Our Spot?"

"Fine," he gave in. "We can go to Our Spot."

She broke away from him, scrubbing at her eyes. "I'm going to take a quick shower. I hate crying; it always makes me feel so gross." She reached up, pulling the elastic from her hair. Chance watched it tumble down around her shoulders. "I need to wash this day off me."

"I'll be downstairs, then," he said, heading toward the door.

"Make sure Jack cleans up that mess in the living room," she added as an afterthought. "That was a disaster down there."

Chance swore he would, and then he was gone.

His phone buzzed in his pocket: a message from Levi, asking when he was coming home. *It's funny*, he thought as he looked down at it, I'm *the one ignoring* him *now*. In a way, it had been easier when he knew there would never be an answer. Levi became less of a person and more of an outlet, more of a nonentity that he could vent to. He was the void, and Chance was always screaming into it. Now he was here, had heard all of Chance's insecurities, and wanted to face them.

Jenny came downstairs a few minutes later, her hair still wet.

"You ready?" she asked.

Chance's phone buzzed again, but he ignored it.

"More than you know."

CHAPTER 23

Jenny

Jenny said good-bye to Jack, giving him a twenty for pizza. "Mom will be home soon," she warned him. "This room needs to be clean by then."

"Aren't you supposed to be doing my chores?"

She glared at him. "My boyfriend broke up with me. Clean the damn living room."

"Yes, ma'am," Jack squeaked, setting to work picking up his trash.

Chance led Jenny from the room and out the door. She felt like she was operating on autopilot, her legs moving of their own accord. Mentally, she was still in that parking lot.

There's probably an alternate reality where that's always happening, she thought. *Somewhere out there is a world where that scene never stops.*

Her feet carried her down the driveway, past the place where she and Chance had had their snowball fight and past where she'd had her first kiss with Drake. *So many memories in so little time.* She reached out to open the passenger-side door, but Chance beat her to it. She raised her eyebrows at him but otherwise said nothing as she slipped in. Chance let his fingers trail on the hood as he made his way around to the driver's side.

They rode in silence for most of the way. She tried her best not to think about what had happened. She stared dreamily out the window, the way she used to when she was little. She would always imagine a version of herself running alongside the car, doing flips and tricks over all the obstacles in the way.

"Don't let him get you down." Chance broke the silence.

"It's hard not to." Her voice trailed off. It wasn't worth it to point out that she actually hadn't been thinking about Drake then. "I thought things had been going well."

"I know." They were finally making it out of the city limits, which meant that they were almost there. "But we're not thinking about him tonight, remember?"

"You're the one who brought him up," Jenny pointed out.

"Whatever." Chance turned onto the dirt road that led to Their Spot. "The fact remains that tonight isn't about him."

"Ugh, men. As soon as a girl goes silent, you assume she *has* to be lost in thought about one of you."

"Oh God," Chance groaned as he killed the engine. "You're not going to start hating men, are you?"

"Oh, yes, I am" was her sarcastic reply. "I'm even going to hate you eventually, so watch out." She wrenched open her door and gave him a fake smile. "Enjoy tonight while it lasts. I'll hate you in the morning."

"Whatever," he called after her. She was already racing toward the barn, out of earshot. She longed for the comfort of being out in the middle of nowhere—for the freedom of being in a place that belonged to her and Chance alone. The real world didn't exist in Their Spot.

"I've missed this place!" she exclaimed, turning back to grab his hand. "I haven't seen it while sober since God knows when."

"It's missed you, too." He grinned, gave her hand a friendly squeeze, and pulled her into a side hug.

She squirmed away, moving to sit in the middle of the floor. She placed her hands in her lap and looked up expectantly.

"Where's my pirate hat?" she asked, wide-eyed.

"Are we still doing that?"

"I know it's been a while. But still, it's Share Time. So bring me my hat. We're doing this right."

"Yes, ma'am." He saluted, making his way to the trunk in the back. He returned with both the hat and the bottle of Absolut.

"Thank you." She pulled the triangle-shaped hat onto her head, content. The hay felt itchy against her bare feet, her shoes abandoned by the door.

Chance sat cross-legged, facing her.

"You first." He pried open the bottle.

"Well, my boyfriend dumped me. Quite publicly, actually." She passed him the hat.

He nodded and took a swig, passing the bottle to her. The foul substance had just touched her tongue when he said, "My mother left and Levi is back."

Jenny nearly spit out the drink she'd taken, her eyes wide.

"What?" she sputtered. "Since when? What happened?"

"She left yesterday . . . or maybe it was this morning? All I know is that I woke up and she was gone. So, I called Levi—no answer, of course. Then he was just *there*, standing in the living room as if nothing had happened." He took the bottle from her, taking a long drink.

Jenny just stared at him blankly. *This* was what he had been dealing with? And he had kept it to himself until now? He had rushed over and comforted her, all the while dealing with *this*? She suddenly felt ashamed of her own pain. Here she was upset over a breakup, of all things, while her best friend was dealing with *this*.

"What did Levi say?" she asked. "Where has he been?"

Chance shrugged. "No idea. I didn't talk to him. I went to you instead. I'll deal with him eventually."

Her guilt increased. Chance had waited years for this, and he blew it all off just to comfort her. She took the bottle back from him.

"Chance, you *have* to talk to him at some point." How could he just walk out after waiting all this time? Didn't he *want* to work things out with his brother? "You've been waiting for this! You've wanted to talk to him all this time and you blow it off?"

"I've decided I *don't* want to talk to him, okay? I thought I did, but now I have no idea what to say to him. It turns out I'd rather not know why he chose to abandon our family." He looked so lost, and he wouldn't meet her eyes. "It's been *years*, Jenny. I was starting to forget what he looked like, for God's sake, and now he's just here. I can't believe it took both our parents running away for him to finally remember I exist."

"That's fair," Jenny said after a while. "You don't have to face him if you're not ready. Do you want to stay at my house again?"

But in her head she was already crafting a plan to get the two brothers together. She was not going to let Chance waste this opportunity. She knew he'd eventually regret not trying to fix things.

He shook his head. "No, someone's got to keep coming home. It might as well be me."

They fell into silence. Jenny wanted to say something, but nothing sprang to mind.

She wished real life was scripted. Then she'd always have the perfect thing to say—every response handcrafted for the situation and no awkward silences. As it was, her mind was blank.

Chance lay back on the ground. "Look at the stars," he said, pointing upward.

"I can't focus on them. You're distracting me." She pulled the pirate hat from under his head so it wouldn't be squished.

"I distract you?" he asked, a smile creeping into his voice.

She moved to lie beside him, setting the bottle to the side. "Sometimes."

He turned his head to look at her. Her face was inches from his, way closer than she expected. Lying like this with Chance was different than lying with Drake, she realized. With Drake it had been awkward and mechanical. But when she lay with Chance, it was electrifying. Every nerve was alive and well, finely tuned to each move the blond made. They could lie side by side without touching, and she'd still feel more alive than she did with anyone else.

"You know I love you, right?" she said suddenly. She wasn't sure if she meant platonically or romantically, and she didn't care. She just needed him to know.

"What do you mean?" he asked cautiously.

She felt her face flush. "That I'm not going anywhere. I'm not going to abandon you. I want you to know that you're the best part of my life, Chance. You're my best friend." She yawned, realizing just how exhausted she was. "What did you think I meant?"

"That," he explained. "You just caught me off guard."

"Oh." She turned toward him, her eyelids already heavy with sleep. "Well, aren't you going to say it back?"

"Does it need saying?" He placed his hands behind his head as he looked back at the ceiling.

"I guess not." She curled up against him, her head resting on his arm. "G'night, Chance."

"Good night, Jenny."

She drifted off a few minutes later, lingering in that space between asleep and awake, where she couldn't tell what was real and what wasn't. She thought she heard Chance whisper, "I love you, Jenny," before feeling the lightest pressure of his lips against her forehead, but she wasn't sure. Then her dreams dragged her into unconsciousness, and none of it mattered anymore.

JENNY WAS UP before Chance and slipped out of the barn just as the sun was rising. She stood by the door, looking out into the surrounding field, taking in the way the sunrise turned the sky various shades of orange and yellow. *It's so beautiful out here*, she thought. She loved being so removed from the real world, as if she and Chance had stumbled upon their own pocket of the universe. Had yesterday really happened? It was hard to think about the awful things Drake had said when she couldn't even see civilization for miles. *Maybe none of that existed and it was all a dream.* She had almost convinced herself of it when her phone alarm went off.

"Shoot," she mumbled, turning it off. *I have to go to school today. I can't be the girl who disappears after she's dumped.* Then she remembered her plan from the night before, the one to get Chance and his brother to talk. She didn't have time to worry about the hell that awaited her at school, not when Operation Chance and Levi was a go.

She rushed back into the barn, accidentally stumbling over Chance with her momentum.

"Ow, what the—?" He rolled onto his back, blinking up at her sleepily. "Jens?" He squinted in the light, his voice slow and sleepy.

"It's seven fifty, Chance!" She offered her hand to pull him up. "School starts in ten minutes!"

This was step one of the master plan: Freak out about being late for school.

"So what?" He ignored her hand, sitting up gingerly. "Let's just skip today. We can sit here, share . . . drink. . . . What's wrong with that?" He reached up, pulling her down into his lap. His arms wrapped around her waist and his head buried itself in her shoulder. "Five more minutes."

"Chance?" She pulled away to look him in the eye. This was *not* part of her plan. "Get up and quit playing around. We need to get going!" She showed him the time on her phone.

"I wasn't planning on going to school today," he admitted. He looked away from her, his eyes cast downward. "Um . . ." He cleared his throat. "I was planning on staying here."

"We have to! Can you imagine the rumors if we're both absent today?" She was already halfway out the door, rushing to the car. "Come on, Chance, we need to hurry!"

"Fine!" he said, following her slowly. "Let's get going."

"Wait, our clothes," Jenny said, looking down at her T-shirt. "We slept in a barn and, frankly, I smell like it. I have to change."

"This is getting more complicated by the minute," he muttered as he unlocked his car. "I can run us by your place."

"No." Jenny shook her head, her wild curls flying everywhere. "Then my mother would know I spent the night with you somewhere without her supervision."

He started the car. "What do you want to do, then?"

Step two: Get the boys together in the same place.

Jenny met his eyes. "I was thinking that we could go to your place?"

"Fine," he said begrudgingly. "We'll stop by my house."

Jenny pulled the visor down to inspect herself in the mirror, cringing in horror as she saw the rat's nest sprouting from her head. She looked over at Chance, staring at his perfectly flat hair with envy.

"I hate you," she informed him. "Like, colossally hate. Like, with the passion and intensity of a thousand burning suns."

"I doubt that. Just last night you told me you loved me."

"That was the alcohol talking."

"You barely had anything to drink."

"I'm a lightweight."

"Yeah, but not *that* much of a lightweight." He turned onto the main road. "We have ten minutes until we get to my house, where you can shower."

Which would be step three: Disappear long enough for the boys to talk but not long enough for them to, like, get into a fight or anything.

"Which puts us twenty minutes late to school," she complained, keeping up the worried charade.

"Our Spot is twenty minutes from town. What do you want me to do, Jenny? Fly? Teleport?"

"You don't have to be a smart-ass," she snapped.

"I forgot how grouchy you are in the mornings." He flipped on the radio. "No more talking until we get some coffee in you."

"Excuse me?" She struggled to be heard over the music that now flooded the car.

"I'm serious!" he called over his music. "I don't want to hear another peep until we get to my house and can caffeinate you!"

"You don't want to hear another peep? Who are you, my mother?" she retorted.

"Shut up, Jenny." He turned his music louder.

CHAPTER 24

Chance

Ten minutes later they pulled into Chance's driveway. Chance killed the car, silencing the music.

"Finally," Jenny muttered, earning a "Shh!" from Chance. She shot him a glare as she climbed from the car.

He led the way to the front door, fumbling with his keys, slightly aware that Jenny had never been to his house before.

"I don't know what we'll find in here," he said as he swung the door open.

They both froze in the doorway, unsure of how to react to the scene before them. Levi—the legendary, enigmatic, elusive Levi—stood by the counter, clad only in his boxers. When he turned to see who had walked in, he almost dropped the jar of peanut butter he was eating from.

"Shit," he said, wiping his hand on his boxers. "Chance? Aren't you supposed to be at school?"

"Aren't you supposed to use a spoon or put that on a sandwich or something?" Chance quipped, motioning to the jar in his brother's hand. "I mean, Christ, I eat out of that, too."

Levi rolled his eyes, setting the jar aside. "I honestly didn't expect to see you. I kinda thought you weren't coming back, since you never answered any of my texts."

Chance stared at him in disbelief. "Feels kinda shitty, doesn't it?"

Levi ignored that, looking past Chance to the girl standing behind him. "Who is she?"

"She's my friend Jenny." Less than a minute in his presence, and Chance already felt like punching him. He had been right to run out the day before. "We're not staying; we're here to get ready for school."

Levi ran a hand through his feathery blond hair, looking from his brother to Jenny. "What's going on?"

Chance ignored him, turning to face Jenny. "The bathroom is down there, first door to the right." He pointed down the hallway. "You can wear one of my shirts."

Chance stayed silent until Jenny turned into the bathroom, then he whirled around to face his older brother. He might as well do this now.

"What are you doing here, Levi?"

Levi gestured to the jar on the counter. "Eating peanut butter in my boxers. I thought that was obvious."

Chance glared at him. "I meant here at home. Why are you back here?"

"You're the one who called me, bro. You asked me to help you. So here I am, helping you."

"I meant for you to call me back, not show up out of the blue uninvited!"

"What can I say—I couldn't stay away, I couldn't fight it!"

"Okay, Adele, I'm serious." It was so like Levi to treat everything like a joke. He never took anything seriously, always making puns or references. Chance was sick of it. "I've been trying to reach you for months. You jumped ship years ago to play college student, and now you show back up like it's nothing?"

"I think I preferred the silent treatment," Levi muttered, his good-natured smile sliding off his face. "It's not nothing, Chance. I had some things happen to me. College, and Anna. I was going through stuff, too."

"Oh right, like running off to college without a word and then 'taking a semester off.' That's what you said you were doing when you called—when was it, oh yeah, last *March*—wasn't it? That you were thinking of taking a break and maybe you'd visit soon?" Chance asked bitterly. "Does your girlfriend know you can never commit to anything?"

Anger flashed in Levi's eyes, his fist slamming down onto the counter just like their father's did whenever he was mad.

"I will *not* tolerate you speaking about her like that." He seemed surprised at his own anger, stepping back from the counter. "I'm not mad, Chance. I'm just . . . I'm a person, too, you know? I was their kid, too; I went through all that you did. I'm not the enemy. Just let me explain."

Chance wanted to ask about what had happened, but he could hardly see through his anger. "How about we don't speak at all?" he said.

Levi sighed, marching from the kitchen down the hallway to his bedroom. "I can't talk to you, not like this."

Chance sank down onto the nearest barstool, his head in his hands. This wasn't how his first real conversation with Levi was supposed to go. *Why do I fuck up everything I touch?*

Levi reentered the room, now clad in a T-shirt and worn jeans. "Okay, *now* I can talk to you." He looked down at Chance, his expression softening. "Who is the girl?"

Chance glanced down the hallway to the bathroom. He could still hear the water from the shower running. "Her name is Jenny. She's my best friend."

"The one you talked about in your messages?" Levi moved into the kitchen to sit across the counter from Chance.

You mean while you were ignoring me? Chance nodded.

"She's pretty," Levi said.

"She's amazing," Chance said quietly.

"What?" Levi asked from his seat at the counter.

"She's amazing, all right? She's my best friend. I can't imagine what I'd do without her."

Levi smiled knowingly. "Oh, so you're kind of in lo—"

"Shut up," Chance cut him off.

"Fine, live in denial," Levi gave in. "I don't care. It's your life."

"What am I supposed to do?" Chance asked, exasperated. "Risk fucking it all up? Like everything else?"

"She spent the night with you, so you guys must be pretty close. What's going to get fucked up if you just go for it?"

"I can't. She literally got out of a relationship yesterday. I can't go after her."

"Don't tell me you don't know how." Levi rolled his eyes. "Even I've heard all about your reputation."

Chance took a deep breath, trying to explain. "Jenny is different. She's my *best friend*. Everyone has been walking out lately, but Jenny . . . she's the *one constant* in my life. She can walk into any room ever and be the only person I see. I could be having the worst day of my life and then just see her smile—it doesn't even have to be directed at me—and suddenly I feel great. She's my best friend . . . *just* my best friend. I *need* her to stay."

Levi gave his younger brother a knowing look. "I think you're already fucked. No offense."

"I don't need this from you," Chance muttered, running a hand through his hair.

"Look at the mess you've gotten yourself into without me here to guide you," Levi went on, not a drop of irony in his voice.

This set Chance off. "Considering that you wasted your money and dropped out before your sophomore year, I'd say that you leaving for college was bad for everyone." He couldn't keep the bitterness out of his voice and then, to drive it home, he looked toward their parents' room. "Most of all them."

Levi reached out to ruffle Chance's hair, his voice quiet. "I'm sorry that you had to go through that alone. I can't imagine what it was like here when they split. I never thought they'd actually do it. I can't make it better, but—"

"No, you can't. You didn't have to become just another weapon in their arguments." Chance shook his head. "I spent most of my time at Jenny's and most of my nights at the old barn."

"I'm sorry, all right? I didn't mean—"

"I don't want to talk about this." Down the hallway, he heard the shower shut off and breathed a sigh of relief—they'd be leaving soon.

"Where Jenny's concerned, I think—"

"I don't want to talk about that, either," Chance cut him off. "Can you write us an excuse? Something like 'car trouble' or 'family emergency'?"

"I can say that I fell down the stairs and that you and Jenny helped nurse me back to health in two hours."

"Can you be serious about this?"

"Fine, your car broke down in the driveway and you had to wait on a mechanic."

Levi scribbled the note and slid it across the counter.

"Thanks." Chance picked it up.

Jenny ran into the room, dressed in a T-shirt and faded jeans, her wet hair in a messy side braid.

"We've got to get going!"

They pulled into the school's parking lot fifteen minutes later, struggling to find an empty space.

"Sophomores shouldn't be allowed on-campus parking," Chance mumbled as he circled around for the third time. Jenny was starting to get fidgety, so he decided to screw it and park in the teachers' parking lot behind the main building.

"You're going to get a parking violation," Jenny said, getting out of the car.

He couldn't even pretend to care. He circled around to stand next to her.

"We're late, remember?" He pointed at the building over his shoulder. "Shouldn't we, I don't know, go to school?"

"I'm not the holdup," she pointed out.

He grinned, taking her by the elbow like any old-fashioned gentleman would. "Come now, we hath class to partake in."

She busted out laughing, pulling her arm away. "Why, my lord, you move so fast. I do fear I have a case of the vapors coming on. I may swoon."

He gestured for her to go ahead. "After you."

She took off toward the aging building, quickly gaining a lead on him. He hung back, watching the way her hips shook when she walked.

"Hurry up!" she called over her shoulder. "I should be halfway done with Chemistry by now!"

"You're welcome, then." He jogged the distance between them. "I saved you from ninety minutes of boring."

The lobby was empty when they walked in, the cool air stuffy and unsettling. There was something about school offices that made the hair on the back of his neck stand up. Jenny bit her lip, looking around nervously as Chance pushed past her, taking the lead.

Mrs. Carroll sat at the receptionist desk, strumming her maroon nails on the tabletop, looking bored as hell. She rolled her heavily lined eyes when she saw Chance approach.

"Did your grandmother die again?" she asked, her tone less than thrilled.

Chance pretended to be taken aback, laying a hand on his chest in mock outrage.

"How could you say such a thing?"

Jenny cleared her throat behind him. "We had car trouble."

Mrs. Carroll's eyes slid from Chance to Jenny. She pulled out a pad of paper.

"Like I even care. I retire in a month, then I'm done with this." She scribbled two excuses and held them out.

"Thanks, Mrs. Carroll." Chance took them from her and winked. "Happy early retirement."

"Get out, before I decide you're lying." The old lady turned to her computer, dismissing them.

"She's just as friendly as can be," Jenny said sarcastically as they slipped out the door. "We could've said anything and gotten away with it."

"Next time, let's say we were off hunting ghosts or fighting evil wizards. . . ." He trailed off when he noticed Jenny's glare.

"There won't be a next time, Chance. I've decided that I can't let my life fall apart just because of what's been going on."

"I know. I'm only teasing."

Jenny grabbed his wrist, turning his watch up to face her. His skin buzzed where she touched him.

"I've got to go." She dropped his hand, hitching her purse up her shoulder.

"Stay out of trouble!" he called after her as she rushed away.

"That's my line!" she called back before rounding a corner into the Science hall.

CHAPTER 25

Jenny

After Science, Jenny skipped the antidrug assembly in the auditorium, not ready to be surrounded by whispering people in a dark room. She had felt people staring at her all during class, their curiosity spurred by her late arrival and obviously male clothes. She could still feel people's eyes on her as she ducked out of the crowd, heading toward her locker. *Maybe I can hide in the bathroom or something.*

There were still a few stragglers left in the hall, begrudgingly heading toward the assembly. She passed the front office just in time to catch Drake and a few of his friends exiting. Panicked, she threw herself around the corner of the Math hall, just out of sight.

"I'm fucking over it, man," Drake was saying, his voice growing further away. "This morning was the last straw. I can't believe she had the nerve to show up with him like that. I knew she was lying."

Jenny's heart sank. Any happiness left over from the night with Chance was ripped away, leaving her shaking. So it was still going to be like this. Class had ended two minutes ago, and the news of her arrival had already spread to Drake. She couldn't blend into the background and fade away anymore. Drake was going to make sure that everyone noticed her.

She couldn't ignore it anymore or push it away to focus on Chance. She was alone, listening to Drake talk crap about her, and all she could do was take it. This was her reality; this was her life. She waited until his voice faded away, still hidden behind the corner.

"What are you doing?" someone asked from behind her.

She whirled around, coming face-to-face with Kelsey.

"Hiding," she said. There was no point in lying.

"From Drake?"

Jenny nodded.

Kelsey nodded, too.

"Okay." She sidestepped Jenny, pausing before she disappeared around the corner, then reaching back to grab Jenny's arm. "Come on." She dragged Jenny to the nearest girls' bathroom.

Kelsey took one look at Jenny—who jumped up and sat on a sink, her legs swinging—and let out a sigh.

"You're not doing well, huh?"

Jenny shook her head. "People keep looking at me, Kelse. They keep talking about me. I can't take this."

Kelsey hopped up onto the sink next to Jenny. "Goddamn rumors." She sighed. "Want me to beat everyone up? Because I will. I pack a mean punch."

"No." Jenny wiped her eyes. She hadn't even noticed when she started crying. "Thanks for offering, though."

"I've never seen you cry so much before." Kelsey reached out a tanned arm and shook Jenny's shoulder. "You're stronger than this, Jens. I know the attention is tough, but it won't last forever."

Jenny leaned into her friend's touch, taking comfort from it. "I'm tired of it already. I was hoping it would've blown over."

"I'm afraid your absence this morning only fueled the flames. I'm just saying that maybe ditching half of the day with the guy you're being accused of sleeping with wasn't the best idea."

"I don't want to see anybody. I'm done with people. The parking lot incident filled my social interaction quota for life. Chance kind of forced his way into my house. I just went along with it. I don't want him to worry; he's got enough going on as it is."

"We have to keep low for now, but eventually something more exciting than which boy you're with will come up, and everyone will forget," Kelsey told her.

"Why can't I go five minutes without my life being reduced to being with either Chance or Drake?" It was starting to grate on her nerves. She was more than what boy she was seeing.

"That's what grabs people's interest, though. They don't care how smart or talented you are, only who you're getting it on with."

"Silly me, I guess all that time I put into becoming top of the class was a giant waste."

"It's a sad reality, Jens."

Jenny knew what Kelsey was saying was true. "If you force your way into my house, I'll hang out with you, too."

"I'll remember that next time."

Jenny repressed a groan. "No, there will not be a next time. I'm done with this. Everything with Drake has taught me that I just don't date well. I'm undateable. I am the queen of being a lonely cat lady and I am okay with that."

Kelsey laughed. "Melodramatic much?"

"I'm just saying I'm done with this petty stuff." She would lock it all away. She wouldn't let herself feel a thing anymore, not for anyone.

"You should've expected petty when you chose to date a hipster who sings about his feelings with confusing metaphors that everyone thinks are deep but are actually super cliché," Kelsey huffed.

"Hey, aren't boys in bands hot?" Jenny defended.

"Yeah, when they're all guttural and passionate; not when they're whiny and crying into a microphone about how they miss the press of your soul on their being. What does that even mean?" She dug her day planner from her backpack. The thing was bursting with pamphlets and other scraps. Kelsey never let a second go unplanned. "By the way, I've finally decided on an event."

"Event?" Jenny watched her flip through page after scribble-covered page.

Kelsey was too busy checking out her plans, not even looking up from her planner. She scanned the page until she found what she was looking for, and then thrust the book under Jenny's nose, pointing to an afternoon a month away. The words *Pine Grove Bake Sale* were written in Kelsey's neat handwriting.

"The event you're going to help me with. I've scheduled a PTA bake sale, and you're exactly the kind of student the overbearing mothers would want helping."

"Isn't your mom a PTA mom?"

Kelsey nodded. "Dillard's pantsuit and all. Which is why I know

you're the kind of teen they want there. My mother is always lamenting that I'm not more like you."

"I keep telling you, if you hold your tongue, adults literally fall at
your feet."

"Teach me your ways, master. Let me be your apprentice," Kelsey
mocked, bowing.

"I'm sorry, but it's too late for you. You're already officially labeled
a bad seed."

"Curse my witty sarcastic mouth, curse it, I say!"

Jenny laughed. "Seriously, I'm not the bake sale type. I'm the
'hiding and eating all the peanut butter cookies' type."

"We can't sell peanut butter cookies because of allergies."

"See, I would suck at helping you," Jenny countered. "I'd accidentally poison everyone."

"I'll make room for you at our booth." Kelsey scribbled Jenny's
name into her planner.

"I'm so glad you listen to me."

But she was teasing. She'd promised to do an event with Kelsey,
and she wasn't going to back out. Kelsey was the only one who didn't
make her sad right now, the only person who didn't set her on edge.
She was the only one not involved in the Chance/Jenny/Drake drama.
The bell rang, and they both reluctantly made their way to class.

THERE WAS NO way she was going to brave the cafeteria yet, so
Jenny headed toward the library for lunch.

Chance found her there, and Kelsey quickly followed. Before long,
it became a routine of theirs. Jenny was grateful for it, even if she kept
thinking about how many people cut through the library just to stare.

Things weren't great, but she loved their little trio. She hoped they knew it.

Chance and Kelsey were a dream team to have around whenever someone said something bad about her within earshot. They both jumped to her defense, sending the offender off crying. Chance's glare and Kelsey's sharp tongue quieted down as many rumors as they could. Eventually things started to die down. Slowly but surely, things returned to normal.

Kelsey had been right: Another big story broke the next week, and everyone who was anyone could do nothing but talk about how Margaret Lester had gotten knocked up by her college boyfriend.

"I feel bad for Margaret and all, but I'm kind of glad this happened," Jenny said the day after the news broke. She looked across the library table at Kelsey. "Does that make me a bad person?"

Kelsey shook her head. "Nah, it's only normal to be happy that the spotlight is off you now, regardless of how it happened."

"That's true," Chance agreed. He sat at the end of the table, feet propped up, earning a glare from the librarian. "If you feel too guilty, you can lend me and Kelsey to her as bodyguards."

"You two do seem to make a good team," Jenny agreed. She was happy to see them getting along. It never occurred to her to mix her worlds before, not like this. It had always been school *or* home, Kelsey *or* Chance. Maybe *this* was the type of branching out she was supposed to be doing, not forcing herself to go to parties with a boy in a band. This felt easy and *right*.

"Hell yeah we do," Kelsey said. She and Chance high-fived. "Does this mean we can go back to eating in the cafeteria?"

Chance nodded. "I hope so. The librarian really hates me." He waved at the woman, who only glared harder.

Jenny watched them, smiling quietly to herself. She knew these two people understood her. They accepted her, warts and all. She hoped that this newfound peace could last forever.

IT SEEMED THAT things were, indeed, too good to be true.

It was a week after the Margaret Lester fiasco, and the day had started innocently enough. Jenny walked into the cafeteria before school, minding her own business. Chance hadn't shown to pick her up so she caught a ride with her mother instead. He'd texted something about missing his alarm. She noticed every eye turn to her, quietly following her every step as she made her way to her usual spot.

"I heard that Drake caught them in the act," someone whispered behind her, making the hairs on her neck stand up. *That* definitely wasn't about Margaret Lester. "Chance just kept going."

"Well, I heard that she confessed because she couldn't handle the guilt."

"No, you're both wrong. Chance told because he didn't want to hide anymore. A cold-hearted queen wouldn't confess." *Cold-hearted queen?*

"Oh please, that's all bullshit. Obviously Drake got tired of her. I mean, everyone knew."

Jenny tried her best to tune them all out, focusing on searching the room for her friends. Her hands shook.

Ignore them, she told herself, but it was impossible. *I thought this all ended weeks ago.*

"I don't understand why he's writing about her anyway. I mean, she's boring and plain." Cue the laughter.

"You all need to shut up before I shut you up," a familiar voice interrupted, silencing the gossiping people. Jenny's head jerked up, turning to see what was happening.

Kelsey stood behind the offending gossips, her hands on her hips. Her blond hair was pulled back and her eyes were angry. She stood at her full height, which was quite intimidating. She whipped her eagle eyes around, glaring at each person.

"If you say one more word about this stupid shit, I'll drag you around back and shave your heads."

Jenny couldn't fight a smile at that.

The group dispersed, and Kelsey made her way to Jenny. "What is going on? I thought everyone jumped ship to talk about Margaret?"

"Your guess is as good as mine," Jenny said. She already regretted going into the cafeteria. People kept looking at her, making her skin crawl. Maybe Chance would have answers. She craned her neck, looking all around for him.

"You look like you're having an aneurism," Kelsey observed.

"I'm looking for Chance," Jenny said.

"He's probably still parking his car."

"I'll keep looking." Jenny walked away, still feeling uneasy.

"Don't forget about the bake sale!" Kelsey called after her. "It's this afternoon!"

"I'll be there!" Jenny promised as she set off to look for Chance.

CHAPTER 26

Chance

C hance was in first block when he found out. He was running late, still getting used to his new schedule even though it was nearly a month into the semester already. He stumbled into Sociology, earning a glare from the teacher. He slipped into his seat, noticing that more people than usual were staring at him. Hadn't this all stopped a few weeks ago? He looked around, people averting their eyes as he did so. Something was up, and he was going to figure out what.

He cornered Danny Jennings after class. "Danny!" he called, jogging to catch up to him in the bustle of the hall.

Danny squirmed uncomfortably, trying not to look at him.

"Hey, Chance. I have to get to class—"

"I'll be quick, then. Why are people staring at me again?"

Danny managed to look even more uncomfortable, a feat Chance didn't think possible.

"I don't think I should be the one to tell you—"

That set his alarms off. "Tell me what, Danny?"

"Can you promise not to shoot the messenger?" Danny said at last, pulling his phone from his pocket. "I know you don't like it when people insult her, and I swear that's not what I'm doing."

"Danny, I'm not going to hit you," Chance swore, taking the phone the smaller boy offered.

A YouTube video was pulled up. Chance could barely make out the sound over the cacophony of the hallway around him, but he heard enough. The image of Drake onstage definitely gave him a few clues. His blood boiled as he watched the video, his fist tightening around Danny's phone. The video was titled "Cold-Hearted Queen."

How could Drake do this?

"Please don't break my phone," Danny said, pulling it out of Chance's grasp. "It was posted sometime last night, I'm not sure when. I don't know any more about it. A friend sent me the link this morning."

But Chance wasn't listening. The breakup in the parking lot was one thing—it could have easily been written off as an oversight of passion. It was believable that he didn't choose that venue; it was just where he was when the breakup occurred. But this? Writing a *song* about her? That was cold. That was calculated.

He hoped to God that Jenny hadn't heard yet.

He took off down the hall. There was no way he could make it to her next class before the bell rang, which meant he had to wait until lunch to talk to her. He made his way to class, glaring at everyone who met his eye.

Someone snagged his sleeve, pulling him toward the lockers.

"Masters, did you see?" Kelsey asked, her phone in hand. He didn't have to look to see that she had the video pulled up.

He nodded. "Does Jenny know yet?"

"I have no idea. Neither of us knew this morning, but Glenda Hargrove just sent me the link." Kelsey was so mad she was shaking. "This is some teen-movie bullshit," she said. "I can't believe he wrote a stupid *song* about her."

"Really?" Chance asked. "*I* can. This is exactly the kind of thing he'd do."

"What do we do?" Kelsey asked. "How do we protect her from this?"

"We can't." As much as it hurt him to admit it, he had to. This was outside of their control. They couldn't do anything about it. "We just have to be here for her."

"Can we at least beat up Drake? Because I would very much like to punch his face."

Chance liked the sound of that, but he knew it wasn't an option. "I think that would make everything worse."

"We're the Jenny Wessler Defense Force; we have to figure out some way to fix this." Kelsey had given them that nickname back when this all started. "We weren't even there when she found out."

"*If* she's found out." Chance wasn't sure what would be worse for him: knowing she found out alone or watching her find out in front of him.

He found out at lunch.

JENNY HADN'T HEARD about the video yet. Chance could tell from the confused way she stumbled through the crowded cafeteria, avoiding every stare. He and Kelsey exchanged a knowing look as Jenny approached the table.

"Do you guys know what's going on?" she asked once she was close enough not to be overheard. "What renewed everyone's interest?"

Kelsey made a face. "I only heard second block, I swear." She pulled the sleeves of her sweater over her hands nervously, looking everywhere but at Jenny.

A look of panic crossed Jenny's face. "What is it?" She looked between Kelsey and Chance before locking her eyes on him, knowing he would answer. "Chance, what happened?"

"The Bleeding Axe Wounds had a gig Saturday night," he began, watching as she quickly connected the dots. With a deep breath, he continued. "They played at the Cyber Bean again. I only heard about it this morning."

"I heard it from Glenda Hargrove. She sent me a link to the video on YouTube." Kelsey hesitantly held out her phone for Jenny to take. "Go ahead and watch it."

Jenny took the phone, and Chance had to fight the urge to look away. "This one is about my ex-girlfriend!" Drake's staticky voice called through the speaker. Chance leaned forward, watching the video as well: a grainy image of Drake bringing the microphone to his lips with a dramatic flourish and beginning to sing.

"I let you play me like a violin but it turns out I was only ever second fiddle, my cold-hearted queen."

Tears sprang to Jenny's eyes as he kept singing, the video pixelating as the person filming began to thrash.

"Did you ever look at me with love? Deem me worthy of your attention from above?"

Chance never wanted to see her so distraught, to see the pain that he saw now reflected in her face. Murderous rage filled him as Jenny continued watching the video.

"Was I only a passing fancy—a distraction for below the waist? If you saw me out in the crowd, would you recognize my face?"

Video Drake pulled down the neckline of his shirt, showing off the sparrows tattooed along his collarbone.

"Tell me, darling, do you even know what happy looks like?"

"This is what he's been doing," Jenny said, so quietly that Chance barely heard her. "He's been crafting more ways to destroy me while I was still trying to pick up the pieces from last time." She thrust the phone at Kelsey, unable to finish the video. "Take it away."

"Are you okay?" Chance reached out to put his arm around her shoulders. "You look like you're going to be sick."

She shook her head, not looking at him. Chance would've given anything to know her thoughts right then. Was she angry? Sad? She shrugged his arm off, staring down at the table.

Chance looked around then, searching for one person in particular. Many people looked away as Chance met their eyes, but one person didn't. Drake was a few tables over, staring right at Jenny. He looked torn, half risen from his seat, as if about to walk over. Then he met Chance's eye and sat back down, his jaw set. The two glared at each other for a bit before Jenny stood, drawing Chance's attention.

"I can't be in here," she whispered, on the verge of tears. She quickly fled the room, Chance and Kelsey hot on her heels.

Jenny stopped in the empty hall, propping herself against a row of lockers. Kelsey wrapped her in a hug as she began to cry.

"I didn't want them to see me, not like this," she sobbed. "I don't want anyone to see me."

"It's okay," Kelsey said in a soothing voice.

Chance felt powerless as he watched the scene in front of him. *I'll get him back for this*, he swore. *No one fucking hurts my best friend.*

CHAPTER 27

Jenny

Jenny was a mess. A stumbling, bumbling, blubbering mess. She was made of nerves and tears, and nothing in between. She had started counting down the days until summer so she wouldn't have to be gossiped about anymore and could fade back into obscurity. She had never felt like this before. Heartbreak always seemed so fascinating on TV—romanticized and deep. Teens in too much eyeliner and expensive clothes always sat in the rain, smoking themselves to cancer, lamenting about the poetic beauty of a broken heart. Jenny was quickly realizing that was bullshit.

Heartbreak was hell. Breakups were messy. Pain was real and raw and there was nothing romantic about it. There was nothing beautiful about crying herself to sleep. There was nothing deep in the way she visibly flinched when someone said Drake's name, images of people staring and laughing assaulting her from all sides.

People were cruel, another truth that Jenny was learning. It was easy to see someone take abuse on TV and wonder why they let it affect them, but it was another thing entirely to experience it first-hand. Insults, rumors, and lies slithered out of mouths with forked tongues, snaking their way through the school, spreading their poison. Everyone thought they knew what was going on; everyone felt informed enough to put in their two cents, no matter how unwanted it was. Chance and Drake were celebrated, Jenny was a pariah. She was the whore sleeping with them both—the villain in the story.

Once the tears started, she couldn't hold them back—they fell hot and quick. Kelsey started rubbing small circles on her back. Jenny was ugly sobbing and she didn't care.

Fuck them; fuck them all.

"How many views?" Her voice was raspy, her throat raw. How many more people were judging her now?

"That's not important." Kelsey pushed Jenny's sweaty hair back from her forehead. "You have to go to the nurse."

She didn't want to. She wanted to know how many people had gone to that show or watched that stupid video. She thought of every-one in class huddled around that phone. She thought of all the stares and the whispers. Everyone knew. The hallway felt like it was grow-ing smaller and smaller, the lockers all around on each side pressing in. She could barely breathe, her lungs burning.

Kelsey and Chance helped her walk, one at each elbow. She wanted to shake them off, to tell them that she could make it on her own. She hated being weak. She hated needing help. Together, they walked her to the nurse. She still couldn't believe what was happening. All she wanted was to fade away. Why was she constantly being brought back into the public light?

They led Jenny into the waiting room, which the nurse shared with the guidance counselor, and the secretary motioned for them to go ahead down the hall to her office. The nurse—a perky redheaded woman—made her lie down on the uncomfortable cot that they kept in the corner. She felt weak, like it was letting Drake win. Thinking about his satisfaction when he found out his song sent her to the nurse made her stomach turn even more.

"Do you think she should go home?" Chance asked, not taking his eyes off her even for a second.

The nurse looked down at Jenny, studying her closely. "I think so," she said at last. "I think she needs a mental health day."

Jenny shakily sat up, the room spinning around her. That wretched song kept playing on a loop in her head.

"I'm fine, really," she said. She didn't want to run. She didn't want to be a coward.

"I'll take her," Chance said. "I'm her ride."

Not true, Jenny wanted to say.

The nurse looked skeptical. "I can't excuse you both."

Chance shrugged nonchalantly, reaching out to help Jenny to her feet. "Then count me truant, I don't care. She needs rest."

Running away had made everything worse before. "I don't know," Jenny said, her throat scratchy.

"You can go, Jenny," Kelsey told her, her voice soft. "Literally no one will hold it against you if you ditch. That whole ordeal was rough. I'll kick anyone's ass if they say anything."

Chance nodded. "I believe it."

Jenny heard a noise behind her, the sound of shuffling feet. She turned just in time to see someone racing from the hallway back into the waiting room, their giggles trailing behind them.

Were they seeing if I was really in here? The thought disgusted her. She couldn't take this, not right now. She reached out, tugging on Chance's shirt.

"I'll go," she said at last.

"SO, YOUR MOTHER'S AT work?" Chance asked as they pulled into her driveway. She nodded as she unbuckled her seat belt. "Let's head in."

Her house was silent, which she found weird. It was usually bustling with people now that Phillip was a near-permanent fixture.

"How about we watch *Buffy*?" Jenny asked as she tossed her bag onto a chair. *Anything to take my mind off that stupid song.* She still couldn't believe he had written about her. "We can finish season six and wallow in our misery."

"I'm not miserable," Chance pointed out. She didn't believe him. She knew he was still struggling with things at home.

"Fine, we can wallow in *my* misery." She made her way to the TV and plucked out her *Buffy* DVDs. "You know you love the Buffy and Spike relationship, don't even pretend."

Chance laughed, throwing himself down onto the couch. After putting in the first DVD, Jenny sat on the other side of the couch. By the time the first episode ended, they had moved closer, Jenny leaning her head on his shoulder. She liked it best when they were like this.

The episode where Dawn accidentally trapped everyone in their house because her sister wouldn't pay attention to her had just ended when she looked at him, her expression thoughtful.

"Chance, can I ask you a question?"

"Wasn't that a question?" he replied. His sarcasm earned him a kick to the shin.

"Humor me."

"Fine, O Violent One, ask away."

"Why haven't you talked to Levi yet?"

Chance turned away, making a face. "Not now, Jenny. Today we're focusing on you."

"I'm serious, Chance, why haven't you? He's been home for a while."

"I'll talk to him when I'm ready." He looked down at his hands, folded in his lap.

"Well, when are you going to *be* ready?" She tried to look him in the eye, but he stood up, pacing the room. "Chance, you have to work things out with him. He came home for you."

Chance sat down in the armchair by the door, his head in his hands. "Jenny, no, I can't do this right now, okay? I'm getting there, slowly I admit, but it *is* happening. I'm not ignoring him; I'm just not ready to bare my soul to him yet, okay?"

"You can take your time. Just don't wait until it's too late." She got up, but he wouldn't look at her, not even when she moved to the very end of his chair. "Chance."

"Jenny, no." He still wouldn't look at her.

"Chance, please."

He didn't respond this time.

"I'll make you talk to me," she vowed before sitting down in his lap.

He reacted at once, yelling, "Get off, you're heavy!" He attempted to push her away.

"Aha! You talked!" She clung to him as he squirmed beneath her. "I'll forgive you for the heavy comment since I did pressure you about family things."

Her heart was pounding fast from their proximity. This was meant to be playful and innocent, but it was anything but. It did nothing to calm her. His scent made her head swim; their contact made her feverish. But God, she wanted to forget her pain, even for a moment. She had to get her easy relationship with Chance back.

"Whoa, off you go, seriously." He grunted as he playfully tried to push her out of the chair. Instead of letting go, she stubbornly clung to him like a baby, resting her head on his shoulder and readjusting herself in his lap. She needed comfort.

"Sorry I brought up your brother," she mumbled into his shirt, her warm breath brushing his neck, his body shivering beneath her. "Oh, and you smell nice," she added as she sniffed his collar. "You smell like sandalwood."

"Thanks." He readjusted her in his lap, placing a kiss on her forehead. Finally, after a few quiet moments had passed, he told her, "Levi is cooking dinner tonight. He wants me to come, but I don't know. We've never eaten together as a family before—why start now?"

"You should go," she told him. She didn't understand. Chance had been so upset at his brother; why wasn't he talking to him now that he had the opportunity?

"I don't want to hear him talk about a life that I'm not in—a life he built by abandoning our family. Realistically, I know Levi isn't to blame for everything, but I've been blaming him anyway. I can't suddenly stop now that he seems to be doing better."

"I get it," she said. "But, seriously, you should go. If anything, get it over with so you can move on."

"I'll think about it," he told her. "I still have a few hours."

CHAPTER 28

Chance

Chance was dozing off, Jenny still in his lap, when his phone buzzed. Jenny nudged him in the shoulder. "Chance."

"No," he said groggily, arms tightening around her waist. He wanted to stay here, cuddling and comforting her. He didn't want to check his text—which was most likely from Levi—and have to leave this warmth for the coldness of home.

"Chance, you have to."

He met Jenny's eyes. She obviously wanted him to do it; shouldn't that be enough? Even if he found out that his brother had left because he didn't give a shit, he'd still have Jenny to comfort him. They could be miserable together.

"Fine."

He pried his phone from his pocket. Sure enough, it was a text from Levi, asking if he'd be home for dinner soon.

"I'll go," he told Jenny. "But it's not like I'm going to be happy about it. I'm going to text you to complain the whole time."

Jenny smiled. "I wouldn't have it any other way. But, seriously, this will be good for you. One of us needs to have something good happen to us right now."

"What are you going to do?" he asked her. He didn't want to leave her alone to wallow.

Maybe she can come with me. She could be the buffer between me and Levi.

"Kelsey has that PTA bake sale thing this afternoon. I wasn't looking forward to it, but I am now. It'll be a good chance to take my mind off things."

"Oh." There went his buffer plan. "I never would've guessed you'd be the one actively seeking personal interaction for comfort."

Jenny laughed. "I know, right? It's like I'm growing or something."

He was proud of her, even if that meant he was truly going to have to face dinner with his brother alone.

HE PULLED UP to his house, killing his car. It was back to parking in the yard again to make room for Levi's car in the driveway. He didn't want to go in the house. He didn't want to deal with any of this. Leaning back in his seat, he looked up at the ruined upholstery above his head. He was going to have to get out of his damn car and face his older brother, for better or worse.

The scent of something wonderful greeted him when he stepped into the house. Levi stood in the kitchen over a skillet, stirring a bunch of vegetables. He cursed loudly as he stirred too vigorously and a few rolled over the side of the pan and onto the stovetop.

"Can you hand me a napkin?"

Chance reached over the counter, grabbing a napkin. "Nice to see you, too. I had a great day. Thanks for asking."

Levi put down his spoon, glaring at his younger brother. He looked a hot mess, with sweat gluing his hair to his forehead. "I forgot that being a smart-ass runs in the family."

Chance ignored him. "What are you doing anyway? Since when do you cook?"

"It's an interest I picked up at college. It's vegan shepherd's pie." Levi gestured to the skillet.

"We're not vegan," Chance pointed out.

"Anna is. I learned how to cook it for her. She's worth this mess." He grinned at Chance. "Can you believe I'm cooking for someone?"

Levi kept doing things like this, and Chance supposed they were meant to come off as buddy moments, but they only made Chance angry. Levi couldn't make a few jokes and assume that everything was going to be okay; Chance wouldn't let him off the hook that easily.

Levi walked over to the bar, grabbing a bottle of red wine and pouring it into a measuring cup. "Do you want to help?"

"It's best if I don't."

"Or I could help?" suggested a voice behind them. They both whipped around to the living room, taking in the woman who had just entered. She stood in the doorway, tall and sure. Her dark hair was in a braid to the side, like a line drawing Chance's eyes from her round brown eyes to her smooth dark skin. She wore a maroon T-shirt and worn jeans, with her head cocked to the side and a wide grin spreading across her face. "Close your mouths, boys, you're drooling."

"Anna, you're here early." Levi recovered first, straightening up.

"Actually, I'm on time," she corrected. She hung her keys on the hook by the door. "Also, your door was wide open. I don't know what kind of small-town Mayberry place this is, but pretty sure that's begging for someone to walk in and rob you blind."

"And yet you're the only one who walked in." Levi crossed the room and engulfed her in his arms, lifting her into the air momentarily.

"It smells great in here" was her response.

Anna was pretty, and the effect she had on Levi was almost palpable. He looked at her like—

Well, like he loved her.

"I'm cooking," Levi admitted proudly, looking down at Anna. He leaned down and kissed her.

Chance looked away awkwardly. It wasn't like he hadn't seen Levi kiss someone before—his big brother had never been discreet in his numerous affairs. But it was different with Anna. He wasn't just kissing her, he was communicating with her. It wasn't a kiss that was a means to an end; it was a kiss with meaning behind it.

Okay, now that *is uncomfortable.*

Chance cleared his throat. "I'll just go to my room."

Levi sheepishly stepped away from his girlfriend. "Sorry about that, bro. I'll rein in my raging hormones while you're present. Now come and meet my girlfriend, Anna."

"How was school?" Anna asked.

"It sucked," Chance told her. He wasn't trying to be difficult, at least not with Anna. She didn't deserve his angst.

"High school always sucks," she said, walking toward the kitchen counter. "Why did today in particular suck?"

"My best friend's douche ex wrote a song about her."

"Shit," Anna said. "I was not expecting that. I was expecting, like, a bad test or something. I can help with tests. I can't help with douchebags writing songs."

"He hasn't even mentioned the best part," Levi told her. "The best friend? Yeah, he's in lo—"

"Levi," Chance warned.

"Well, you *are*," Levi said. "The sooner you admit it to yourself and everyone else, the sooner you can make your move."

Chance groaned. "For the last time, I'm not making a move. Besides, I don't even know what move to make."

"Kick the ex's ass, duh," Levi said, as if it were obvious.

"Don't do that," Anna said quickly. "Definitely do *not* do that."

Levi went on, "You have to make your move. It's what comes next. What you do next is very important, so it has to count. Listen to my sage advice and kick his ass."

"Your advice is not sage, Levi. You just like to hear yourself talk." His brother's advice was always "Go for it." Chance couldn't use that. He couldn't go for it when there was nothing to go for. Everything was pretty simple: Stay friends with Jenny, or make a move and lose her. Only one option kept her in his life.

"That's how these stories go." Levi ran a hand through his unruly hair. "This is the only path."

Chance stared at him like he'd lost his mind. "Everything doesn't fit nicely into your tropes."

"Yes, it does."

"You should listen to him—about the girl, anyway, not the

punching. He's weirdly clairvoyant about these types of things," Anna confirmed.

"See," Levi said triumphantly. "Anna agrees with me."

"She's your girlfriend. She has to."

"Not true," Anna assured him.

"*Really* not true," Levi added. He stepped away from her, returning to the kitchen to pour veggie broth into the pan. "Why don't you two set the table while I finish cooking?"

Chance didn't want to, but he decided Jenny had been right—it was better to do this all now and get it over with.

"I don't mind," Anna said, walking over to check on what Levi was doing. "What do you say, Chance, show me where everything is?"

"Sure," Chance said.

"Look at you two, getting along already." Levi wrapped his arms around Anna's waist, resting his head in the crook of her neck. They were happy in the way his parents never were. They were probably the first happy couple to ever be in that house.

It's weird to see that peace in this house of horrors, Chance thought as he retrieved the plates from the cabinet.

He didn't know what to do with a happy relationship. He had never been around one before. Relationships were made up of yelling and screaming, throwing fits and furniture. That was all he had ever known, and yet Levi had found some way to circumvent that.

Chance tried to pry his eyes from the scene in front of him. It made his insides churn to see his brother so at ease and connected—so content in the moment.

Anna took the plates from him. "So you have girl trouble, huh?"

"You could say that," Levi snorted from the kitchen.

"Aren't you supposed to be busy right now? Isn't this the time for me to talk to your brother?" Anna called out, not even looking over at her boyfriend.

"It's nothing," Chance told her. "How did you and my brother meet?" That was an innocent question, right?

"Freshman seminar," she said. "He sat in front of me. I couldn't take my eyes off his hair."

"Women do love the hair," Levi said wistfully.

"He's going to keep doing that," Chance told her. "He's never been able to butt out of a conversation."

"Oh, trust me, I know. That's how we met. He kept turning around to talk to me and my partner."

Chance could easily picture that.

"I'll be right back, guys; don't go talking behind my back," Levi told them as he set his spoon down and disappeared toward his room.

The silence was heavy. Anna fiddled with the silverware.

Chance looked down at his feet. "What has Levi told you about me?" he asked quietly.

Anna didn't look up, clearly uncomfortable. Chance knew what she was going to say: His brother hadn't mentioned anything more than the fact he had a younger brother.

That's because it's all he knows about me.

"Look, he said that you were in high school and you guys weren't close." She finally looked up, meeting his eyes. "I'm surprised he brought me home at all. He doesn't really talk about any of you."

"He's always been good at adapting and moving on," Chance replied bitterly.

"That's not true." She reached out to place a hand on his shoulder. "Why don't you talk to him about this? He has more answers than I do."

Levi waltzed back into the kitchen, grinning. "How are you two doing? Getting along, I hope."

"We're sharing embarrassing stories about you," Chance said, causing Anna to laugh. "I'm telling her about everything you used to do as a kid."

Levi cringed. "Please don't do that."

Anna moved to stand by Levi, looking over his shoulder. "How's it coming along?"

Levi poured his vegetable mixture into a glass pan. "I think we're ready to go."

"It smells good," she told him. "It's way better than the last thing you made."

"I've been practicing."

Chance got to his feet, making his way toward the couple. "How did this whole cooking thing start?"

Levi shrugged. "No one cooks in this house. Have you ever noticed that? It didn't really occur to me until I was on my own, but we don't. We're not even encouraged to do it. It was like, unknowingly, it was something we weren't allowed to do. I started going over to Anna's apartment, and I suddenly realized I wanted to try new things—things I hadn't had the freedom to experience before."

"We're allowed to cook," Chance said. It was preposterous to say they weren't. There were no rules against it.

"Really?" Levi asked, slipping on an oven mitt. "What would happen if they were still here and you asked if you could make dinner?"

Chance didn't even hesitate. "They'd probably get annoyed that I was bothering them in the first place. Mom would be angry, because I threw off whatever vague dinner plans she already had for the night, and Dad would nitpick everything I did. They probably wouldn't even eat it."

"So you wouldn't do it, would you?"

Chance shook his head, realization dawning. "Because it isn't allowed."

"Exactly." Levi spooned some food onto his plate. "I didn't realize it either. There's a whole world outside this house, Chance. There's a world outside of *them*. It takes some getting used to," Levi told him.

Anna looked between the two. "Should I go?" she asked. "If you guys need time to talk about things, I can disappear for a few."

"No, it's all right," Chance said. He was finding that he quite liked having Anna near. He turned to Levi. "I still can't believe you cook."

"I'm thinking about taking some classes," Levi told him. "Maybe check out culinary school if I get good."

Culinary school? Levi was making plans again, just like before. He had an entire world locked in his head, full of choices and paths. Chance didn't have that. He had no plans or goals. He couldn't see beyond his own front yard. If his brother was doing so well on his own, then why even come back? It was clear that their parents, and even Chance, were holding him back, so what was the point?

His brother pushed a plate in front of him. He looked down at the golden vegetables perfectly cooked in their broth, and his appetite died. Levi had made the right choice leaving them, he realized. There was nothing for him there in that house. He was holding Levi back.

It's my *fault*, Chance realized.

He heard a roaring in his ears. *I was the one who couldn't stop our parents fighting. I was the one who drove them to run away. I was the reason Levi stopped calling. I was the reason Drake broke up with Jenny. Everything bad that's been happening has been because of me. Not Levi,* me.

He pushed himself away from the table and stormed out the back door and onto the deck. He braced his hands on the railing and looked out into the backyard, hoping the fresh air would calm his racing heart.

CHAPTER 29

Jenny

Jenny had been okay while Chance was there but now . . . now she felt alone. Truly alone. And it was actually a pretty sad feeling.

She pulled out her phone, finger hovering over the text icon. She was going to text Chance and see how the dinner was going. She almost pushed the text icon; she swore she was going to—but the YouTube icon was calling her name.

She pushed the big red square and typed in the name of Drake's band. There, curled up on her couch, she watched his video again. She took in the way he stumbled onstage, screeching out his whiny lyrics. *This* is what he had been doing while she was waiting for her life to return to normal. Now, here, alone and away from the bustling cafeteria, she had to admit that the song was catchy. If it hadn't been about her, she might've even liked it.

She watched it three more times, watching the view number climb each time she refreshed. How hilarious would it be if the band got recognition because of this stupid video? If she, the one who never wanted to be seen, was immortalized this way?

Ain't that just the way?

The silence of the house echoed around her each time the video ended. She couldn't stay here alone, not this time. She couldn't hide away in her house for days on end. She didn't *want* to. So she didn't.

Kelsey picked up on the second ring. "Wessler? What's up?"

"We have a bake sale this afternoon, don't we?" she said. "I was wondering if you wanted any help setting up."

"Oh." Kelsey sounded surprised. "I was sort of under the impression that you weren't coming."

"What, why? I promised, didn't I?"

"Well, after everything that happened . . ." Kelsey trailed off. "Don't force yourself, okay? I know you've had an overwhelming day—"

"Kelsey, I *want* to go. I don't want to be cooped up in my house alone right now. Let's go force some pretentious mommy bloggers to buy overpriced organic snacks."

"This doesn't sound like you. I was expecting you to quietly withdraw from school and homeschool yourself until you graduated."

"Always the drama queen, aren't we?" Jenny replied dryly, getting to her feet. "I don't want to hide. I want to hang out with you."

"I *am* a ray of sunshine in your dark life," Kelsey admitted smugly.

"You're something, all right."

"I'll swing by as soon as I can."

Jenny hung up, smiling to herself. The silence resumed as soon as she did so, and it was as overwhelming as before. She shook it off, going upstairs to change her clothes.

This is going to be fun, she told herself. *This is what I need.*

THE BAKE SALE looked like even more of a nightmare than Jenny had expected. It was big, for one thing, with large tables set up like a hallway and bright yellow and black tablecloths—the elementary school colors. Tons of annoyingly eager PTA moms bustled about in floral-print dresses and perfectly coiffed bobs, barking out orders at the volunteers. The worst part was that it was outside, in the school's front yard, right square underneath the flagpole.

"PTA moms make me so uncomfortable," Jenny whispered to Kelsey as they faked smiles at everyone they passed. Walking on the sidewalk between the tables was like a catwalk, and every busybody was judging them. "They're so pushy."

"I know, right? I have a theory that they're made in factories, like Barbies. Mass produced, already equipped with a kid whose life they can meddle in."

They spotted their booth halfway down the catwalk. Kelsey's mother, Beverly, stood behind a table with a yellow tablecloth, arranging trays of lemon bars as if she were defusing a bomb. She wore a mauve pencil skirt and a floral-print blouse buttoned up to her neck, her blond hair tumbling in waves down her back. She smiled as they walked up.

"You're late."

"We're here now; in the end that's all that matters." Kelsey grinned.

Beverly tapped her pointy-toed shoes impatiently. "Look at this." She gestured to her table. "They gave us a yellow table."

"Yes, Mom, I can see that. What a horrendously nauseating shade of yellow it is."

Beverly waved off her daughter's remarks. "We can't have a yellow table. I'm selling lemon bars, for goodness' sake!"

Both girls looked at her as if she had lost it.

"Lemon bars are yellow! Now we have too much yellow!" Beverly struggled to keep her voice down, her eyes darting to the booth across the sidewalk. "I know that Linda Mae assigned us this table on purpose. She was the one who took down what everyone was bringing."

Jenny looked over her shoulder to take in the scheming, deceitful Linda Mae. The woman looked like any other overbearing mother—her sandy hair was permed and pinned close to her head, and her outfit looked like it had walked right off a JCPenney mannequin. She had a black tablecloth, and lemonade set up in a punch bowl with fancy glasses to dip it out with. Her main attraction, though, was a big lemon cake in the middle of her table. The yellow and the black really did seem to reek of school spirit . . . or at least of desperation.

"She stole my yellow-on-black idea," Beverly continued, bringing Jenny's attention back to her.

"Those are the school colors, Mom," Kelsey pointed out dryly. She pushed past her mother and settled in behind the table. "You're not the original Bumblebee, so you can't claim the idea."

Beverly put her hands on her hips and shook her head. "Lord knows what I did to deserve you. I bet Jennifer here never smarts off to her mother the way you do." But her tone was soft, teasing. They were always like this, bickering out of affection. Jenny didn't quite understand it, but she found it endearing.

Kelsey let out a laugh. "Love you, Mom."

Her mother stuck out her tongue, the first Kelsey-like act Jenny had seen her do.

"Love you, too." She ruffled Kelsey's hair before heading off.

"Hey, Kelse?" Jenny circled around the table, moving the black cash box from the extra chair before sitting down. "Didn't you help organize this event?"

"Uh-huh," said Kelsey.

"Doesn't that mean *you're* the one who gave your mother a yellow tablecloth?"

Kelsey grinned. "Would you look at that, so it does." She opened the cash box, producing a bunch of little note cards that listed the price of things in neat cursive script. "I bet these are scented." She raised one to her nose and made a face. "Yup. I would've done the exact same thing."

"You had to get your love of organization from somewhere," Jenny pointed out. "Your level of preciseness is born, not made."

Jenny watched Kelsey set up the cards in neat rows in front of every tray. Soon, middle-aged women, dragging bored-looking kids, began popping by every few minutes, demanding to know exactly what the ingredients were.

"I don't let my Tommy have sugar."

"I refuse to let little Samantha eat anything that isn't organic."

"Are these healthy?"

Jenny started to feel bad for them. The majority of the kids weren't even allergic, just forced along on whatever crazy fad their parents were following.

She was glad it was so busy; it gave her little time to think about everything that had been going on. It was exactly what she had wanted. She was winning all around.

"Where is your little sister, anyhow?" Jenny asked after a balding man pulled his son away from the table because the colors "gave him a headache."

"Piano lessons, I think." Kelsey shrugged, reaching out and plucking a lemon bar to snack on.

"Your mom will kill you," Jenny warned.

"Nah, it'll be gone before she even sees. Besides, I'll smell her perfume for miles before she shows up." Kelsey took a huge bite. She gestured across the aisle as she swallowed. "Look at how people are fawning over Linda Mae's lemonade. The ice she's using is frozen lemonade with, like, rind in it."

"You have got to be kidding me."

"I kid you not, my friend." Kelsey sighed, reclining back in her chair. "Welcome to the world of competitive moms."

"Where is your mom, anyway?"

"Double-checking to make sure everything is going smoothly. She's like the me of the PTA moms—they respect *and* fear her," Kelsey said, polishing off her bar and reaching for another one. "Damn woman is also an amazing cook."

Jenny rested her chin in her hands, watching the people mill about. It seemed that almost everything on the black tablecloths was lemon flavored, so their table's traffic started thinning out rather early. Her stomach grumbled, demanding food, so she grabbed herself a bar, too.

"Welcome to the dark side. We have reasonably enjoyable baked goods," Kelsey laughed, nudging her shoulder.

Jenny nodded, her mouth too full to respond.

Kelsey reached out and grabbed one of the price cards. Flipping it over, she scribbled: *On break for ten minutes. Walk away.* Placing it back at the front of the table, she turned to Jenny expectantly, folding her hands in her lap like a therapist.

"So, spill. Tell me everything."

"About?" Jenny asked around a mouthful of lemon bar.

Kelsey raised an eyebrow, "C'mon, Wessler, spill."

Jenny swallowed, setting down the rest of the bar. She still didn't really want to talk about it. The last hour and a half had left her feeling pretty fine, and thinking about it now was only going to make her sad again. But she owed her friend something. Surprisingly, what came out wasn't a rant about the song.

"Would you say that I'm . . . distant?"

"Hell yes," Kelsey answered without hesitation. "Where did that come from?"

"What do you mean, 'Hell yes'?" Jenny demanded, taken aback.

"I mean you're as distant as can be. I never know where you are. You've always been that way." Kelsey shrugged, taking the rest of Jenny's abandoned bar and popping it into her mouth. "You've been like that ever since I can remember. It's a part of you; nothing you can do about it."

"Are you saying you think I'm stuck-up?"

"No, just that you're very wrapped up in your own little Jenny Land. You're reserved, you know that."

"Drake . . . he called me cold-hearted and incapable of love. But I thought I was giving him enough. He didn't see it that way. If he missed it, then does everyone else?"

"I know you're trying, Jenny. It's obvious. Drake didn't understand how you are. He wanted more from you." Kelsey laid a reassuring hand on Jenny's arm, giving it a friendly squeeze. "You're hard to get close to, it's true. To be honest, it wasn't until Masters appeared that I realized you were capable of more. I thought maybe something was wrong with *me*, since you never got close to me."

Jenny's eyes widened. "Kelsey, no, I love you." Did everyone in her life think they didn't matter to her? "It's this stupid thing in my head, keeping me from everyone. I never wanted to be a burden to you—to be an annoyance. So I kept to myself."

Kelsey looked at her incredulously. "Wessler, your friends are the people you're *supposed* to burden with that stuff. That's why you have friends, so you don't have to go through anything alone. I guess you've always had Chance, though—why didn't you ever tell me about him? I've been scrambling for months now trying to figure out if I was just some giant joke to you." Kelsey placed her chin in her hand, looking at Jenny expectantly.

Jenny felt a newfound appreciation for her friend. How could Kelsey stick by her when, by the sound of it, Jenny was unresponsive to everything? What kind of strength and determination did that take?

"It's complicated," she said. She couldn't tell Kelsey the truth, could she?

Well, why can't *I? It's just as much my secret to share as Chance's.* If Kelsey blew up and got mad at her for it, then she deserved it anyway.

"Actually," Jenny continued, "no, it's not. I didn't tell you about Chance before this year because we made it all up. Every single memory was a lie. He's as new to me as he is to you."

Kelsey stared at her blankly, blinking in silence. "Why a lie?"

"It was for our class assignment."

Kelsey burst out laughing, shocking Jenny.

"Are you serious?" she wheezed. "It was all a lie. I can't believe this!"

Jenny didn't see what was so funny. "Kelse—"

"I was worried over nothing!" Kelsey giggled, reaching out to place her hands on Jenny's shoulders. "You made a new friend! I thought you were hiding something, that you were never as bad as I thought, but that's not true. You're just getting better in your own weird little way. Jenny, you *made a new friend*!" Her eyes went wide then, realization dawning. "Jenny, you and Chance are close, right?"

Jenny was afraid her friend was having some kind of breakdown. "Yes—"

"You love him, right? He's your bestie?"

"Yes, but Kelsey—"

"And he knows this? He knows you love him?"

"I'm pretty sure, but what does that have to—"

"Then it's not you, Jenny. It's *not you*. Both Chance and I—your new friend and your old friend—are aware of how much you care and how hard you're trying. You're not really cold and distant to us. *We know.* Which means that the problem isn't you, it's Drake. It's *not you*."

Appreciation flooding her, Jenny stared openmouthed at her friend. She flung herself from her chair and threw her arms around Kelsey's neck, sending them both tumbling to the ground.

"I love you!"

"Always forever."

Jenny nodded. "Near and far."

"Closer together." Kelsey laughed, pushing Jenny to arm's length and looking into her eyes. "I must know you, Jenny. How else would I know you'd get my sucky nineties song references?"

A prim *ahem* sobered both girls immediately. They looked up to find Beverly standing over them, arms crossed and pink lips pressed into a thin line.

"Are you two done? We still have lemon bars to sell."

"Nobody wants your lemon bars, Mother. Everyone here is selling them." Kelsey stood, brushing dirt off her jeans. "We fell out of our chairs; you know how it is."

"I think you're right." Beverly reached out and picked up a bar. She examined it before taking a bite. "We might as well pack up."

"Look at you, Mom, breaking the rules and eating your own merchandise."

"It's not like you two haven't been eating them, too."

"We haven't. Right, Jenny?"

"Not a single one," Jenny swore. She held up her right hand. "Scout's Honor."

It was clear that Beverly didn't believe them. "Well, eat some more. I want it to at least *look* like we outsold Linda Mae."

The rest of the bake sale passed uneventfully, with Linda Mae obviously earning the most money. Beverly fumed the entire meeting, while everyone rushed around gushing about how amazing the lemonade had been. Kelsey and Jenny snuck away once the cleanup started, giggling the entire run to the parking lot.

"Mom and I are going to have to start planning the next fund-raiser immediately. We'll beat that Linda Mae yet," Kelsey laughed, sliding into the driver's seat.

Jenny chuckled, buckling her seat belt. She hadn't felt this good in forever. "You have to keep that Linda Mae from usurping your mom's PTA power."

The car roared to life as the girls quieted down. "You gonna be okay now, Wessler?"

Jenny didn't know the answer to that question. "I have no idea."

Kelsey studied her quietly for a moment. "Have you finished crying about Drake yet?"

Jenny focused on the frog keychain that dangled from the rearview mirror, swinging like a pendulum. "Yeah."

"Are you sure?"

Jenny looked at her. "Yeah. It's not even a good song, is it?" There was only so long they could avoid the topic at hand. "Sure, it's catchy. It draws heavily on that pop-punk I-don't-need-you-or-this-town mentality, but it's not *good*. It's not going to go viral or anything."

Kelsey glanced at Jenny before gluing her eyes back to the steering wheel. "I mean, do you even miss him?"

"Shouldn't I? We broke up, and I—" She couldn't say out loud that she'd loved him. It felt wrong.

"Are you upset because he broke up with you or because of the *way* he broke up with you?" Kelsey tore her gaze away from the parking lot, briefly meeting Jenny's eyes. She was oddly serious about this.

The way he'd done it was horrible, no question. And the aftermath was even worse. It was true that she couldn't separate the two in her mind. But would she be happy if they were back together? Or if they'd never broken up at all? She looked down at her hands in her lap, wondering if maybe she had always been going through the motions. "Can't it be both?" Jenny asked hopefully.

Kelsey shook her head, just once, and sighed. "I don't think so, Wessler, not this time."

CHAPTER 30

Chance

Chance heard the door open behind him, quiet footsteps making their way toward him.

"Don't," he said before Levi could say a word. "I don't want to talk about this, not with you." *You, who I'm holding back.*

"Then we won't talk." Levi leaned against the railing, searching his pockets. He produced a pack of cigarettes. They were Marlboro Reds, just like when he was younger.

"I didn't know you still smoked," Chance said, watching as his brother shook one out and placed it between his lips.

"Barely." Levi brought a lighter to his lips and lit it, taking a drag. "Anna hates it so I've cut down considerably. When we first met, I chain-smoked like a madman. I still find it comforting."

"In about twenty years, the cancer won't be comforting."

Levi just looked at him.

"What do you want?" Chance asked, turning away. "I came out here to be alone."

"I know. Anna made me follow you," Levi said, exhaling, the smoky tendrils twisting toward the sky.

Of course he didn't do it on his own.

"You know everything isn't half as complicated as you're making it out to be, right?" Levi went on, staring out into the backyard as well. "You're seventeen years old, so you're a ball of anger and hormones, but I swear things calm down when you're older."

"You're only twenty-three," Chance pointed out.

Levi shook his head, letting out a noise of frustration. "That's right. I'm practically still a kid myself, Chance. I'm just a selfish kid."

"Right, so I don't really want to take your life advice."

He saw the words hit home, saw the way Levi's eye twitched at his tone.

"I'm trying the best I can."

"I know." Chance could give him that much.

"I want to say that I'm sorry," Levi began, resting his hands on the deck railing. "I also want to say that I'm the worst brother in the world. I know that I left you here. I wanted *out*, Chance. I couldn't stay here anymore. All my friends were suddenly talking about college and I thought, 'Hey, there's an idea I never considered before. I can use it as an escape.'"

Chance looked at him, taking in how old he looked. Levi had always seemed so much bigger to Chance—larger than life, almost. But now, standing side by side, Chance was nearly as tall as he was. "Why didn't you tell me you were leaving? Why did you just . . . disappear?"

"You know our parents. They wouldn't have let me go. They would've thought me doing anything with my life—anything other than sitting in my room and being their chew toy—was a huge fucking inconvenience to them. They weren't going to stop being horrible, so I had to be the one to do something about it. So I did. I left, and let me tell you, it felt amazing." He ashed his cigarette, looking out into the backyard. "And once I was gone, I couldn't bring myself to ever come back."

Chance flinched. "I'm glad leaving me behind was so amazing for you."

His brother sighed, turning to look at him. "Chance, it wasn't about you. I was so focused on *getting out* that I never once stopped to consider that I was sentencing you to the same thing I was running from."

"And then you dropped out." It was surreal. He had wanted to have this conversation for forever, but now that it was going on he just wanted out of it. *I don't really want to know*, he thought.

"No, I did not freaking drop out. I'm taking a break, all right? I've never had so much freedom before. I can do whatever I want, Chance. So I want to muck around a bit and see what's out there before I go back to school. There's nothing wrong with that." He let out a humorless laugh. "I was a shitty brother; I get that. It was dumb for me to expect I could come back and start over with you."

"Do you *want* to start over?" Chance asked, hopeful despite himself. "I never thought you cared."

"Of course I cared!" Levi snuffed the rest of his cigarette out on the railing. He looked at it, all crumpled and broken, before flicking it out into the yard. "When you called me, I was ashamed that I had left you in the first place. How could I do that to you? How could I be so like *them*?"

Chance had never seen his brother unsure—never seen him waver in anything before. It was surreal to hear about his regrets.

"You're not like them," he said quietly, looking down at the unfinished railing below his hands.

His brother shook his head. "Yes, I am. You needed me and I wasn't there. I bailed, just like they did."

"There's a difference, though," Chance said, finally looking up at him.

"I don't think so."

"But, Levi, you *came back*."

That brought his brother up short. Levi recovered swiftly. "I still left you with them."

"Yeah, and I really needed you. But you still came back when I called."

"I know you needed me." Levi rested a hand on his brother's shoulder. "I should have been there, but I can't change the past. But listen to me: Everything isn't cut and dried, okay? There's always a third option. I thought it was either run off and be free or stay and be miserable, but that's not true."

Chance paused. He had never considered that there was a possibility that Levi and he could make up and get out together. "What exactly are you saying?"

"Anna's roommate is moving out at the end of term, and I'm looking for better employment. I'm going to move in with her. There's an extra room, Chance. It's yours if you want it."

Anna popped her head out of the door then, her dark eyes curious. "Is everything okay now?"

The brothers looked at each other, a silent moment passing between them.

"I think so," Levi said at last, before turning to his girlfriend. "I asked Chance to move in with us."

Anna's eyes lit up. "Really?" she asked.

"I haven't decided yet," answered Chance.

"I'd love to have you. It's not only your brother who wants you there," she assured him, moving to stand between the two brothers.

"I'll think about it," Chance told them. "I promise I will."

So it wasn't all his fault. He wasn't holding Levi back, Levi was pulling him forward. *It's nice to have a third option*, he thought as he watched Anna and Levi talk excitedly about their apartment. *If only everything worked out so well.*

CHAPTER 31

Jenny

Jenny thought about what Kelsey had said all night. She had liked Drake, really—hadn't she? But she had never loved him. Maybe she could've grown to, but he'd cut it off all too soon for that. She wasn't mourning their relationship. It was the attention and the rumors that were eating away at her. If he had just broken up with her in private, over the phone or something, she would've been fine. But not like this.

She thought about it as she walked into school the next day. It was as she was walking through the cafeteria that someone started playing the stupid song. That stupid catchy vindictive song. She stood there, fuming. Anger coursed through her, hot and thick, burning its way through her veins.

She had finally had enough. She wasn't going to wait for Drake to disappear and for things to go back to normal. She wasn't going to let him continue to walk around hurting and humiliating her. She was going to march right up to him and demand answers, demand an apology. She deserved at least that much.

He wasn't in the cafeteria, though she looked everywhere. She wormed past groups of people giving her dirty looks, ignoring them completely. Nothing was going to distract her. She scanned the crowds, looking for the boy who was a head taller than everyone else. She was practically dizzy from looking when she spotted Emelia sitting at a table by herself. Jenny ran toward her, slamming her hands down on the table when she got there.

Emelia looked up, started, her long hair in her eyes. "Jenny?"

"Where's Drake?" Jenny demanded, unconcerned about how crazy she sounded. "Have you seen him?"

Emelia looked around, confused. "Err, I think I saw him heading toward the library?"

Jenny was off like a rocket, flying out of the cafeteria and down the hallway. She didn't even slow down as she raced past the principal's office, the doors to the library in her sights. She burst through the doors, every head turning to look at her.

It was as she was walking past the computer desks that Max Gregs decided to open up his big mouth.

"Look, it's the cold-hearted queen," he sneered to his buddies.

Jenny paused, her heart pounding. Normally, she would slink away, head down and face red, but not today. Not right now. "Excuse me?" she asked. "What did you say?"

It was clear that they hadn't expected her to react. The other boys looked away, turning back to their computers as if they hadn't spoken.

"If you're looking for someone new, I would love a little freak like you."

Jenny's back went rigid, her hands shaking.

Before she could even get a word out, Drake appeared from across the library and grabbed Max by the collar of his shirt.

"What did you just call her?" he hissed into the guy's face, fire in his eyes.

"Nothing, I'm sorry!" Max squealed, working his way out of Drake's grip. He ran from the library faster than Jenny thought someone that beefy was capable of.

"I don't need you to defend me," Jenny snapped. She found her bravado slipping now that she was face-to-face with him. A wave of tiredness washed over her, engulfing her, the nerves from what just happened finally catching up to her. She sank down into one of the computer chairs. "Not after everything."

"No, I suppose you don't." He settled into the chair next to her, his hands on the table. "I guess I overreacted."

"You guess?"

It was surreal sitting next to him and just talking. There was no longing in her chest, no secret desire to be in his arms once more. There was only hurt from how he had treated her, embarrassment, and tiredness. She was *so* tired of worrying about this, about everything.

"You do realize that this is my first breakup, right? And you've made the whole thing public. You wrote a freaking song about me and started all these rumors, then have the nerve to defend me after not listening to a word I said? I'm trying not to be upset. Do people not have anything better to talk about than my supposed affair with

Chance—which never happened, by the way—or our failed relationship? It's all pointless and meaningless. I don't even care anymore."

That wasn't true, but she wished it was. She'd give everything she had to not care.

"Ouch." Drake winced. "You're still as cold as ever, I see."

Her head shot up. "Excuse me?" Did he seriously have to sit here and insult her? White-hot rage returned to the surface. "I gave you everything!" she said loudly, her voice like a gunshot in the quiet library. Everyone turned their heads to see. "I gave you everything I had! What else do you want from me?"

"I just wanted to matter to you!" he responded, voice lower than hers. "It was like I was talking to you through glass the entire relationship. Meanwhile, Masters was your golden boy. You always looked so happy with him and you always smiled when you talked about him. I felt like I couldn't ever reach you because you were always buried in Chance fucking Masters. Were you ever even happy with me?" His voice grew softer. "Are you ever even happy at all? Because you give off this air of not really caring about anyone or anything."

"Chance has nothing to do with this," she said quietly. "And of course I was happy. You don't really know me at all."

"Chance has everything to do with this!" he exploded, tugging at his hair with both hands. She was surprised he didn't beat his fists on the table. "He was the only thing that could get through to you. I was screwed from the start. You've had Chance Masters swimming through your veins since the day you met him. You don't let anyone but Chance in. I felt it the whole time—our first date, when we'd talk on the phone, when you'd come backstage after shows, even when we slept together—you were never all there. It was like I was only ever getting half of you. But you gave him one hundred percent—you obviously did. He didn't have to repeat something five times to make sure you were paying attention. He didn't have to—you know what? No, I'm not doing this." He sighed, defeated.

"I don't even know what you're talking about. I tried so hard to make us work. Yes, I was happy . . . I think I was happy. . . . I *wanted* us to be happy. Is that what you want to hear? Because I don't understand this!" Tears prickled at the corners of her eyes. *I will not cry*, she vowed. "To be honest, what happens with Chance has nothing to do with you. You're the last thing on my mind when I'm with him."

"Did you say that to convince me you aren't cold? Because it didn't work." He leaned forward, his face close enough that she could see the holes where his old lip piercing had grown in. "It's shocking to realize how little I meant to you."

"What do you mean by that? You meant a lot to me, Drake!" she hissed, conscious of the librarian throwing angry glances their way.

"Really, then how come you ran into the arms of your best friend?" He didn't sound angry, just curious. "Maybe I handled the breakup poorly. I wrote a song because I wanted to see you react to something I did. I was your boyfriend, and yet you couldn't spare two seconds for me."

She opened her mouth to protest but froze, letting his words sink in.

"I'm sorry." The funny thing was that she meant it. "I never wanted to hurt you." It didn't excuse his actions, but it made them more understandable. She started to stand, tired of it all.

"Don't." Drake reached over and grabbed her arm. "Don't apologize." He gave her a sad smile. "If you don't apologize, I can pretend you're super broken up about me and hiding it really well."

Tears sprang to her eyes as she tried to pull away.

She didn't want to think about this. She didn't want to keep making a scene here in the library. She pushed it all down and buried it away, just as she had with her crush on Chance. She didn't care if Drake thought she was distant. She didn't care about any of it. Kelsey had been right: He didn't know her, not really. It was as simple as that. The people who really mattered knew how she felt.

"Wait," Drake asked her. "Please don't run away."

"Are you kidding me?" someone loudly exclaimed from behind them.

They turned to find Chance standing in the doorway. "Are you seriously making her cry right now?"

"You don't have to yell. We're in a library" was Drake's snarky reply, his hand still wrapped around Jenny's forearm.

Chance ignored him, turning to Jenny. He looked good today, but then he always looked good, with his shaggy hair and faded jeans. "Is he hurting you?"

"No, and I'm not crying." She blinked away the tears in her eyes as she jerked her arm free. "We were talking, but we're done now. Can we please just leave?"

Chance looked at her for a second before turning back to Drake. "You need to back off," he hissed.

"I don't think so." Drake moved to step between them and the doorway, purposely blocking their path.

Jenny could feel something bad starting, the air crackling with tension. *Oh my God, not now.* She placed a hand on Chance's chest, trying to steer him toward the other exit. Everything had been wrapping up nicely, but now it was unraveling fast.

Drake zeroed in on Chance. Any truce they'd called before was over now that Chance had gotten him riled up. "You never came between us before, Masters." He smirked wickedly. "What were you doing the whole time I was seeing your girl?"

"I am not Chance's girl! I don't *belong* to anyone."

"I was getting on with my life, because that's what regular people do. This obsession you have with making her miserable is not normal." Chance lunged, straining against Jenny's hold on his collar. "If you think acting like an asshole is endearing, it's not. I know her, and I've been with her a lot longer than you have."

"You know her better than me, huh?" Drake asked. "That's funny, because I happen to know her pretty well. And I know the only kinds of girls that hang around you are whores and sluts. Yet somehow I thought she was different. I was wrong. Of course I was. I mean, look how easily she gave it up."

Jenny froze—how dare he throw something like that in her face?— and Chance broke from her grip. One second her hand was on his chest, pushing him back, the next his fist was ramming into Drake's smug face. Jenny jumped out of the way, tripping over her own feet; she crashed to the ground as they crashed into the reference shelf. She scrambled to stand, grabbing at whoever's elbow she reached first, trying to pull them apart, to no avail.

Girls in teen movies always gushed about having boys resort to blows over them, but this was no picnic. Jenny winced as blood erupted from Drake's nose and Chance reared backward to land another blow.

A small crowd gathered around, watching the two roll from the reference section to the new arrivals. Books tumbled to the ground and the noise was enough to bring the librarian out from the back room to see what was going on. She took one look at Chance perched over Drake, holding him by the collar of his bloodstained shirt, before running to the checkout desk and frantically buzzing the office over the intercom.

Jenny's eyes scanned her surroundings, looking for anything to help stop them. Everyone was gathering, staring from the fight to her; some people had even taken up the creative chant of "Fight! Fight! Fight!" Her gaze rested on a stack of reference books the boys had knocked over, and she decided that desperate times called for desperate measures. She lifted one of the heavy tomes above her shoulder. She tried to wait until Drake pinned down Chance, but Chance wasn't letting up at all. She didn't care anymore, not right then. Let people stare, let her blush permanently stain her skin, she just wanted them to *stop*.

Just like that Jenny Wessler lost it.

She closed her eyes and started chucking dictionaries.

CHAPTER 32

Chance

The first dictionary launched into the fray and connected with Chance's side, knocking him over and giving Drake enough time to work in a punch that split open the blond's lip. It took Chance a few seconds to realize what had happened. One second he'd been grappling with Drake, and the next something heavy had hit him, pain exploding all down his side. He reeled back, looking around just in time to catch Jenny heaving another dictionary into the air.

What. The. Fu—

Another dictionary came sailing through the air, catching Drake in the small of his back. He crumpled like a pile of rags.

Chance stopped, still trying to process what had happened. He'd seen Jenny crying and Drake was there and suddenly all the anger and angst of the past few months had broken through. He hadn't meant to do this. Chance—confused, blood dribbling from his busted lip, pulsating with pain—looked at her. Drake picked up the offending dictionary, looking as if he thought it had fallen from the sky.

"You are both so stupid!" Jenny yelled, her anger boiling over. She reached out to grab Chance by the shirt and dragged him away from her ex-boyfriend. "You stupid boys! I can't believe you two right now!"

She looked down at Chance, and he realized he had never found her as hot as he did right then. He had never seen her angry before. Her eyes were on fire, her hair wild, and her skin flushed. She was vivid, passionate, and *wonderful*.

"I don't need you fighting my battles! And you—" She whipped around to face Drake. "Aren't you a pacifist? What the hell do you think you're solving with this?" She clenched her fists at her side, seething. "I should leave you both here to kill each other!"

Everyone stared at her, wary that she was going to start throwing dictionaries again at any minute. Chance's anger evaporated, shame flooding him.

"Jens—" he began, but she silenced him with a glare.

"First off, Chance, I hate violence."

A glance to the front of the library told Chance that the librarian was now watching through her office window—no doubt waiting for the principal or resource officer to arrive.

Great, as if the librarian didn't hate me enough already.

Jenny went on. "How many times have I told you that I hate fighting? It is literally the dumbest thing you could do."

"Yeah, but he—"

"I don't want to hear it!" She whipped around to face Drake, wincing at the blood that poured from his nose. "Second off, I have not slept with Chance. But you know what? His presence alone made you so insecure about your ability to keep me interested that you left like a scared little boy. He's that much of a threat to your manhood—not that there's much of that anyway."

Drake brought the hem of his shirt up to stem the gushing blood. "I think he broke my nose," he wheezed.

Pathetic, Chance thought. *I didn't hit you* that *hard.*

"Good, I hope he did." She glared at the people still gathered around. "What the hell are you looking at?" she demanded, throwing her arms wide. "Haven't you ever seen a girl lose her temper before?"

The crowd scattered.

"Well, thank you for that insightful speech, Miss Wessler," a voice rang out from behind her. Her arms fell limply to her sides. Turning slowly, she saw that Principal Rickman had entered the room, Officer Pullman right behind him.

Well, shit.

"SUSPENDED FOR THREE days," Principal Rickman repeated in his monotone voice. Chance sat in the uncomfortable chair across the desk from him. It wasn't Chance's first time in the stuffy office this year, but it was definitely the most trouble he'd ever been in.

"I don't know what possessed you to act out in such a way, but we do not tolerate solving problems with our fists in my school, understand?"

Principal Rickman was a portly man with a flab of skin that hung down under his chin and wobbled when he talked, making him resemble a turkey. Chance tried not to stare as he nodded.

"Very well, then, you're dismissed. Send in the other boy."

Drake sat out in the hallway, slumped in one of the miniature plastic chairs. The nurse had given him a rag to help stop his nosebleed, and Chance was delighted to find it was still pressed to his face. He would smile if his fat lip weren't pulsating with pain. Drake definitely had a better right hook than he'd thought.

"You're up," he said in a clipped tone.

Drake nodded before rushing past him and into the office.

Chance stood for a minute in the silence of the empty hallway. Everyone else was in fourth block. He looked down at his injured hand. The nurse had bandaged him up to the best of her ability, but the skin broke open when he moved it, rapidly soaking the bandages.

"Watch out for infection," she had warned. "You might even want to look into getting stitches."

Yeah, right.

"I'm fine," he had assured her, and she had sent him on his way.

He checked his phone, spying a text from Jenny. Right after the principal had walked in, everything had happened in overtime. The resource officer had restrained both the boys—even though the fight was over—and held them as the principal escorted Jenny to the counselor's. She was gone by the time he got to the office.

Her text read: *I've got detention. We'll talk about this later.*

Whatever, he didn't need her to tell him that what he'd done was wrong. He already knew that. There he'd been, thinking about third options, everything finally falling into place—and then there was Drake, spoiling the moment like he always did.

I guess it's not meant to happen, he considered as he dialed Levi's number.

"Well, well, well," Levi said in a pompous voice. "I've been expecting you, Chance. You can't see it, but I just flipped on the lamp here, all dramatic."

Chance groaned. "The school already called you, didn't they?"

"Yes. I was waiting for you to come home so I could surprise you then, but this works, too. I'm also wearing a bathrobe and holding a glass pipe."

"Dude, that is not the right pipe for the situation."

"I found it under my bed. I'd forgotten all about it." Levi laughed. "It was the best I could do on short notice. The next time you get into a fight at school, I'll make sure to run to the costume shop first."

Chance ignored him, getting straight to the point. "Am I in trouble?"

"Trouble? I'm proud. You punched a guy in the face. I heard him whining that you broke his nose. This was the douche ex, right?"

"Yes, and I did *not* break his nose."

"That's disappointing," Levi sighed. "Tell me all about it."

Chance wasn't used to getting to explain himself. Whenever he messed up, his dad yelled until he was blue in the face, then his mom stepped in and grounded him. Well, if they even noticed he'd messed up at all.

"Drake was making her cry. Then he said some disgusting stuff about her. I snapped. I couldn't help it." After all these months of Drake being an ass, Chance couldn't hold it back anymore. He'd had to punch the guy.

"Good for you. I knew you needed to do this. Doesn't it feel better now?"

"Honestly? Not particularly. It's a hollow victory."

He felt empty. Any satisfaction he felt after sinking his fist into Drake's face evaporated once the fight was over. The adrenaline left, and so did his fury.

"Is it because of Jenny? Is she okay with you breaking her ex's nose?"

"Of course she's not. She'd livid. Also, I didn't break his nose," Chance insisted.

"What did Jenny do?"

"Pelted us with dictionaries and screamed that she hated us. I feel bad about that part." He touched his busted lip. "I think I ruined any potential third options."

Levi scoffed. "No way. You've only improved your chances."

"You can't possibly know that."

"It's how the story goes," insisted Levi. "You defended her honor. Now she has to love you."

Chance recalled Jenny's expression as she'd glared at him and Drake. "She doesn't *have* to do anything."

"Seriously—"

"Levi, no," Chance interrupted, his voice stern. "I messed up. I need to deal with it. I constantly screw up all my chances."

He needed to go away, to think about what he'd done. He couldn't sit there and listen to Levi spout his optimistic bullshit. He needed to plan out his next move, to figure out what to do.

He needed to figure out how to fix things. All he could see was Jenny's face, twisted in rage. He hung up on his brother, walked to his car, and drove away.

CHAPTER 33

Jenny & Chance

I still can't believe him!" Jenny said for the umpteenth time that day as she stormed down the street after school. "I can't believe either of them!" She didn't even care that she was talking to herself in public. *Let people stare*, she thought. She'd already gotten enough attention from throwing dictionaries. She hadn't even thought about what everyone around her had been thinking; her sole focus had been to keep the two idiots away from each other. *I was so angry that my mind went blank.* It was so freeing not to care, to just let go and let herself feel something raw and real.

People kept whispering about her for the rest of the day, but she couldn't bring herself to care anymore. *Finally.* There were more important things, such as finding Chance and giving him a piece of her mind.

She couldn't even fathom the level of stupidity that drove Chance to start a fight. She'd had the rest of the school day *and* detention to stew over it and work herself up all over again. She wasn't as angry as she had been, but she was still righteously pissed.

He won't even answer his phone, she fumed as she made her way onto Chance's street.

Chance's car was nowhere to be seen as she approached his house, but that didn't stop her. Jenny stormed up the drive and knocked loudly on the door. Someone had to be home, and they would give her answers.

The door opened just enough for Levi to stick his head through, his blond curls wild.

"Hello?" he asked. "Jenny?"

Jenny stood there, hands on her hips. "Where is Chance?"

Levi opened the door wider, stepping outside.

"He's not here," he told her. He stood so much taller than she did that she had to crane her neck to look him in the face. "He didn't come home. He said he needed to think. I think I know where he is, though."

"So do I." There was only one place Chance would go to escape it all. "Can you give me a ride?"

Chance's Charger was parked outside the barn when Levi pulled up. Jenny's adrenaline was pumping, urging her to tuck and roll out of the car and sprint toward the barn. The car had barely stopped before she hopped out.

"Thanks for the ride!" she said.

Her legs carried her past Chance's car and sent her hurtling through the barn doors. Chance looked up, startled, from his perch on the table. The pirate hat sat on his head, and there was a fresh bruise blossoming on his chin. The sight of it only made Jenny angrier.

"Jenny?" he sputtered, jumping to his feet. "How did you—"

"Chance—" She paused, taking him in, softening her tone. She couldn't yell at him, not when he looked so sad.

"I'm sorry, okay?" he said, his expression doleful. "I know today was a disaster, but—"

Quite the understatement.

"No, you don't get to talk right now," Jenny said. She struggled to keep her tone even, to quell her anger, but hearing him try to make excuses set her off again. "This is *my* turn." She reached out, snatching the hat off his head and shoving it onto her own. "Drake wasn't hurting me, Chance. We were talking it out. We were coming to a freaking truce, okay? Then you had to come sweeping in like some knight in rusty armor and save the day. I *do not* need saving!"

"He was making you cry!" Chance defended. He glowered at her, taking a step forward. "I couldn't sit by and watch him make you cry! You should know that about me by now."

"You didn't even know the situation," she insisted. "You stormed in without even thinking. I can't believe that you would act so . . . so . . . *horrible!*" she said, for want of a better word.

The word hit home all right, causing him to take a step back. He roughly snatched the hat away, pulling it down onto his own head.

CHANCE NEEDED HER to get it. "This is exactly the kind of thing I do, Jenny. I'm going to protect the few people I have in my life. If that comes as a shock, then you obviously don't know me."

She threw her hands up in frustration, turning away from him. "That's crap, Chance, and you know it. You just don't want to take responsibility for your actions."

Chance had to laugh at that. "I'm taking full responsibility for my actions, trust me. I know I screwed up. Why do you think I'm here? It's because I'm trying to figure out how to fix yet another mistake."

He wanted her to calm down, to sit at the table and let him explain things. He didn't want this to be a fight. He didn't want her to get mad and leave like his parents had done.

Jenny kept shaking her head. "This isn't fixing your mistakes, Chance. This is hiding."

That hurt like a blow. "Why stop there?" he said, spreading his arms, ready for an attack. "Tell me what you really think, Jennifer."

"Fine." She took the hat back, shoving it on. "I will."

"I'M ANGRY AT you, really truly angry at you! But that's okay, because I can *be* angry with you and *not* abandon you. I *do* know you, Chance. I know you perfectly well. I have *feelings* for you. Real genuine feelings, and I buried them away like I do everything else because I know how you are." Her heart was pounding in her chest, and she felt like she was going to hurl any second. "I know you don't have those feelings; you don't do relationships. So I hid my feelings away, knowing it would make you uncomfortable to know the truth. I pretended that I felt nothing when we kissed. I dated Drake, I watched you date countless girls, and I kept it all to myself because I knew we weren't like that."

Chance looked at her, his expression unreadable. "You have feelings for me?" he asked uncertainly. "You—hell, Jenny, you've got it all wrong."

She folded her arms over her chest, not sure whether she liked the way he was looking at her. Their voices seemed so quiet after all her yelling.

"I'm *not* wrong," she insisted.

Chance took back the hat.

HE COULDN'T BELIEVE it. All these months of torture had been for nothing. "Jenny," he said again, his voice soft. "You've got it all wrong."

"I don't want to hear it, Chance." She tried to step away from him, but he caught her wrist. "Let me go," she said, breaking free. "I already know how you feel. I *heard* you tell a girl that you don't date."

What is she even talking—oh. Oh my God.

Chance remembered. He remembered trying to find Jenny so he could confess everything, brushing off the girl who'd come up to him. He remembered letting that girl down gently, telling her he didn't do relationships. He had shot himself in the foot without knowing it.

"Jenny, no, I told that girl that because I wanted to let her down easy."

"Why would you want to let her down easy?" she asked, disbelief clear on her face. "She was gorgeous, just like the other girls."

"Because I had just made out with you the day before!" he yelled. "I let her down because I wanted to be with *you*, Jenny! I was going to tell you in class that I wanted to give it a try, but you made it clear you felt nothing for me. Then you started dating Drake, and my parents left—it wasn't the right time. I couldn't push my feelings on you."

Jenny blinked up at him, befuddled. "Wait, you like me?"

"Yes, Jenny. Everyone knows." How could she not know? How could she be so blind, so set in her view of him that she couldn't see? Why else would he punch someone for her? "You became the only good thing in my life. You still are."

"You mean to tell me that this entire time, we've both had feelings for each other? That we wasted all these months with other people, playing games for no reason?"

Chance took off the pirate hat, letting it fall to the ground without a second thought. "I don't know, Jens."

She looked around. "What do we do now? We just admitted that we have feelings for each other. We can't go back from this. We can't cover it up with a make-believe story and pretend it didn't happen. Chance, this is real, what do we do—"

There was only one thing he wanted to do—something he had been wanting to do for months. He closed the distance between them in three steps, his hands flying to either side of her face, his lips crashing against hers.

The kiss caught her off guard, and she stumbled in his arms. She recovered quickly, her hands sliding up his chest and twisting their way into his hair. He was kissing her and it was everything. Part of him couldn't believe it, while other parts were pressing her closer.

This is real, he kept reminding himself as she sighed against his lips. *This is real and it's incredible and wonderful and, holy crap, this is happening.* He felt her fingers knot into his hair, dragging him closer still, her hips rotating against his.

This is real.

This is happening.

IF THEIR FIRST kiss was amazing, then this was nothing short of incredible. She never wanted to stop kissing him—to feel any sort of space between them ever again. Her anger had melted into lust, and it demanded to be satisfied. Months of longing sprang to the surface, egging her on as she pushed up the hem of his shirt, her fingers exploring his warm skin.

Hands were exploring with mouths close behind, Chance's body practically scorching hers where they met. She wanted him *closer*. He pressed his lips to the hollow behind her ear, making her gasp. This was Chance, *her* Chance.

There was no leverage to gain, nothing to prove. They had laid their emotions out on the table. Unlike with Drake, she wasn't doing this to prove a point or settle an argument. She wanted to be with Chance, to be as close to him as possible. There were no ulterior motives here; there was only Chance, Jenny, and an unbearable need growing inside her.

I want this. I want him.

She knew it with such conviction that she didn't even pause when he raised his shirt over his head, only rushing to get hers off as well. His lips made a fiery trail down her neck to her collarbones, and all she could think was—

This is how it's supposed to be.

He wanted *her*: sarcastic, anxious, smart-mouthed her. Not some girl he wanted her to be. Chance saw her as she was, as she would always be. No one in the world knew her better. It all felt so right.

He pulled back, his eyes boring into hers, and asked, "What do you want?"

All she could do was pull his face back to hers, whispering, "You."

CHAPTER 34

Chance

We can't go back, Chance thought the next morning, looking at Jenny curled in his arms. The night before, they had lain there in silence, staring up at the stars, until she drifted to sleep, a dreamy look on her face.

Now the worry set in, curling into the pit of Chance's stomach. His mind was in overdrive, trying to process what had happened.

I had sex with Jenny. We can't go back from this.

He had done it—he had crossed that treacherous line. He couldn't help but run every possibility through his head, thinking of everything that could go wrong.

She could change her mind. She might be using me as a rebound. We might not fit. We could let the awkwardness eat away at us until there's not even a friendship left.

Chance couldn't hide it—he was petrified. He had never been with someone who meant anything to him. Love had always been a game, trying to live up to the legend his reputation painted him as. It had never been real—not like this.

I love her, he realized. *I am in love with her.*

There are always third options, he reminded himself. Levi had told him that, had said it applied to everything. Yes, they could revert back to how it was, or they could fall apart, but they could also make it work.

Jenny lifted her head, looking up at him with bleary eyes.

"Chance?" she asked, her voice thick with sleep. "What—?" She broke off, her eyes growing wide. She slowly looked down at his bare chest before snapping her eyes back to his.

"Good morning," he whispered.

She was uncomfortable, he could tell. He felt any hope he'd mustered crash and burn.

She regrets it. She regrets me.

Jenny sat up gingerly, covering her chest with the blanket. Her hair was wild, the way Chance liked it best, sticking up every which way. She looked around for her clothes, not looking back at him.

Chance sat up, too, finding his pants on the pallet. Her underwear tumbled from the blanket as he picked up his pants. Wordlessly, he handed them to her.

They dressed in silence, unsure of what to say.

I have to do something to fix this, Chance thought. He knew it was now or never. *The past. We always fall back on the past.*

"Remember when—" he began, his voice unnaturally loud in the silence.

Jenny looked over her shoulder at him, quizzical.

"When . . ." He trailed off, his mind blank. "Remember when . . ."

He couldn't do it. Nothing sprang to mind. The effortlessness of their stories escaped him, leaving him speechless. There were no more stories to tell, no more past to lie about.

Jenny continued to stare at him for a beat, her expression almost pleading. But he couldn't fix this. He didn't have the words to say. He didn't know what to do anymore.

"I guess we should go," Jenny said at last, turning away from him.

He watched her walk out of the barn and into the bright morning light.

CHAPTER 35

Jenny

She wanted Chance to say something, to fix this. Everything had been so perfect, but now it was ruined. Jenny walked to the car, her limbs stiff and awkward.

I slept with my best friend and now everything is weird. Maybe he'd changed his mind? *Did this mean nothing to him?*

She wished she could take it back, stuff the words back in her mouth. She'd known it would end up like this, but she had told him her feelings anyway. She had realized as he had kissed her, his body moving against hers, that they could never go back from that.

She had never loved Drake—that had only ever been wishful thinking. She had been trying to force her puzzle pieces into the wrong puzzle, never realizing the right one had been there the whole time. She remembered how everything with Drake had been lacking and how everything with Chance had always been fireworks. She knew now why love was always equated with heat and burning. Drake had been as fleeting as a flickering candle, snuffed out in seconds. But Chance? He was as all-consuming and unstoppable as a forest fire.

And now it was all slipping away.

She climbed into his car, her hands shaking. She had to break the tension, do something to fix this. She looked everywhere but at him, focusing on anything she could while he started up the car. She stared down at her scuffed-up shoes, tracking mud all over the floorboards. She could hardly see the stain from where she'd dropped her first beer anymore; it had been so long ago. And then she knew what to say.

"Remember when I dropped my first beer?"

"Oh God, you looked so distraught," Chance said, laughing at the memory. "I wish I could've taken a picture of that face. It was priceless."

"You're the one who simply handed it to me, even though it was slippery."

"Don't put this on me; you're the one with butterfingers."

"I wouldn't have dropped it if you hadn't—" Then she stopped, because it occurred to her that she wasn't lying. This wasn't a fake memory, made up on the spot.

It was real. *This* was real. They were real.

Chance's laughter dried up, too, the same realization dawning on him as well.

They had a past now, weird and convoluted as it was. They had been each other's everything: best friends, confidants, lovers. Now it was time for them to take the last step.

"Can you believe we'll be seniors next year?" Jenny asked, settling back into her seat.

"Oh God, imagine how dramatic *that'll* be."

Jenny nodded. "There will be a new transfer student who comes between us, throwing our relationship into jeopardy."

"We'll make up before Christmas, though—"

"—so you can take me ice-skating."

"Then we'll be the shining example of the perfect couple on Valentine's Day, when I present you with a dozen roses during home room."

"We'll be so sickeningly lovey."

"They'll have no choice but to vote us Cutest Couple."

"We don't have yearbook superlatives, Masters."

"They'll create them, just so they can name us Cutest Couple, Wessler."

"Of course, you'll ask me to prom in some ridiculous way."

"Skydiving," he informed her. "You have to act surprised, though."

"Oh, I promise. Then we'll kiss on the stage at graduation."

"Oh God yes, we'll be the reigning monarchs of PDA."

Jenny liked the sound of that future. As they sped off toward town—back toward their real lives—Chance reached over and took her hand. She liked the feeling of it in hers. It might not always have been there, but she knew that it would be from now on.

Their past might be fake, but their future was real. It was theirs to build. It was real, unscripted, and unplanned.

And she was going to experience it all with Chance by her side.

Acknowledgments

It's funny because I've always imagined writing this page. I've wanted to be an author for as long as I can remember, so naturally, I always imagined who I'd list in my acknowledgments. The list has evolved so much over time, as people come and go from my life, but I think I've finally figured it out.

First, I'd like to thank the wonderful Swoon Reads community, especially the readers who helped this book get noticed. Holly West is probably the best editor around, and I'm totally not biased at all, I swear. She made every part of the journey a joy, and I'm forever grateful for her help and insights. This book would not exist the way it is now if it wasn't for her. Thank you to everyone on the Swoon Reads team. A huge thank-you (and a lifetime's worth of appreciation) to Jean Feiwel, for giving this book a chance. Also, a huge thank you to Liz Dresner for designing such a beautiful cover.

I have to thank my family—Mom, Ashley, Lisa, Papa, Popo, Grandma Pitcock, and Anita—for always supporting me no matter what. I love you guys so much. Meme, I wish you were here to see this. I miss you every day.

Thank you to everyone who has helped me grow and change as a writer. The first story I ever wrote was a Harry Potter fanfic with my middle school best friend Autumn, and it was mostly in chatspeak. I think I've grown a lot since then. Thank you to Mrs. Stacks for welcoming me into the BHS writer's circle. Thank you to Rae Davis for always being there for me to bounce plot ideas off of and give criticism. Thanks to Erica McDaniel, for always being up for an emergency midnight walk across campus so I could rant about my newest book idea. Also to Dr. Marck Beggs for being an awesome Creative Writing professor and publishing my work in the *Proscenium*. Megan Bray and Peter Wilson, for being the first people ever to read my book. I don't know where my writing would be without any of you, and I'm so grateful.

Thank you to my best friend Grace Raines, the absolute light of my life. Also Jordan Nett, Lauren Forthman, Kasey Perry-Lovell, Joel Beck, Randy Perry-Johnson, Julie Torix, Christen Brown, and countless others who have stood by me for all these years. I love you all. Thank you for putting up with me.

And thank you to you, the reader, for picking up this book and giving it a chance.

FEELING BOOKISH?

Turn the page for some

Swoonworthy EXTRAS

Chance and Jenny's Playlists

CHANCE'S PLAYLIST

1. "Barlights" – fun.
2. "Somebody's Heartbreak" – Hunter Hayes
3. "A Drop in the Ocean" – Ron Pope
4. "Hey Jealousy (cover)" – Hit the Lights
5. "King of Wishful Thinking (cover)" – New Found Glory
6. "7 Minutes in Heaven (Atavan Halen)" – Fall Out Boy
7. "You Found Me" – The Fray
8. "Bad Blood" – Bastille
9. "Everybody Talks" – Neon Trees
10. "Brighter Than Sunshine" – Aqualung

JENNY'S PLAYLIST

1. "Oh No!" – Marina and the Diamonds
2. "Something That I Want" – Grace Potter
3. "Closer" – Tegan and Sara
4. "Everything Is Embarrassing" – Sky Ferreira
5. "Pumpkin Soup" – Kate Nash
6. "Thinking of You" – Katy Perry
7. "Torn" – Natalie Imbruglia
8. "Shake It Out" – Florence and the Machine
9. "State of Grace" – Taylor Swift
10. "Parachute (acoustic)" – Ingrid Michaelson

A Coffee Date

between author Tiffany Pitcock and her editor, Holly West

Getting to Know You

Holly West (HW): What was the first romance novel you ever read?
Tiffany Pitcock (TP): I think it was *All-American Girl* by Meg Cabot. It quickly became my favorite book. I used to check it out from the middle school library constantly.

HW: I love Meg Cabot. She's lovely. Who is your OTP, your favorite fictional couple?
TP: Lily and James Potter. I know they're Harry's parents and they die before the books even start, but I'm in love with them. I fell in love with them in the flashbacks all through the series. I love that "I hate you . . . oh no I don't" type of relationship. I've read so much Marauders Era fanfiction that it is ridiculous. It's to the point that I only care about *Harry Potter if it has something to do with the Marauders.*

HW: Do you have any hobbies?
TP: I do a lot of crafts like painting, drawing, etc. I have no idea if I'm any good at them, but I enjoy myself. I love gardening, too. I collect *Beauty and the Beast* merchandise and copies of *Peter Pan*. Oh, and I collect comic books, particularly the 1990s run of *Robin*.

HW: And my favorite question: If you were a superhero, what would your superpower be?

TP: I've never actually given this question serious thought. I've always been partial to telekinesis, but that seems a little too outgoing for me. Probably invisibility. I'd love to be able to go around and observe without being observed. I like to people-watch. Plus, there are about a thousand-and-one different times in my life that I've wished myself invisible.

The Swoon Reads Experience

HW: What made you decide to post your manuscript on Swoon Reads?

TP: I had just finished writing *Just Friends* for my creative writing class (it was my final project) and I decided, hey, why not. It seemed like fate. Even if I was never chosen, it would still be great to get feedback and connect to readers.

HW: What was your experience like on the site before you were chosen?

TP: I loved the site. I loved reading other manuscripts and seeing what people liked and what they didn't. For me, the best part was receiving feedback. I don't have the privilege of being near any writing or critique groups, so being part of a community that gave positive criticism was a huge help for me as a writer. I think I still have a document somewhere where I saved every comment I got so I'd know how to fix things later.

HW: Once you were chosen, who was the first person you told and how did you celebrate?

TP: My college roommate. I actually found out three days before my twenty-second birthday, so I told her and we went out to a celebratory birthday/book dinner with my best friend.

The Writing Life

HW: When did you realize you wanted to be a writer?
TP: I don't think there was ever a defining moment. I've always wanted to be a writer, since before I can remember. That was always my answer when people asked me what I wanted to be. I wrote stories back in first grade. When I was eight, I promised my best friend Kasey that I would dedicate my first book to her. One of the best moments of my life was getting to call her last year and tell her I can finally make good on that.

HW: Do you have any writing rituals?
TP: I have to be alone. I mean, totally alone, like no one else can be in the house. If I even know someone else is nearby, it's a distraction for me.

HW: Where did the idea for *Just Friends* start?
TP: I was a junior in high school and had just broken up with my first boyfriend, who had also been my best friend at the time. I was also trying to watch as many classic teen movies as I could, because they were my escape. I have to say it was the movie *Reality Bites* that inspired me the most. There's this scene where Winona Ryder's character yells at Ethan Hawke's about ditching her after they finally hooked up, particularly the part where she says that he can mess around with

everyone else but how dare he mess around with her. So many teen movies focus on that fragile line between friends and lovers and I wanted to explore a relationship where crossing that line could really be a disaster. My original intent was to, I guess, kind of deconstruct those types of narratives, which is why I gave them the fake past. My original idea was *really* dark, though. Chance and Jenny never even got together. I think someone had a kid and they never spoke again. Luckily, that version never got written.

HW: Do you ever get writer's block? How do you get back on track?
TP: Yes, all the time. I try to skip ahead to a scene that I really want to write—even if it doesn't actually fit in the story—and write that instead. It's like a reward. Sometimes I get bogged down and I just want to have a little fun, so I'll write a scene where the characters just talk or dance or do something stupid, and that helps. I have about twenty different scenes of Chance and Jenny just hanging out that'll never see the light of day, but they helped motivate me to finish.

HW: And now we are all dying to see those scenes! What's the best writing advice you've ever heard?
TP: To just write. There's a section on Meg Cabot's website where she says the difference between writers and people who want to write is that writers actually find time to write. I think that's true. You just have to push through it, even though it's hard. Write now, edit later. Get the ideas on paper first, and then see what you're working with.

Just Friends
Discussion Questions

1. If you were to create a fake past for yourself and your friends, like Jenny and Chance, what would it be?

2. Did Chance and Jenny's fake past help or hurt their relationship? How would things be different if they had dropped the lie?

3. The book makes use of dual points of view to give an inside look into both Jenny's and Chance's heads. Are there any scenes you would've liked to see from the other's point of view?

4. Throughout the novel, Chance struggles with his relationship with his older brother Levi. Do you think he was right to be as angry as he was? How would you have handled the situation?

5. In the beginning, Jenny has a hard time connecting to other people and showing her emotions. Do you think that changed over the course of the story?

6. When Jenny overhears Chance say that he doesn't do relationships, she's crushed. How would you have reacted in that situation?

7. Both Jenny and Chance choose to date other people in an effort to "get over" their best friend. Do you think this was a smart plan? What would you have done?

8. Drake reacts badly to his breakup with Jenny. Why do you think he was *so* upset? Do you think he had genuine feelings for her? Or was he just in love with his idea of her?

9. At the end of the novel, Levi offers to let Chance move in with him. Would this be a good move for Chance? Why or why not?

10. After they get together, Chance and Jenny find it hard to make up a fake past. Why do you think that is?

I KISSED MAX HOLDEN.
IT WAS A TERRIBLE IDEA.

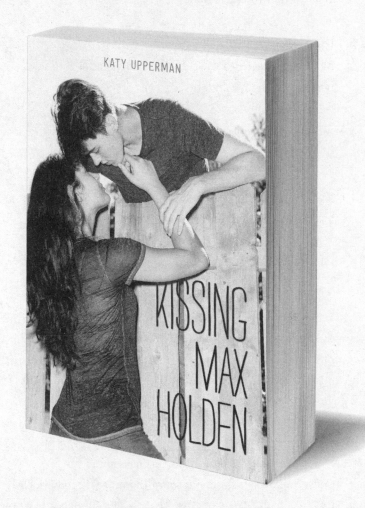

KATY UPPERMAN

KISSING MAX HOLDEN

After her dad catches her making out with the bad boy
next door, Jillian swears she'll stay away from him.
But not kissing Max is easier said than done. . . .

*H*E TUCKS A LOCK OF HAIR behind my ear. "You really committed to getting crazy."

"Thanks mostly to your mixology."

"Yeah, well, it was cool having you as my partner in crime." He glances at the ceiling and his face changes. He takes a slight step to the right, eyes alight. He gives a nod, indicating I should shift too. I do, confused but intrigued. He looks up again, meaningfully. I follow his gaze.

A sprig of green with waxy white berries, attached to the archway with a festive red bow.

"You know what this means?" Max asks slyly.

I give a laugh that comes out sounding more like a bark. "Mistletoe is a parasitic shrub," I say, because that's a fact he needs to know *right now*. "It's also poisonous—eating it can make you really sick."

"I'm not offering you a taste, Jillian." And then, incredibly, "You don't want to kiss me?"

I prop a hand on my hip. "How drunk are you, Holden?"

He gives my question a moment's consideration before saying, "Not nearly as drunk as I was last time we kissed." He rubs his hands together, like he's prepping to discuss plays in a midfield huddle. "Let's do this before someone comes upstairs."

God, he's serious. "What about Becky?"

He snorts. "Since when do you care about Becky?"

I don't *care* about her, but when I think about what Max and I did on Halloween, I feel guilty, and ashamed, and I wonder why he's pegged me a willing collaborator in his two-timing.

Partner in crime, he said. Is that who I want to be?

Just as I'm remembering my morals, deciding to put a stop to whatever the hell this is, I make the mistake of looking up. Max is sort of gorgeous with his hair all spiky, his lips turned up in a hopeful grin. All kinds of alluring. All kinds of kissable.

I've had a lot of rum.

I shut out the siren in my head, the one that's wailing, *Bad idea! Bad idea!*, and take a tiny step forward. Mistletoe—it's tradition. Besides, tonight's about letting loose, right?

Oh, Max smells good, very good, a clean, woodsy scent that reminds me of pine needles and hiking and moonlight. His eyes are smoky like always, but there's something different about them, too, something inviting. He blinks languidly and everything—my knees, my pulse, what's left of my resolve—goes weak.

"Jesus, Jilly, you look terrified. We don't have to."

"No, I'm fine." And I think, maybe, I am.

He rests his hands on my shoulders. "You're sure?"

I nod.

I close my eyes.

I wait an immeasurable moment.

Max's lips touch mine.

He kisses me—*really* kisses me—warm and soft and leisurely, and I kiss him back, leaning into his chest. I feel him smile. He skates his hands across my shoulders, under my hair, along my neck, until his calloused palms cradle my face. I shiver, delighting in his tenderness.

He pulls back, and for one horrible second I think it's over. But then the softest groan escapes him and he walks me backward, presses me against the wall, and opens his mouth over mine. He tastes like chocolate and beer and I wonder: Will I ever get to kiss him when he's sober?

I shove that musing out of my head, content to focus on the here and now.

Max Holden is kissing me like it means something.

Like he wants to keep kissing me, forever.

Check out more books chosen for publication by readers like you.

Tiffany Pitcock

TIFFANY PITCOCK

is a young writer from Benton, Arkansas. She studied English at Henderson State University but has been writing stories for as long as she can remember. She is a fan of reading, cats, staying indoors, and TV dramas. Being published is a dream come true for the girl who spent her high-school nights scribbling out plot ideas wherever she could. *Just Friends* is her debut novel.

Find her online at
Maybe-This-Time.tumblr.com.